FINN'S CLOCK

Dean Whitlock

Thetford, Vermont

Published by Boatman Press, LLC, Thetford Center, Vermont

This is a work of fiction. It represents many months of thought, writing, and rewriting. If you like it, please tell your friends. Thank you.

A historical fantasy set in a time when steam was threatening sail, when factories were displacing workers, when the immigrants were Irish – unwanted and under threat, but determined to make their place here. It's 1853. Young Finn O'Neill and his father are boatmen on Boston Harbor, rowing a small boat for a "chronometer man," who adjusts and repairs marine chronometers for incoming ship-masters. One fog-bound morning, a sea-going Chinese junk sails into the harbor, bearing mysteries and magic.
Young adult, Fantasy, Historical Fantasy

ISBN-13: 978-0-9909025-6-0

Other books by Dean Whitlock

Sky Carver *(first in the Carver's World Series)*
Raven *(second the Carver's World Series)*
Fireboy *(third in the Carver's World Series)*
Iridescence and other stories
The Man Who Loved Kites *(a chapbook of the novelette, also in Iridescence)*

For Rich and Ella.
And for Ross.
They have all been for Ross.

Prologue

I WILL NEVER FORGET the moment I first saw the *Hang-Jinhe*, no matter how many decades have passed. Who could forget such a thing? Or such people? Mr. Lawson, and his unbelievable Chinese clock. An-Ming and Peter. Wang and Hu-Lan and Captain Li. If I close my eyes I can see their faces sharp and clear, like they were standing right by me. All the others, too: old Robert and his daughter, Eleanor, and her husband, Jacob Sands. Billy Adams. The tall thug whose name I never knew. Good old Pat Delany. And the family, of course: Ma and my little sister Bridget. Grace and Molly. Even Tim, though he'd been dead four years already.

And Da. Sure I'll never forget Da, how he drank and brawled, how he cursed and cuffed, how he argued and fought, with us and for us. How he died, despite the clock. Alive and dead, he's right there at the heart of me, though it took all the others to help me see it. All those people aboard the Hang-Jinhe, and all the people swept up in the wake of her coming.

The year was 1853. September the twelfth, it was, just two days past my 14th birthday. The time was early morning, very early. A cold fog had settled over Boston that night, thick as a wet pea coat. It did strange things to sound, as fog will, and from our little boat we could clearly hear the rattle of wagon wheels on the cobbled wharves that lined Boston Harbor, the hawking and spitting of the longshoremen waiting in line for a chance to work that day, the bell of the early horse car tram on State Street. Yet the creak of our own oars straining against the oar-locks, and the ripple of blade and boat through the water were muted. The fog allowed us only the faintest hint of dawn. I could make out my father's broad back where he sat on the middle thwart, pulling easily on his oars. Beyond that, not a blessed thing but fog.

I was pulling from the forward thwart, and Peter Jenkins was seated in the stern, minding the tiller. It was Da telling Peter which way to steer, of course. Da had been a boatman on Boston Harbor going on ten years now, and for quite a few before that in Dublin. And finally he was letting me row with him. Peter wasn't a boatman, he was what came to be called a chronometer man, the first in Boston, I believe. He worked for the company of Wm. Bond and Son, which was famous back then. Da and I would row him out into the harbor every morning to find inbound ships that needed to have their clocks and chronometers serviced. Peter was seventeen, and he'd been working the job for hardly six months. Not to say he wasn't a fine man with a clock – he soon showed just how fine – but he wasn't a boatman.

I had been working full days with Da only since finishing school that spring, but I'd been living on and by that harbor for as long as I could remember. Small as I was, I could easily handle our little canoe, which is what the sturdy, sleek rowing craft were called then in Boston. I knew the difference between a brig and a snow, no matter they both had two masts and square sails. I could tell a ship-rigged three-master from a bark, and a bark from a barkentine, in the dark. I knew the names of the merchant houses and most of the ships that flew their flags. I could recite the list of the dozens of wharves from South Boston all the way up and around, through Boston and Charleston and over to East Boston. In September, 1853, all of 14 years old, I thought I knew Boston Harbor and the life on it as well as any man could.

Until that fog blew in. Oh, I had a good idea where we might be, but Da, he knew exactly. And it was just like him to say to me, "Now then, where are we, Finn?"

I was tempted to say, "Boston, Da," but you never knew with Da. A joke could get you a laugh or a box on the ear. So I said, "Off Foster's Wharf, sir."

It was close, but not close enough for Da. "All right then. How far off?"

"Near a hundred yards?" I ventured.

"Tim wouldn't have had to ask," he said.

I gritted my teeth. In Da's memory, Tim had never done anything wrong. "One hundred yards, give or take . . . two." I was bluffing, and he knew it.

"Direct Mr. Jenkins to the number six buoy then," he said. "We'll wait out the fog there."

"It's hard to believe a fog this thick will lift before noon," Peter remarked.

"It'll lift in the hour," Da assured him. "What's our heading, Finn?"

I tried to measure the set of the tide by the weight of the water on my oars, the sound it made on the hull. I could tell better from the smell of the mud flats off South Boston, a reek strong enough to overpower even the coal smoke and sewer stew the city sweated out every minute of the day. The tide was still ebbing. No wind to speak of, so it was just us and the tide to worry about. The number six buoy was off the southwest tip of Bird Island, a good mile away. If I was right about that one hundred yards.

I prayed I was. "Steer to the east, please, Mr. Jenkins," I said, and after a dozen more strokes, "Now straight ahead, please."

"Straight ahead it is, Mr. O'Neill," he replied. I liked Peter for that: he always treated me like he did Da. Well, not quite like Da – we all knew who was boss on that boat. But, still, like a man. I wasn't big like Da, nor tall like Peter himself. In fact, I was a bit of a runt. But I was a strong runt even then. I pulled my own weight, and Peter respected that. I always liked to think that Tim would have liked Peter, and the other way round.

We rowed for a while, and I kept looking over my shoulder for any sign of the buoy, a tight red bundle of spars that marked the east side of the channel. A dark form loomed out of the fog, a small brig at anchor, the riding light at her stern hardly more than a gray glimmer. I studied the play of the water as it slipped past her hull, trying to calculate the tide again. I wondered, had she anchored in the channel or outside? Then she disappeared as sudden as she had come, and we were back in the fog world, the not-world, with nothing to see but a bit of ourselves. I took another glance over my shoulder.

"A little more east now, please," I told Peter. I studied Da's back, trying to see what it might tell me about my choice, but it just shook a little as he stifled a cough. The rough sound of it hurt, but I didn't say anything. Da would rather hear a bad joke than have you mention his cough. He spat over the side and didn't miss a stroke. And two, and three, and I was beginning to think I'd got it all wrong, that we were halfway to Castle Island, when Peter said, "There's the buoy." I could tell from the sound of his voice that he was just as relieved as I was.

We were right on it, we were, and all it took was a wee nudge of the tiller to bring us alongside. Da and I backed water, and Peter managed to grab one of the buoy rings on the first pass. I shipped my oars, reached behind to snatch up the painter – that's the rope fastened at the bow – and handed the end back to Da, who tied us neatly to the buoy. Without a word to me, as usual, but I knew he knew what

I'd done. I had found the buoy, and there we were, all secure and resting in the current, with our bow facing back the way we'd come. I breathed a little lighter. We had a view of the inner harbor and a long view out through the Lower Middle channel into President Roads, ready to spot any new ship that came in or had slipped in during the night. Not that we could see anything in that fog.

"Should I blow the horn, Mr. O'Neill?" Peter asked. He lifted the fat brass tube of the fog horn toward his lips, but waited for Da's word.

Da coughed again and cleared his throat before shaking his head. "There's nothing moving but ferries till the fog lifts, and we're well out of their way. We'll be having quiet. My head hurts enough without the horn."

I thought it must hurt like perdition, given the state he'd been in when he staggered home last night, but I knew better than to mention it.

"Besides," Da added, "it's lifting."

Peter caught my eye and raised his brows. He was a skeptic about many things, Peter was, and not afraid to say so. "Either your eyes are better than mine, or that headache has made an optimist of you, Mr. O'Neill."

But even as he said it, a breath of wet breeze put a wrinkle in the gray blanket. The fog folded and rolled, and shades of real light leaked through, the first we'd seen since yesterday evening. As the breeze picked up, the fog swirled and shredded and streamed away like the vapor it was, letting in beams of bright September sun, just topping the height of Governor's Island to our east. And there to the south, anchored in a shaft of that sunlight, was the *Hang-Jinhe*!

Chapter 1

FAITH, BUT SHE WAS fine! She was a junk, a genuine sea-going Chinese junk. Peter gaped. I must have, too. I know my heart soared at the sight. Only one other junk had ever graced Boston Harbor. Six years before, the *Keying* had stopped in on her way to England from Canton, and I still remembered the crowds and hullaballoo. And Da rowing the whole family out to see her on the water. It was the last time we'd all been in the boat together. Before Tim died.

The *Hang-Jinhe* was much like the *Keying*, though a bit smaller, one-hundred-twenty feet on deck at most. Her hull curved up high at either end in a broad moon shape that looked as though it could hardly stay upright on the water. Her bottom paint was bright yellow, and it came well up her broad planking. Her topsides were a deep brown-red, almost the color of rust, only brighter, more like varnished blood. She had six square gunports, painted white with a red Chinese letter on each one. Her rail was carved in steps and filligrees, and her bow had a blunt transom with painted eyes. Her sails were furled on her booms, but flags flew from all three masts, the biggest and brightest being a long, streaming, swallow-tail on her mizzen, just lifting in the freshening breeze. There was a smaller broad pennant at her forepeak, sky-blue with golden, long-legged birds flying into the wind. But on her main flew a common flag: a white cross, diagonal on a blue field, with a single white star in the upper quarter. It was a house flag, like any you'd see at the maintop on a Boston merchantman, the ensign of the company that owned her. In some ways, it was the strangest thing about her.

"Whose flag is that, Da?" I asked.

"I'm not sure," he said slowly. "I recall one like it; Lawson and Sands, I believe. The house changed soon after we arrived. Sands died. Or maybe it was Lawson."

"The same Lawson and Sands who founded the Harbor Bank on State Street?" Peter asked. "Whyever would their flag be flying on a Chinese junk?"

"Can't say," Da allowed. "Let's go ask."

I'm not sure who was more excited, Peter or me. We slipped the line and had our boat turned and flying over the water in a trice. Peter held firmly to his top hat with one hand and steered with the other. I set my mind to rowing, hard as it was not to sneak a look over my shoulder. The *Hang-Jinhe* wasn't the only ship anchored in the harbor. Boston was a busy port, with two-dozen arrivals on a slow day. Two dozen more cleared outbound for the foreign trade or coastwise or for California. Their masts forested the wharves, and still there wasn't room. The rest waited in the harbor or out in the broad spread of the Roads. That's where we looked to find them, before any of the other boatman could.

But that morning, we only cared for the *Hang-Jinhe*. She hadn't been there the evening before. She must have come in with the fog, though it seemed to me she'd slipped in on that beam of sunlight. And we would be the first to reach her side. Peter was the only chronometer man working the harbor, but there were plenty of other boatmen working for chandlers and boarding houses, trying to sell supplies or lure the crew away to a different ship. It was hard to get in close enough to state our business once that pack started circling. I took a quick look around. There was only one other canoe like ours near enough to give us a run. And wouldn't you know, it was Billy Adams, a nasty piece of work, if ever there was one.

"Da!" I said.

"I see him, boy," Da replied. "Lay to those oars."

Da set a quick, strong pace, and we covered the quarter-mile like we were leading a race, which it was, really, with the *Hang-Jinhe* for trophy. I don't know if Adams had seen us, but he was rowing like he wanted to jump right over us. We matched him stroke for stroke, though it left me sore winded when we finally drew up and shipped oars, a good hundred yards in the lead. Peter steered us near and stood to hail the ship, but they had been watching. Before he could say a word, a high voice called out.

"Go away, boarding-house runners! Our crew is content!"

Peter's mouth hung open. It was a girl's voice. A Chinese girl. She was standing by the rail, glaring down at us, flanked by a pair of scowling Chinese fellows who would have given a Broad Street brawler a moment's pause. A half-dozen others peered at us from the high decks at bow and stern.

"Don't stand there like a ninny, Mr. Jenkins," Da said. "Tell them who you are."

Peter cleared his throat and called out, "I am not a runner, ma'am. I represent the firm of William Bond and Son, of Congress Street."

The girl wasn't impressed. "Do not need chandler, nor anyone like that. Go!"

"I am not a chandler or other peddler," Peter began, but Da cut him off. He always did think Peter put too much store in the formalities, from his top hat on down.

"Would you be needing service for your chronometer, ma'am?" he bellowed.

The girl looked taken aback. She had a quick palaver with the fellow on her right, who seemed inclined to disagree, but she hailed us again. "Did you say 'chronometer?'"

"Yes!" Peter replied quickly. "I can clean, balance, adjust, and reset all makes, from Britain, France, and the United States. I can also offer new—"

"Yes yes. We can use you. Please, come board here."

She said something else to the right-hand fellow, who yelled a few words. Right off, a couple of crewmen opened a gate in the railing and dropped a ladder over the side. Da and I sculled our canoe close to the hull, and Peter grabbed his case and scrambled up.

Just at the top, he turned and said to Da, "Mr. O'Neill, if you don't mind, I would appreciate some company this time, yours or Finn's."

I would have paid a gold dollar for that chance, and Peter knew it. I tried not to look too hopeful, because Da had the right. He set down his oars and started to stand, but a fit of coughing took him.

I reached out to steady him. "Are you all right, Da?"

I think he'd have hit me if he could've. Instead, he just sat back down and motioned angrily toward the ladder.

"Yes sir," I said. "I'll keep close watch, I will." And I scrambled up after Peter.

Close-to, the girl was simply beautiful. I noticed right away that she didn't look the same as the two Chinese fellows beside her. Not that they looked like each other – one was tall, the other short; one round-faced, the other sharp and heavy-eyed – but they both looked more Chinese than she did. She was small, no taller than my sister Bridget, who was only twelve. Her hair was black and shiny and hung in a long, straight braid. All the crew wore braids, too, but hers hung all the way down to the small of her back. And she was even wearing loose pants, under a long shirt or jacket, almost like the men's. But there was something about the arch of her nose and the shade of her skin that set her apart.

Sure, Peter noticed. He yanked off his topper and actually bowed. "I am Peter Jenkins, ma'am," he said, "and this is Mr. O'Neill, my boatman." I knuckled my own cap.

She bowed, a jerk of a motion. "Ann Lawson," she said, which answered part of the question about the house flag but brought up a fistful more. "This is Li Jia-Hai." The man with the long face stuck out his hand, grabbed Peter's, and shook it once, stiffly, like it was a trick he had just learned. Peter was left with his hand hanging.

"You repair clocks?" the girl went on, not bothering with the round-faced fellow. I took him for the bosun. Or maybe a bodyguard; he had the look. All of the other sailors were staring at us, too. It made the back of my neck tingle.

"Marine chronometers, ma'am," Peter said, holding his hat to his chest.

"Yes, we have. And others. Please come." She started toward the high stern castle.

"Excuse me, but is Mr. Jia-Hai the captain, ma'am?" Peter asked, stepping quickly to keep up.

"Li. Mr. Li," she said. "Yes, Li is captain."

"Ah. And are you the, ah, navigator?" Peter was speaking very carefully, trying to figure this pretty girl out, and obviously afraid he'd insult her. His hat was still pressed to his chest, as though stuck to his heart.

"Of course not. My father is."

"Ah. Perhaps I should confer with him regarding the chronometer and, ah, clocks?"

"He is not to be bothered. He steered in last night, now sleeps."

That right there impressed me. Boston Harbor sits inside a maze of islands, small and large. Even the senior pilots of the Marine Society would have waited till the fog burned off.

She took us to a companionway that led under the poop deck. The entry was low and narrow, as on any ship, but its frame was carved all over with vines and birds and even

Chinese dragons, done up with some kind of oriental lacquer, just like the fancy plates and boxes and such you'd see in the windows of the auction shops. Peter had to stoop as we went along a short passageway lit by a skylight, also carved, and into a small cabin in the stern quarter. Two windows looked out over the water and the ships clustered in the harbor, and Boston itself in the distance. The sun was gleaming gold on the State House dome high on Beacon Hill.

"There," she said, pointing to an ornate table against the inner wall. A plain foot-wide box chronometer sat on one end of the table, next to a half-rolled chart, a sextant, and a dark set of parallel rules. What captured Peter's eye, and mine, too, was on a shelf above the table. Two larger clocks stood there, side by side. Both were at least two feet high, with carved, lacquered cases, like you'd see on a grandfather clock, except for the size and the Chinese carving. The top third of each case was wider than the bottom and had five sides. I could see three of them, and each held a broad, white clock face, painted with birds, animals, dragons, symbols, all like the carvings on the boat. But none of the faces had hands. Nothing was moving. The plain chronometer ticked; the two fancy clocks on the shelf were still as death.

"Can you fix?" she asked.

Peter was staring at those Chinese clocks so hard, I thought he didn't hear her. Finally he muttered, "I don't know, miss. I'll have to look inside."

"Be most careful!" she said. "Do nothing you aren't sure of."

"Oh, of course not," Peter said, turning toward her. He froze. The round-faced bosun, or bodyguard, was standing in the doorway, arms crossed. "Absolutely not," Peter added.

"Good. You understand." She crossed her arms, too, and stood there waiting, like she planned to watch his every move.

Peter gave her a strained smile, put his case and his hat on the table, and reached for the right-hand clock.

"Not that one," she said. "No longer of use. Only the other."

"Ah," Peter said, and he carefully hefted the other clock from the shelf. I could tell it was heavy. I hurried over and moved the chart and sextant to the side to make more room. Peter set the clock gently on the table. He wiped his hands nervously on his coat tails, tried another smile on her, with no more effect than the first, and opened the front panel on the base of the clock. Inside hung a brass grid of some sort, and behind that a pair of dark weights on gleaming cords. I swear they looked like real gold. Peter studied them for a moment, peering inside to see what they connected to up top.

"Can you fix?" she repeated.

"I believe so," he said. He slid the clock around, revealing a fourth clock face with no hands, and studied the fifth side, at the back. It had a carved wooden panel instead of a face. He pressed a bright brass latch, and smiled when the panel popped open. Gears and wheels gleamed at us. "I will have to study the clockwork to be certain. And, if some piece has broken, I would have to have it special made. Do you know anything about its function?"

"No!" she said, very quickly. "It is father's. He will—"

She was interrupted by a hail from the water. Then someone yelled from the deck. She muttered something that sounded like a curse.

"Must go translate. Look, study, but do not—" The hail came again. Her scowl deepened. "Be careful!" she repeated, and hurried out.

Peter watched her go. "Well," he said. "This is quite a situation, eh, Finn?"

"It is," I replied.

He shook himself and turned back to studying the

clock. "Look here, Finn!" he exclaimed. "It has an anchor escapement shaped like a dragon! And this armature—" He indicated the brass grid in the lower compartment. "—is actually a pendulum. The tubes and cross-bracing must provide some compensation for temperature, don't you think?"

"If you say so," I replied.

Peter chuckled. "Forgive me, Finn. I tend to forget that not everyone shares my enthusiasm for such mechanics."

He was right about that. Ma was after me time and again to ask Peter about clocks, to get interested. "He'll need an apprentice some day," she'd say. "It'd be a fine career, more certain than rowing a boat, and a lot more dry." Here was the perfect chance to start asking. Truth is, I had been waiting all my life for the chance to row with Da. Now that I finally had it, I wasn't at all interested in clocks. Even that odd Chinese one.

It had an interesting look, I had to admit, though not for the gears. "Is that really gold?" I asked, pointing at the cords and weights.

"I wouldn't think so," Peter said. "Although it certainly looks like it."

Then my eye caught on something else. In the heart of the workings, centered behind the several faces, was a gleaming red crystal, dark as a ruby and big as the end of my thumb. Like a big tear of blood. It made my own heart skip to see it. Like the two were connected somehow. If only I'd known.

"Look at that!" I exclaimed, pointing into the works.

A harsh cry stopped me cold. "What are you doing! Get away from that!"

Chapter 2

THERE WAS A WILD man standing in the doorway. He looked and sounded like an American, but he was wearing Chinese clothes and had such a fierce expression that I thought he might jump us. The bodyguard hovered behind him, looking very worried. That made *me* even more worried. Peter stepped to my rescue.

"He wasn't touching anything, sir. He was merely pointing."

"Who is he? And who are you?" the old fellow demanded. And he did seem old right then. Frail, too. Bowed by some weight. He had a thick head of hair, but it was silver and tangled and stuck out in odd shocks. His cheeks were gray, his nose a sharp hook of a thing, his eyes deep and yellow as old teeth. His gaze wavered from Peter to me and back. Uncertain he was, as though he thought he should know us. I'd seen the old folk look like that. His voice was strong, though. "Well? Speak up!"

"I am Peter Jennings, sir, a chronometer man, working for William Bond and Son, and this is my boatman, Mr. O'Neill. The young woman – your granddaughter, perhaps? – she asked me to examine this clock to see if I could determine why it had stopped."

"My granddaughter?" The old man turned to the bodyguard and asked him something in Chinese. The bodyguard replied, nodding. He seemed even more worried.

"Hah!" the old man remarked. He turned back to us, and the bodyguard relaxed a little. "I've heard of Bond and Son," he said. "Well regarded. What have you found?" He crossed the small room unsteadily. I had to skip back to keep out of his way.

"Ah," Peter said. "Well, not knowing the precise function of the piece, I couldn't be certain . . ." He paused, and I think he was hoping the old man would shed some light on the workings of the clock. It didn't come. Peter turned back and studied the clock again. "I couldn't be certain where to find the most likely source of wear or a breakage. It has no hands, so I assume the faces must revolve." The old man grunted. "Has it been stopped long?" Peter asked.

"A few days," the old man replied. "Maybe a week."

"Did you forget to wind it, sir? Or did it stop of its own volition, as it were?"

The old man bent over alongside Peter and peered into the works. They looked like two scrawny hens wondering at a duck egg. "We went through a bit of heavy weather, not the worst we'd had, but the seas were vexed. It stopped in the midst of the heaving."

"Ah, not surprising with weights and a pendu . . . Ah! Is this . . .?"

Peter reached inside and plucked at something. I heard a distinct click. He gave the grate of the pendulum a twitch, and the clock started. *Tick . . . ka-tock, tick . . . ka-tock . . .* The pendulum swung a steady beat, about once a heartbeat, and two of the faces began to turn, one fast, the other slow. I figured the other faces were moving, too, but not fast enough to show.

"Glory be." The old man brushed both hands back through his thick hair, gave out a great sigh, and straightened up. He was almost as tall as Peter. "What was it?"

Peter was still studying the innards of the clock. Without looking up, he held out a tiny brass pin, hardly a half-inch long. "This was lodged in the gear train," he said. "It must have worked loose from some part of the casing. Ah, yes." He took something from the very bottom of the inner compartment, beneath the beating pendulum, and turned to the old man. "Here's a little piece of wood, a bit of carving it would seem. A repair, perhaps? Whatever, the piece came loose, the pin fell into the gears, and the clock stopped."

The old man took the pin and the bit of wood in his palm. He weighed them with a look of shock. "Done in by a curlicue, and a broken one at that. How ridiculous." He closed them in his fist, then slipped them into one of the pockets on his Chinese jacket. "I should carry them with me as a sermon against vanity. Well done, young man. You've earned your fee and then some, I daresay."

"Thank you, sir," Peter replied, "but it was simply a matter of taking a close look."

"With sharper eyes than mine."

"And I haven't even glanced at your chronometer yet. You are the navigator, I take it? Miss Lawson's grandfather?"

"Her father, yes. How impolite of me. Matthew Lawson." He held out a hand and they shook. I was taken aback to think the old man could be father to such a young girl. I was even more surprised when he offered his hand to me; so surprised it took me a moment to take it. He had a firm handshake. "Forgive me for not introducing myself," he said. "I'm afraid I've been too long away from the company of Americans, and too distracted by . . . that."

He gave the clock another heavy look, and I thought he must be a little mad. I couldn't imagine caring so much for a timepiece, even if it did have gold cords and rubies in it. Peter seemed to understand him, though.

"It is an amazing mechanism, sir," he said. "Having it stop must have been very disappointing. I could clean and lubricate it, but I'm not sure I could determine how to adjust it."

"I can take care of the adjustment," Lawson said. "But cleaning and lubricating – would you have to stop it for any length of time?"

"Two to three hours, I suppose. Perhaps a little longer," Peter replied. "The mechanism is complex. Not too small, which is a help, but I did notice some surprisingly rough work in places." He bent back to the clock. "Was it made in China?"

"Yes."

"Wonderful," Peter muttered. "Shall I work on it?"

There was such a note of hope in his voice that I was beginning to worry he'd caught the old man's madness. Before Lawson could reply, his daughter rushed in. I had to skip out of the way again.

"Father!" she snapped. "Why are you not in bed?" She turned to the bodyguard and started to chide him in a burst of Chinese.

"Let poor Wang be, An-Ming." Lawson said, almost jovially. "I've rested." He gave her a smile like nothing I'd ever got from Da, and looked ten years younger.

She glanced from him to the clock to Peter. I stayed out of the way. "You touched it?" she demanded. "I told you be careful!"

"As I was, Miss, I assure you." The tips of Peter's big ears went red. He held his palm to his chest again. "I did nothing without your father's permission."

"He's right, An-Ming, and what he did was also right. All is well."

"All is not well!" she replied. "We are surrounded by boats, demanding to speak to captain. They try to board, they tempt the crew."

"They tempt the crew?" Lawson asked.

"Offering money for hats, for clothes, for pieces of the ship even! Luring crew away. Worse than you ever described!" She glared at Peter and me as though it was our fault.

"The crew has behaved, I'm sure," Lawson said, trying to calm her.

"Because they don't understand! Only by luck, Hu-Lan is too frightened to come out and translate."

"Please be more careful with your grammar, my dear. And go tell Li I shall come out in just a few minutes to help you deal with them. I have one more thing to discuss with Mr. Jenkins. You should be able to hold off the pirates for that long."

"Perhaps I will have Li run out guns," she replied.

"The guns? That might be a bit extreme," he said. He smiled, and she smiled back. They were nothing alike in looks, except for a common spark in their eyes when they smiled. Then you could tell they were family.

"I will have him wait before firing, but briefly," she said, and she hurried out with a word to the bodyguard. He followed her.

The old man and Peter both watched her disappear down the companionway. Mr. Lawson's face had a fond smile on it. Peter looked bludgeoned.

"We best hurry," Mr. Lawson said, "I daresay she will run out those guns."

"What? Oh, yes, I do believe she would, sir," Peter remarked. "She's quite, ah . . ." His ears reddened again. "Lively. Ah, what was it you wished to discuss?"

"Excuse me, sir," I put in. "Would you mind if I went checking on my da? To let him know how we're getting on?"

"Good idea, Finn," Peter said. "I'll be up as soon as Mr. Lawson and I have spoken." He pulled his turnip watch out of his vest pocket and flipped open the cover. "It's just after seven. We've plenty of the day left."

Mr. Lawson fixed on Peter's watch. "That's a very nice piece; a pocket chronometer, yes? Is it by Bond and Son? How old is it? How often do you have to wind it?"

I left the madmen to their clocks and watches.

I came on deck to find that the sun was bright and warm, and Miss Lawson – Ann or An-Ming, take your pick – hadn't been fancifying. The *Hang-Jinhe* was ringed with small craft, from ship's boats no larger than our four-oar canoe up to broad water boats, cat-rigged with a single big sail in the bow. There was even a pair of hefty lighters with two big sprit sails apiece. There were two or three larger ships moored nearby, but they sat in empty water, ignored as a pair of homely dogs. A schooner – a fisherman by the smell of her – was heading out in the channel, and every man of her crew was at the rail, staring as she slipped by in the light breeze.

I went to the rail to speak to Da. He was lounging on the bow thwart of the canoe with his jacket for a cushion and his broad-brimmed hat tipped back, taking the sun and playing the squire with the other boatmen. Billy Adams was sitting on his oars not two yards off, looking ready to chew nails. I suspected Da had been goading him.

"You heard her, Billy Boy," Da was saying even then. "No one's to come aboard but Mr. Jenkins and my boy, Finn. Back water and don't be bothering the captain and the lady no more. This crew's not going anywhere, particularly not with the likes of you. "

Billy Adams was a runner for Joseph MacLean, who had a big boarding house on Richmond Street. He was a crimp, too, who'd lure sailors in with promises of a soft bed, cheap liquor, and easy women. Then he'd get them blind drunk and sell them out that very night as crew on another ship. And he'd steal their sea bag, too. Now they call that getting shanghaied.

"You're welcome to them, Mickey," Adams snarled. "A bunch of babbling Chinamen is all you Irish deserve. Just watch your back."

"They don't worry me, Adams," Da replied. "Or was it yourself you meant? I can't tell you how much that scares me." He lay back and pulled his hat brim over his eyes.

That didn't strike me as the safest thing to do. Da had worked for MacLean when we first came to Boston. Crimping sailors for a boarding house could pay well, he said, if you didn't mind paying back with your soul. Ma finally made him quit, and now he and MacLean didn't have much good to say to each other. So Da enjoyed giving Billy Adams the shove-off, and wouldn't have turned away from a fight. Adams was a brawler. He hated anyone who wasn't a born-and-bred American. But that time he just spat into the water and pulled away. I gave him a dozen strokes to get well clear before I relaxed.

"Da!" I called down. "Mr. Jenkins says he'll be out in a few minutes with the plan. He's talking with the navigator now."

"Having a good *craic* are they?" A *craic* is a good discussion. Da still spoke a lot of the Irish, even to people who weren't.

"Talking up a storm about clocks, they are," I replied. "There's more than one here needs cleaning."

"Good enough, then." Da put his hands behind his head and settled back in the crook of the bow. "Give a shout when it's news."

I should have gone back into the cabin to join Peter then, but I couldn't help taking a look around the deck. Junks don't have any standing rigging to speak of, even ocean sailors like the *Hang-Jinhe.* There were the masts and booms and halyards, but none of the shrouds and ratlines you'd find on a Boston ship. Miss Lawson and Captain Li had gone up onto the poop deck over the stern house, which put them well above the bustle on the water around them. The sailors were standing here and there, talking and laughing about it all, in Chinese of course. There was a big cargo hatch just forward of the mainmast, and I wandered over to see what I could through the grating. There were guns on the deck below, sure enough. The gun ports weren't just for decoration, like they were on many of the American merchantmen. But there was no one down there getting ready to run them out.

I was bending over to see what else might be down there when someone coughed right behind me. Faith, I jumped. It was the guard fellow, Wang. He'd come up on me so quiet I never even heard him. He gave a sharp nod, all serious in the face. I could tell he was laughing inside.

He pointed toward the poop deck and said, "Ann Lawson, Li, come see?" He pointed to me and back at the poop deck to make sure I got the idea.

I said, "I'll come," and nodded back. He wasn't much taller than me, but he was built like a bear. I think he would've carried me up the ladder if I'd said no.

Miss Lawson and Captain Li were standing at the stern rail. It was the highest point on the ship and gave quite a view. She pointed at a small steamer coming out from Boston.

"They show our family flag. Why?" she asked.

From the low, dark deck house and single stack, I could tell it was the *Andrew Peabody*, one of the small screw tug boats that worked the harbor. Sure enough, I could make out the blue-and-white house flag of Lawson and Sands flying from the staff at the *Peabody's* bow. "I can't say as I know, miss. They must have pulled an old flag out of a locker somewhere."

"Why?"

"I'd guess there's family on board, coming to see why you're flying the flag."

"*Zaogao!*" she muttered, or something like that. She said a few words to Captain Li, who began calling orders to the crew. Then she hurried off, with Wang at her heels. She fairly jumped down the ladder, quick as any sailor in her Chinese trousers, and was heading for the companionway when Mr. Lawson and Peter came out. Maybe it was the kind light of the sun, but Mr. Lawson looked a far cry better than he had down in the cabin. Still too old to be his daughter's father, but not the unsteady gaffer I'd taken him for at first glance.

She pointed out the tug, which was coming on at a good pace. Mr. Lawson turned to look, and stood dumbstruck at the sight of Boston.

"Glory be, just look at it," he said. "I'd seen a painting, but . . ."

"You've been away a long time then, sir?" Peter asked.

"Yes, Mr. Jenkins. A very long time. The dome is quite beautiful, isn't it? And all those steeples; there's half again more than I remember."

I took another look at old Boston. It had never occurred to me that a city would have less than a dozen steeples. And there were six more at least across the harbor in East Boston and Charleston, and a pair in South Boston. And all but two of them Protestant. I guess you could be calling that a lot.

"My memory's of a much smaller place," Mr. Lawson said.

"Father!" Miss Lawson cut into his thoughts. "The steamboat! If it brings old family, we must be ready to greet them."

"You're quite right, An-Ming. I must change. Mr. Jenkins, if you will excuse me?"

"Certainly, sir," Peter said. Mr. Lawson called for Wang and went back into the stern house. Peter turned to Miss Lawson and said, "If there is anything I can do to help, please don't hesitate to ask."

"Your boat could fetch people from the steamboat."

"The *Peabody* can pull up right alongside, miss," I put in.

She translated to Captain Li, but he shook his head and said a few things that added up to a firm no.

"They do it all the time," I told him. "They'll hang thick fenders along the rail and—"

"No!" she said. "Not alongside. We will lower our boat."

"There's no need for that," Peter said quickly. "I'm sure

Mr. O'Neill won't mind. I'll explain the situation."

"We can pay," Miss Lawson said.

"Oh, I'm sure there's no need—"

"That'd be welcome, Miss Lawson," I put in quickly. "You're kind to offer, and I'm sure my Da would be happy to carry anyone you'd like for no more'n a dollar."

"Finn!" Peter exclaimed.

"Spanish or American?" she asked.

"American," I replied.

"Quarter-dollar, American," she countered.

I pretended to consider.

"Finn . . . ," Peter muttered.

"Four bits," I said. "Four bits, American. Half a dollar."

"Done," she said.

It was as much as we'd make in a morning from freighting Peter around. I was beginning to like Miss Lawson, or An-Ming or whoever she was.

The *Peabody* came on quickly, black smoke streaming from her funnel. She wove around the moored ships, sounding her horn, and the small craft did their best to shift out of her way. With a great flurry of white water under her stern, she came to rest within easy hailing distance.

"Hello the junk!" a fellow called. "My compliments to the captain, and might I request permission to ask if I may come on board?"

Miss Lawson frowned. "He asks if he can ask?"

"What he means is, simply, may he come on board," Peter explained.

"*Hao bun!*" She shook her head and stepped to the rail. "Who asks?" she called.

I could see the look of surprise on the fellow's face when he was answered by a girl. I could sympathize a bit.

"Mr. Jacob Sands," came the reply. "I represent the interests of the late mercantile firm of Lawson and Sands. You are flying the house flag, are you not?"

"Yes. Please come, Sands." To me she said, "Go now,

O'Neill."

I skipped down the ladder in a trice. Da was already untying the painter, and we had oars out, shoved off, and were halfway there in less time than it takes to tell.

Mr. Sands was waiting for us with a sour look and total silence. He had the broad, curved mustache of a dandy and was dressed in a trim, pressed suit topped with the tallest hat I had seen. Sure he was no sailor. The *Peabody* was low to the water, like all them tugs, but Sands needed a deck hand to help him navigate the short ladder. He moved stiff as a rusty pump, and he wiped the stern sheets off first with a big, white kerchief, as though they might soil the bottoms of his tight striped trousers. I was holding onto the *Peabody's* planking to keep us steady, and I could feel Da give a bit of a lean just as Sands plopped down. We lurched and Sands grabbed for the gunnels. I had to swallow a smile.

"Sit tight, sir," Da told him. "We'll be having you there quick and dry in an instant."

Sands had thin lips that just about disappeared when he looked down his pointed nose at us. He was one of the gentry, a Boston Brahmin through and through, the kind who didn't speak to Irish unless he had to.

"Ready, Finn?" Da said, and he bent to his oars, short and hard. We skipped away from the *Peabody* with such a jerk that Sands almost lost his top hat.

"Have a care!" he snapped.

"As you're saying, sir," Da replied, but he kept to a short stroke that gave Sands a rough ride back to the *Hang-Jinhe*.

Then there was the ladder, much higher than the *Peabody*'s. Sands made it only with Peter's help from above, while the Chinese crew grinned down on his fumbling climb. I went up two steps behind him, just to make sure he didn't take a tumble and damage our boat.

Mr. Lawson was there with the others by now. He had changed into a suit and looked like a regular American, if not so fancified as Sands. With his neat collar and hair combed, he seemed even younger than before.

"Mr. Sands, is it?" he said, stepping forward with his hand out.

Sands shook it with a look of relief to find someone who wasn't Chinese, Irish, or female. "Yes, sir. Jacob Sands."

"Daniel's son?"

"No, sir. His grandson."

"Of course," Mr. Lawson said, "you'd have to be. I am Matthew Lawson. I knew your grandfather well."

Sands studied Lawson closely. "How did you know him?"

"He was a partner in the firm, of course. Lawson and Sands. But I learned in Canton that the house had closed. Switched to banking. You must be part of that enterprise now."

"Yes, sir. With Mr. Robert Lawson."

Mr. Lawson's face lit up. "Robert? He's still alive?"

"Why, yes sir," Sands replied. "And well enough, for his age. He is my father-in-law."

"Well, well," Lawson remarked. "Family then. I'm doubly pleased to meet you. Please let me introduce my daughter, Jian An-Ming. Excuse me, Ann Lawson."

Sands's smile froze on his thin lips. "Miss Lawson," he said, remembering a bit late to doff his topper. He turned right back to Mr. Lawson. "And how exactly are we related, sir? Are you a cousin of the Lawsons here?"

Mr. Lawson smiled. "Oh, no. I'm Robert's uncle. I suppose that would make me your great uncle by marriage."

Sands worked it out and was shocked at the sum. "Good heavens! You're that Matthew Lawson? I don't believe—They said you were dead, sir. Pirates or something."

"It was a close call."

"But that was . . . Well, you would have to be ninety years old at least!"

"Ninety-one, actually."

Chapter 3

I'D NEVER HEARD OF anyone being that old, outside of the Bible. Da was forty-three. Looking at Mr. Lawson, I could see he was older than that, but ninety-one? Sure, it was hard to believe.

Mr. Sands was having a hard time with it, too. "That's . . . that's simply amazing," he stammered. "Robert will be astounded, to say the least. You must come see him right away."

"I most certainly must," Mr. Lawson said.

They arranged a meeting at the Harbor Bank that very morning. Mr. Lawson offered Sands a tour of the *Hang-Jinhe*, but he gave the crew a wary look and said perhaps later, he needed to notify everyone and get the bank ready. I wondered what that would mean. Dusting off the money? I think he was afraid he'd be held for ransom, or get his fine trousers soiled.

There was more shaking of hands and another tip of the hat to Miss Lawson as Sands took his leave. He managed the ladder well enough, with me above and Da below, and we got him back to the *Peabody* with only the slightest bit of a splash from the oars.

"That there's a regular Englishman," Da muttered as we

pulled away from the tug. It wasn't a compliment.

Back at the *Hang-Jinhe*, Mr. Lawson asked both Da and me to come on board. Peter and Miss Lawson were there, and Wang, persistent as a shadow.

"Mr. O'Neill," Mr. Lawson said, offering his hand. "Thank you for taking on that extra service. If you find it agreeable, I would like to hire you and your son to ferry my daughter and myself to Long Wharf this morning and show us to the Harbor Bank."

"What insult!" Miss Lawson exclaimed. "Inviting us to bank instead of home. We are not merchants, we are family! You are his uncle!"

"His father-in-law's uncle, An-Ming," Lawson said, "and we are merchants, or were. The real point is, he is not convinced I'm not an imposter. Robert will recognize me, I'm sure. Now, Mr. O'Neill, Mr. Jenkins tells me that his employers pay you one dollar daily, and your son half that. I would be able to pay you both that much for your help today while he is adjusting our chronometer. That would be in addition to your usual daily wage, of course."

Da's the man who taught me how to bargain, but there was nothing he could say to that. We were Lawson's for the morning, which was fine by me.

"Captain Li needs to replenish our store of fresh water and food," Lawson went on. "Mr. Jenkins also said you were previously employed by one of the chandlers here. Is that so?"

"I was," Da replied. "James Bliss and Company, for three years."

"Can you recommend us to them?"

"I could put in a word for you, sir. Mr. Bliss is a good man. Treat you honest, he will."

"Excellent." Mr. Lawson beamed. "Would you like tea or water while you're waiting? Heavens! An-Ming, you should be getting ready. You know you can't go like that."

"Father, I—"

"No. We have discussed this already. Please go change."

She went, but the look on her face would've pickled a cabbage, whole.

One of the crew brought up cups of water that had a bit of lemon juice mixed in, and we all drank up. It felt strange to be sipping dainty water with the likes of Mr. Lawson, but he didn't seem to notice so I tried not to. Then he and Peter went back to the clock room. Da took a quick look around and was all for climbing back down to the canoe, when there came a hail from a water boat, looking for custom. Captain Li came to the rail and tried some broken English that didn't do much to clear the air, so Da stepped in, using his cup to show Li what it was all about. Soon enough, Da and the waterman were haggling over a price.

Meanwhile, the crew had brought up a crate and a small box from the hold. Both of them were done up in Chinese lacquer, deep reds and blues and gold Chinese symbols, shining like they'd just been polished with a soft cloth. I couldn't help but wonder what might be in them. The rest of the crew were busy with the ship's boat. It had been lashed bottom-up on the fore deck, a short, blunt-nosed thing hardly bigger than ours, which was only fifteen feet long. Not nearly large enough to hold the junk's crew. An American ship would have carried two or three boats; at least enough to get all the men off if she foundered.

Miss Lawson came back on deck in the midst of all this. I almost didn't recognize her. She had her braid rolled up somehow under a small bonnet, and she was wearing a dress. Not a Chinese robe dress with a high collar, like you'd see painted on a plate or a scroll. This was an American sort of dress, the kind Ma sewed, with a wide skirt and lace and belled sleeves and a tight waist. The only thing Chinese about it was the print: water and reeds and some kind of flowers I'd never seen before. And her face, of course. Even in that dress, she didn't look like an Ann Lawson. She looked like an An-Ming.

Fluttering at her heels was another Chinese woman, in a Chinese dress and a long, fancy version of the overshirt An-Ming had been wearing. She was older, and not nearly so pretty. Flustered, she looked. She was brushing at An-Ming's dress and pulling at the waist, trying to straighten it out, just like Ma did with Bridget every morning. An-Ming spotted Da and Li and hurried right over, spouting English and Chinese all at once. I thought for a minute she would pitch Da over the rail, but once he and Li got a word in edgewise, she stepped back and appeared to let them get on with it. She butted in twice, just as Da was about to close the deal, and I noticed that he got the price down a little more each time. They both knew what they were doing.

Li and the crew were well into taking on water when it was time for us to leave. Mr. Lawson, An-Ming, and the Chinese woman, Hu-Lan, went with Da and me. An-Ming refused any help on the ladder. She wrestled her skirts into a bundle under one arm and skipped on down, grumbling all the while. Da told me to steady the boat and not to look, but we both did. She fooled us, though. She had her Chinese pants on under her petticoats. As for Hu-Lan, Wang carried her down sitting on his shoulder. She crossed her legs, held up her head, and came down like a queen.

Wang could have squeezed in, but he went on the *Hang-Jinhe*'s boat, along with the boxes and a pair of crewmen to pull the oars. An-Ming took the tiller in our boat. Hu-Lan said something that obviously wasn't approving, but Mr. Lawson let her be. We were quite a sight.

The day was hot, too hot for September, but Da kept us at a smart stroke. After all, the whole harbor was watching. By the time we'd rowed the wandering mile through the shipping, we were both sweating. Mr. Lawson stared at the city all the while, as if he'd never seen it before. As we passed India Wharf and approached the long, tall granite row of stores that ran the length of Central Wharf, he exclaimed glory be and said he never guessed so much could have changed. He started pointing out every little difference, which was just about everything.

Da had An-Ming steer us in between Central Wharf and Long Wharf. Both of them were lined with ships and brigs and schooners, all busy putting off or taking on cargo. Every bay in the high, gray warehouses was open and busy. At the outer end of Central Wharf, a team of longshoremen was unloading a great mound of peanuts beside a stack of rough dyewood logs. The Portland steamer was firing up at the end of Long Wharf, and everything smelled of fresh fruit and coal smoke and cloves and horses and sweating stevedores. The appearance of a Chinese rowboat put a stop to all the work. We had everyone's attention as we slipped along the gap between the close-packed hulls. Da and I shipped oars smartly, and we glided to a gentle bump by the ladder up to Custom House Square.

"You first, Finn," Da said. "Make sure folks stay back while we're getting the ladies up."

I did, and sure he was right. The idlers and teamsters and anyone else with more than a moment to spare were crowding the cobblestones between us and the Custom House. Traffic could hardly get by on Commercial Street, which was already crowded with stacks of cargo waiting to be hauled off or loaded aboard. Boxes, barrels, bales, carts, wagons, horses, people – it made for quite a tangle.

I spotted one of my friends from school at the edge of the crowd. Pat Delany it was. He was trying to sell newspapers, without much luck. I gave him a hallo and waved him over. "Give me a hand here, Pat," I said. "Use that donkey voice of yours to help me clear some room."

"What's going on, Finn?" he asked. "Who are these folks?" Pat wanted to be a news reporter. Lord knows he was a good snoop around the neighborhood.

"Mr. Matthew Lawson, come from China with his daughter, Ann," I told him. "He's uncle to the people at the Harbor Bank, and that's where we're headed." I gave him a slug on the arm. "Come on, now. Move 'em back for me."

"You'll tell me more later?"

I gave him another punch. "Not if you don't start yelling."

Pat was a dark, quick lad with a fine set of lungs. He let out his best newsboy bray, and together we managed to clear out a bit of space at the head of the ladder.

Mr. Lawson made his way up then. Luckily, the tide was well on the make, and the climb was only about nine feet. He didn't even seem to notice the crowd at first, so taken he was by the sight of the Custom House dome rising before us on its fat columns. An-Ming came up right after him, with no more than a pause to collect her dress. Every eye was staring at her ankles as she let her skirts fall, and then they lifted to her face. I heard her mutter *wa!* But she lifted her chin and took her father's elbow, as if he were the one who might need a bit of support.

Then we had to wait for the Chinese boat to come alongside, so Wang could step across to ours and carry up Hu-Lan, sitting on his shoulder. That there really captured the gawkers. This time, Hu-Lan was mortified, but Wang glared at them so fiercely that even the boldest shuffled their feet and went back to staring at An-Ming. She nudged Mr. Lawson. He came to his senses long enough to ask folks to give us a little more room, which they did. He may have been away a long time, but he could give orders like a Brahmin when he needed to.

Da and I helped the two Chinese crewmen muscle the crate and box up the ladder, while Wang kept watch over the Lawsons and Hu-Lan.

"Shall I stay with the boats, Da?" I asked, when we were all unloaded.

"I'll do it," he replied. "This is more hullaballoo than I'm wanting today. You show the way and help that Wang fellow keep the dogs at bay." He gave me a shove. "Get on with you."

It wasn't like Da to walk away from the chance for a scrap, but I was happy to be going. I took the small box and led everyone across the square into State Street. Mr. Lawson kept stopping to exclaim over every building – all new to him – but An-Ming pulled him along as best she could. Wang stayed right at his elbow and Hu-Lan tip-toed behind. The Chinese fellows brought up the rear, followed by Pat and a dozen or so other boys and idlers who decided to come along and see where we were going. Boston was a low city then, most of the buildings brick or wood, no more than four or five stories tall. The streets were narrow, with just enough room for a pair of wagons to pass abreast, and the cobbled sidewalks were narrower. We spilled out onto the street, which was just as busy as the wharves. We beat our way slowly against the tide of businessmen, tradesmen, seamen, messenger boys, shoppers, and even a knot of women dressed up in flags for sashes, handing out abolitionist pamphlets.

And everyone of them turned to gawk as we passed by. We stopped more than one horse in its tracks in the busy street. Luckily, the Harbor Trust was only two blocks past the Custom House, right opposite Merchant's Row. Any farther and we might have grown into quite a parade.

The entrance to the bank was done up in polished wood and brass, with etched windows. I hesitated on the doorstep; it wasn't the sort of place I felt welcome. But An-Ming had finally pried Mr. Lawson away from the sight of the old State House up the street, a building he actually recognized. I figured I'd better not give him the chance to snag on some other pile of stone. I managed the door latch with my elbow and went in with the box held high, like one of the Magi. There were two men at dark wooden desks and two more standing behind high counters, all of them in full suits. They looked up and gave me four frowns. I suppose not many Magi wore patched trousers and hand-me-down coats.

The one with the biggest frown growled, "The delivery entrance is in the back alley, you." Then he saw Mr. Lawson and An-Ming and the rest, and changed his tune. He hurried forward, all smiles and greetings, while one of the other men skipped into a side room. Out came Mr. Sands, followed in short order by an older gentleman on the arm of a fair woman in a fine dress. Right away I guessed they must be Lawsons; they had the same beak.

You could see the old gent had once been a bigger, straighter man, but now his suit drooped like a curtain, and he was shaky on his pins. He had a pair of specs clipped on the hook of his nose, and he squinted through them at Mr. Lawson as the young woman helped him along. Mr. Sands had paused in his hello and stood watching, his eyes shifting from the old man to Mr. Lawson and back. As the old gent got closer, and still not a word, Mr. Sands' sour mouth began to show a hint of a smile.

Then Mr. Lawson took a second look at the old gent and gasped. "Glory be! Robert?"

The gent's gaze cleared. He dropped hold of the woman and stepped forward almost briskly, reaching for Mr. Lawson.

"Uncle Matthew! It *is* you!"

Chapter 4

ROBERT LAWSON'S VOICE HELD so much joy that it made me want to laugh outright. It was the oddest thing to see an old, frail gent call Mr. Lawson uncle, but their greeting sealed it for me. Any doubts I might have had about him blew off like the fog. Mr. Sands, he looked about as happy as he had when Da nearly dumped him in the drink. The two Lawsons were shaking hands like terriers at a rat, exclaiming over the wonder. Old Robert Lawson got quite winded by it. He finally let go and reached for the woman's arm again, patting his chest as he did.

"You will tell me how you survived the pirates, Uncle," he gasped. "I insist. But first – forgive me, my manners – let me introduce my daughter, Eleanor Sands."

"I am thrilled," Mr. Lawson said, taking her free hand in both of his. "It is such a pleasure to see family again after all these years. And this is my daughter, Ann."

Mrs. Sands and An-Ming smiled and murmured, sizing each other up the way strangers will who aren't supposed to be strangers. And they couldn't have been less like family. Mrs. Sands was a tall, pale confection beside An-Ming. She had her blonde hair pulled back in a swoop over each ear and tucked into the tiniest lace bonnet, very high fashion for Boston, and she was wearing a white dress with lace all over the bodice and three deep flounces trimmed in pink. It was the sort of skirt Ma, a dressmaker, would call "a right flakey pastry."

"'Ann' you say?" old Robert put in. "And your daughter? Uncle!" He laughed and actually spoke to An-Ming in Chinese. She looked shocked, then broke into a big smile. "Oh, dear," he said. "I hope I haven't come out with something vulgar."

"No, no, your Chinese is most excellent," she said, speaking very carefully. "I am surprised to hear it."

"You flatter me, my dear girl," he replied, beaming. "I barely remember a few words. It is certainly no match for your grasp of English."

"Don't over-flatter her, Robert," Mr. Lawson said, and to An-Ming, "Robert was with me in Canton for two years, learning the business."

"I was there for ten more years after you disappeared, Uncle, and spent half of every day seeking word of you. Or your body, as we came to believe."

"I am sorry, Robert," Mr. Lawson said. "I . . . Well, you know my mournful state when I started that trip upriver. I was wounded in the attack, and was a long time recovering, and then in no mind to hurry back to my old sorrows. Later . . . There's no excuse for it, but I let my heart rule me." He looked at An-Ming with a great fondness. "I fell in love again and, so, rose out of mourning."

Old Robert regarded An-Ming with new regard. "Come here, my dear. I suspect your father may have told you who you are named for? Well, there is something you should see."

He shifted his hand to An-Ming's arm and drew her toward the side room. Mr. Lawson immediately offered his arm to Mrs. Sands and followed. Jacob Sands, still sucking on a stone, fell in behind, and I figured I might as well follow. Curiosity had me by the throat.

The side room turned out to be an office, with a desk and a Turkey rug and a few chairs, but it was the paintings on the wall that Robert Lawson wanted An-Ming to see. Among the scenes of ships at sea were three portraits. One was obviously old Robert as a young man. The other was another Lawson – that nose again – who I guessed must be his father. The third was a family portrait: Mr. Lawson – Matthew, that is – with a pretty woman and a little boy, no more than five or six, I guessed.

"Your father and his first family," old Robert said to An-Ming, pointing to the portrait. "His son, Nathaniel, and his wife, Ann."

"*Aiyo*," An-Ming whispered. She went closer and studied the painting for some time. "So beautiful, Father," she said. "And Nathaniel . . ." She shook her head. "I see now. What loss."

"He was devastated," old Robert told her. "A ruined man, it seemed. After a year and no change in spirits at all, my father urged him to go to Canton, for the business, of course, but we truly hoped it would bring him back to life. It was the yellow fever, you know. First poor little Nate, then Aunt Ann. She went from grief as much as the fever, and we were afraid it would take you, too, Matthew. Then, when you disappeared in China . . . Well, you can imagine."

"Father," Mrs. Sands put in, going to him, "you're upsetting everyone. This should be a happy day."

"She's right, Nephew," Mr. Lawson said. "That was all very long ago. I will always remember them with great love, but the grief has passed. Do you have children, Eleanor? Jacob?"

"Not yet," Mrs. Sands replied, "but—"

"We married late," Mr. Sands put in.

"And they are making up for lost time," old Robert said. "Eleanor is due in January."

"Congratulations!" Mr. Lawson exclaimed, and An-Ming said, "You must be very happy."

"I was both early and late to marriage," Mr. Lawson remarked. "It has been a blessing, a curse, and a blessing again. I am able to treasure all the memories now, as you will some day."

"And what of your present wife, Matthew?" old Robert asked. "Surely you didn't leave her back in China?"

"Jian-Ming died two years ago," Mr. Lawson said quietly.

Well, that tied a noose on things for a minute or two. Old Robert and Mrs. Sands kept saying the usual things – how sad it was and all – and Mr. Lawson and An-Ming kept thanking them and trying to change the subject.

Then Mr. Sands spoke up. "My father-in-law has told us that your son gave him a very humorous pet name, sir. Um . . . What was it?" He waved his hand, as if he were trying to conjure the memory. It seemed plain to me he was still trying to catch Mr. Lawson out as an imposter.

Mr. Lawson gave Sands an ice-cold smile. "*Robber*, Jacob. The entire family called him Robber. Only among the household, of course," he quickly assured Mrs. Sands. He smiled more warmly. "I daresay a Canton merchant might wear that name in public with some contrary pride, but a banker here in Boston? Best we keep it quiet."

"God bless you, Uncle!" old Robert replied, laughing. "I'm sure there are some who use it behind our backs, eh, Jacob?" Mr. Sands forced a smile. "Now, tell us what you have in that big box, Uncle. I'm sure Eleanor is absolutely bursting to know."

"Father!" she exclaimed, blushing. "It's not me bursting, it's you."

That gave everyone an excuse to laugh, and An-Ming obliged the old gent by leading us all back into the big room, where the others were still huddled by the doorway with the crate. An-Ming called them over and introduced Wang and Hu-Lan, who turned out to be An-Ming's *ahma*, which was not just a maid, but also a governess and chaperone and companion, all in one. Wang they called their manservant. Old Robert had to try his Chinese on them, which brought on more smiles, and it turned out Hu-Lan could speak English pretty well. I quietly slipped back beside the two crewmen, but Mr. Lawson even introduced me, as "our boatman and guide."

That brought an awkward nod from the old gent and his daughter, and stone silence from Mr. Sands. An-Ming stepped in again by coming over and opening the box I was holding.

When I saw what was inside, I felt like one of the Magi again. It was a necklace made of dark green jade and a bright red stone An-Ming said was coral, carved into birds and dragons, and divided by brilliant pearls as big around as my fingernails. Well, my little finger at least. An-Ming carried it to Mrs. Sands, who could hardly catch her breath. She was already wearing a fat brooch pinned at her throat, but she made a great fuss of taking it off and letting her father put the necklace around her neck. It showed up grand against the tiny lace and pink trim she was wearing. She gave An-Ming a hug and a kiss on the cheek, which sure made An-Ming blush.

An-Ming recovered by calling the two crewmen front and center to open the crate. They brought out boxes of tea, lacquered bowls and cups, animals carved from ivory and wood, a brass gong cast with long-legged birds, and beneath all that, whole bolts of fine silk in Chinese prints like An-Ming's dress. Mrs. Sands was happy as a child with a Christmas cake.

"I hope you don't already have a home full of such things," Mr. Lawson said. "I learned in Canton that the trade has changed considerably since the Opium Wars."

"It has failed, as far Boston is concerned," old Robert replied, "what with that and the damned auction tax. I don't think there are two houses left in town that still ship from China."

"It's all moved to New York," Mr. Sands explained. "Robert and my father were wise to get out of it when they did."

"It was hard to let go," the old man said. "There's still money to be made in the Mediterranean, the West Indies, South America. Ah, but I was never the seafarer you and Father were. Nor was John – John Sands, that is, Jacob's father."

"I remember John," Mr. Lawson said.

"He passed on rather young, God bless him, almost ten years ago. But Jacob stepped into his role very nicely. Very nicely," he repeated, giving Mr. Sands a smile. "He is our general manager now. And your arrival, Uncle, couldn't be more timely. I'm semi-retired from the day-to-day business, as you can imagine. No, don't try to gloss over my wrinkles with false protests; I know how old I am. And how old I feel. By God, Uncle, I am twenty years your junior, yet anyone looking at us would think it reversed! Must have been those Chinese teas, eh?" He chuckled at his own joke. "The fact is," he went on, "since you are not dead, you are still a partner, and you look in far better shape to be one than I am."

"Lord above," Mr. Lawson said. "It never even occurred to me. No, I couldn't. I—"

"Yes, you must," the old gent went on. "At the very least, you must be on the board, look over the books. We have investments in the railroads – absolutely necessary to survive in this business, you know – and in the new garment factories in Lowell and Needham. New industry, that is the ticket. Watches, for example. We have a share in the Boston Watch Company in South Boston, just began production this year. And then there's—"

"Father." Mr. Sands put a hand on the old gent's shoulder. "He did not come to rejoin the firm, as he himself just stated."

"I grant you, it is an interesting mix of investments," Mr.

Lawson said. "Watches, you say? Imagine that, Ann."

"It's only a very small share," Mr. Sands replied. "Not at all an important part of our portfolio."

"Surely you men can discuss such things later," Mrs. Sands said. "Uncle Matthew, I hope you and Ann will join us for dinner this afternoon, or perhaps supper this evening. I would so like to show you our home, and to hear about your adventures in China."

"You should stay with us while you're here," old Robert said. "You must be tired of that leaky boat after all those months at sea."

"Actually, our home is a bit crowded since Father moved in with us," Mr. Sands said. "But Boston can boast some of the finest hotels in the country. The Revere House is very comfortable."

"No, no," Mr. Lawson said. "Truth be told, I'm quite used to my cabin on the *Hang-Jinhe*. As to your kind invitation, Eleanor, I hope you'll forgive me if I ask leave to postpone it for a day. I have promised Captain Li that I will help him reprovision and repair, and also arrange some shore excursion for the crew. They are far from home."

"Certainly, Uncle Matthew" she replied. "Tomorrow then? At seven? And now I really must be getting Father home for his dinner and a nap."

But the old gent wasn't having it. He brought up the partnership again. "I will not let you off the hook so easily, Uncle. You are a partner, in my mind, and I daresay in the law's eyes as well. You must see the books."

"If you insist, Nephew, but you put too much stock in my business sense. It's Ann who runs the household since her mother's death. Including the investments. She has the head for it."

Old Robert blinked, then laughed. "If that's what it takes to get you involved, so be it! When can you come in, Ann?"

Everyone was struck dumb for a moment, he sounded so much like he meant it. Sands's face went red. Then he spluttered, "Yes, yes, very droll. A good jest. And now, Father, we must let Uncle Matthew get back to his ship to help his good captain."

Finally, we were away, and Mr. Lawson led us straight across the street, dodging cabs and wagons all the way down Merchant's Row to old Faneuil Hall. The sight of the three big market buildings between it and City Wharf gave him a start – he told us they weren't there when he left, nor the wharf neither – but it was the old hall he knew that thrilled him. He wandered in and out of the shops and along the rows of stalls and carts, and just about cheered when he discovered a barrel full of early apples. He had An-Ming buy a sack. Pat Delany, who'd been hanging around scratching notes on a pad, had the nerve to come up then and offer him a newspaper. Mr. Lawson was delighted, and even tipped him a penny. He read the paper on the spot, happily munching an apple.

An-Ming, meanwhile, ordered up a crate of chickens, two small pigs, dozens of eggs, and bushels of squashes and fruit and green goods to haul back to the junk, so everyone in the crew could have fresh food. It was fun to watch her bargain with the startled merchants, put off their guard by the appearance of a Chinese girl in an American dress and bonnet, speaking their own language. Hu-Lan hung at her side, silent and stern-looking, producing coins from a little purse she kept up one of the full sleeves of her overshirt.

There was more than me and the crewmen could carry, so I grabbed Pat and two other boys I knew and promised them each half a penny to help. Da shook his head when he saw the parade coming. But Mr. Lawson gave each boy a whole penny, plus an apple, despite An-Ming's glare. He was just thanking them when a police officer came up, all bustle and stick, to see what we were about. As soon as he saw the Chinese people, he was polite as could be. But he cast a warning eye at Da and me and my friends.

"Keep a careful watch on these Irish," he said. "Don't

overpay them or you'll never be rid of them, until they run off with the work half done."

"Thank you, my good man," Mr. Lawson said, "but I've been well served thus far."

"Whatever you say, sir," the officer replied. "Just keep an eye on 'em is my advice. You boys, get along now. You're done here." He would have shooed me, too, but Da came and stood by me, arms crossed.

"So, it's you, O'Neill," the officer said.

"They are my boatmen for the day," Mr. Lawson said, cutting in. Which was good, because I knew Da was about to say something a bit impolite to the officer.

"Good enough," the officer said. He gave Da a heavy scowl and watched us closely as we loaded the two boats and set off for the *Hang-Jinhe*.

The tide had turned again, so it was an easy row out, despite the cackling chickens and the squealing pigs. The cook must have heard us, because he was waiting at the rail when we arrived. Mr. Lawson went right to the clock cabin, and An-Ming disappeared with Hu-Lan. She was back out in hardly a skip, wearing her Chinese jacket and pants, with her braid down her back, and looking far more like herself.

Da pulled out the bucket with our dinner in it and we ate in silence in the canoe. One of the crew handed down some more of the lemon water, which was nice. Then Da sent me up to check on Peter. There was still time enough in the day to find another in-bound ship, he said. Da was paid regular every day, but my pay depended on how much business Peter got.

I made my way into the stern house and was halfway along the passage when I heard Mr. Lawson say, "Yes, that's right, I left for Canton in 1799. I met Wu ten years later. He saved me from certain death, and while I was recovering, I fell in love with his daughter, Jian-Ming. Wu and I became friends, and he gave me two great gifts: permission to marry Jian-Ming, and this clock."

By then I had come up to the doorway. Peter and Mr. Lawson were both seated at the table. The chronometer was out of its box and lying on its face, back open, showing gears and springs. The other clock – Mr. Lawson's Chinese clock – was open, too. They ticked and tocked in different rhythms.

"Is An-Ming's mother . . .?" Peter let the question hang.

"She died two years ago," Mr. Lawson said. He looked up at the other clock, on the shelf above them. I couldn't help notice it was stopped, and a shiver went down my spine. "We both miss her terribly."

"I'm sorry," Peter said.

Mr. Lawson took a deep breath. "Yes. Thank you. Well, you've done an excellent job with this chronometer, as near as I can tell. As I said, I'm no clock-maker myself. Wu always hired one of the Portuguese or French from Macao. Never the same one. They were of mixed abilities, as you can see from this." He gestured at the innards of his clock. "What do you think? Can you rebuild it along the lines of a marine chronometer? Something truly precise? Something that will last a very long time?" Then he noticed me lurking outside the doorway. "Finn! What are you doing standing there, young man? Come in."

I felt a little guilty, having stood so long eavesdropping. "Da just sent me, sir," I said, making like I had just arrived. "He was wondering when Mr. Jenkins might be finished."

"I just have to close up these clocks," Peter said, "and then a few more minutes to discuss some business." He checked his pocket watch. "Tell your father we might very well have time to call upon another ship or two."

"Yes, sir," I said, skipping out fast, so's not to give them the chance to think about what I might have heard.

Peter was another half hour. I could hear more than one steeple clock ringing as he came out. He checked his pocket watch again and shook his head. The pocket chronometer was part of his toolkit from the Bonds, and he was always timing the other clocks against it. Boston didn't have a noon gun or ball or other regular time signal, so Peter depended on that pocket watch.

Mr. Lawson came out with him and paid Da for our extra bit of work, and we pulled away feeling mighty rich for the day. Da had spotted a new arrival drop anchor a little farther out in the roadway, so we rowed over as soon as Peter had settled himself in the stern. It turned out they had no use for him, but there was another a wee bit farther out, and they did indeed have need of a chronometer man. So Peter got in two that day at full fee, and we were all well paid.

It was going on evening when we finally headed back in toward the wharves. I asked Peter if he was going to be doing more work for Mr. Lawson, and he gave me a look.

"How much did you overhear, Finn?" he asked.

"I heard that he wants you to make a new clock for him," I admitted, leaving out the rest.

"Yes, that's true."

"And will you?"

"I don't know," Peter replied. "I shall have to put it to Mr. Bond. I hope so."

He smiled, and I couldn't resist a bit of teasing. "Are you hoping about the clock or pretty An-Ming?"

Peter's big ears turned bright red under the brim of his topper. "Well, not . . . It has nothing to do with . . . I meant the clock, of course."

"You be minding your own business, Finn!" Da warned. His shoulders shook. He might have been coughing, but maybe it was a laugh.

"Just what does that clock do, Peter?" I asked. "I didn't see hands on it anywhere."

Peter hesitated, and I had the feeling I was about to be lied to. "I don't know for sure," he finally said. "It's more of an astrological clock, marking out the turning of the celestial seasons. Some of the symbols are signs of the Chinese

Zodiac, Mr. Lawson said. I expect I'll learn more if I'm able to do the work."

"Would you be taking the clock to Bond's shop then?" Da asked.

"Oh, no, Mr. Lawson was quite clear about that," Peter assured him. "All of the work is to be done on board the junk. I will still need your services. In fact, I will insist on it."

"Thank you, Peter," I said. Da grunted.

We dropped Peter off at Central Wharf, then pulled around to Lewis Wharf, where we kept our boat. It was coming on dark, and the heat of the day was giving way to a damp night. Da started coughing again, and it took him some time to stop.

"I'm fine!" he growled when it was all done.

"I didn't say nothing, Da."

"Keep it that way. I'll see you back home." He reached for the ladder.

"Da? I should bring the pay home if you're not coming right off."

"Is that so? Well, I'll be giving you something to bring." He raised the flat of his hand.

I knew better than to cringe. "Ma said."

He lowered his hand. "She did, didn't she. All right, then." He counted out half of the coins. "Here's the daily wage from Jenkins. And here's for squiring the crazy gent around." He put another two bits in my palm. "That should satisfy her."

"Yes, sir. Thank you."

He grunted and heaved himself up the ladder. I wondered if we'd see him for supper, or not till we were all abed. There were times when I hated my da, and times he deserved it. That day was a draw.

I set about putting the boat tidy. There wasn't all that much to do, but Da liked it done right. I put the oars together along the thwarts with the tight bundle of the little sail and spars, then pulled the bailer from its nook under the stern thwart. The boat was getting older, like Da, and it took on an inch or two of water through the day. The bailer was a worn wooden scoop, and I always wondered where Da had found it . . . or nicked it. He'd always had it, in every boat I could remember. There was a bit of rag tucked up high in the bow, right under the breasthook. I used that to mop up the last of the water. Da always said a dry boat lasted longer. Faith, Da was more particular about that boat than about his own self.

I draped the rag over the oar-lock, shouldered the oars and sail, and made my way up the ladder. The gear went into the wharfinger's shed, then I headed toward the street. Lewis Wharf was lined from end to end on both sides with ships, their tall masts and long yards sketching crossbars on the twilight. There was one in particular that drew me: the *Flying Fish*. She was a California clipper, long and lean and the tallest ship in the harbor at the time, rigged seven yardarms high, all the way up to skysails. She sailed for the Glidden and Williams line, along with the *Morning Light* and *Spitfire*, and she was bound out for San Francisco in only eight more days. I had dreamed of signing on as a seaman and sailing off to California, where there was gold and open land and a chance to be rich and well-to-do for anyone who could get there, even an Irishman. Until that day, it was all I could think of.

Now there was the *Hang-Jinhe* and An-Ming, Wang and Hu-Lan, and Mr. Lawson and his strange astrological clock. What a news story Pat could make of this, I thought. I put away my California dreaming, for the moment at least, and hurried off the cobbled wharf toward home to tell Ma and Bridget everything that had happened.

Chapter 5

MA WOKE FIRST EVERY morning. She and Da had taken over the side room when Molly and Grace moved out. Now Bridget was sleeping on the bench in what had been their corner of the main room, and I slept on a bench in the opposite corner, with a curtain between us. Both rooms were small, and there was no staying asleep once Ma was up. It was her lighting the lamp and rattling at the stove that got me to stirring. I pulled on my pants and shirt and took the pail down to the alley to get water from the city tap. By the time I got back, Bridget had pulled back the curtain, put away our blankets, and emptied the chamber pot. Ma had the fire going in the stove and the supper leftovers heating up.

I could hear Da breathing heavily in the side room. He'd come in sometime late, trying to be quiet as usual and not doing a good job of it, what with the coughing and the cursing when he banged his shin on Ma's chair. We all pretended to be asleep until he was settled and snoring. Up till then, the evening had been almost a party. Pat Delany came by. Then the Ryans and Dooleys from downstairs and the Dohertys from above and the Baileys from across the hall had all come in to hear me tell of the Chinese junk that had appeared like magic in the harbor. The word had gone round Boston fast as bird song, but I had the real tale. And Da not there to butt in. It made me the chief of the day.

We let Da lie in till the coffee was hot. Or tea, when we could afford it. Sometimes it was just plain hot water, but that wasn't too often. We were luckier than most in the North End in those days. Ma and Da both had regular jobs, and Molly and Grace were out and making their own way, so there were two less mouths to feed. And Bridget and I were adding a little bit, me rowing with Da, and her putting in a few hours with Ma at Mr. Tierney's tailor shop after school let out each day. I had Ma's looks, but Bridget had her skill with the needle and thread. She could have worked full time sewing for Mr. Tierney, but Ma wouldn't let her quit school till she was thirteen, and Da agreed with her on that. They'd made me go all the way through, too.

"It's the only way you'll get ahead here in America," Da would say. "It's not enough to be strong and willing. You're going to have to outwit 'em." It was one of the reasons he never let me row with him before. That and Tim being there already, three years older than me and built big and strong like Da. And even after Tim died, Ma insisted I had to finish school and try to get a job off the water. Da could have over-ruled her, but he didn't. Tim was meant to follow after him. I wasn't, and could never replace him. Da finally did take me on when the rent doubled and there was no job for me after school, but no one could fill that hole in his heart.

After breakfast, Ma and Bridget would clean up, while I put some dinner in the pail for Da and me. Then we'd all leave. In September, dawn would just be paling the sky. We'd thread our way out the narrow lane of Snowhill Place to Margaret Street, then down its steep hill to Prince Street, then along Prince to North Square, joining the general flow of men and women looking for work. We were among the few that always had a job waiting at the end of the walk.

We'd cut through the alley beside the Sailors Bethel, zig and zag, and finally come out Lewis Street right across Commercial from Lewis Wharf.

There was always a line of men ahead of us, at the wharfinger's office and by the ships, hoping to get the nod for shifting cargo. There were never enough jobs to go around, and what there were paid next to nothing, but they were all that most of the Irish could hope for. That or the factories or the digs and landfills, and for some of those you needed money for the ferry or the omnibus. I could feel the hungry stares of the waiting men as Da and I fetched the oars and sail from the shed. A few of them knew him from the taverns and gave a greeting. From most it was no more than a sullen nod. And that was all Da gave back those days when he'd been out late drinking and the results rattled hard in his chest. He'd cough and spit. I'd say a word to my own friends, but I'd stay out of his reach while we climbed down to the boat and set off.

That morning, we found Peter already waiting for us at the end of Central Wharf. He was wearing a pleased smile beneath his topper, and fairly scampered down the ladder.

"Mr. Bond has approved the arrangement with Mr. Lawson," he said, "with the one condition that we spend the first half of each day at our usual round and only work for Mr. Lawson after noon. Mr. Bond says he can't afford to ignore our usual custom outright. That seems reasonable, don't you think? I'm sure Mr. Lawson won't mind."

Da grunted, as if it made no difference one way or the other to him. Me, I felt like cheering.

We rowed out to the *Hang-Jinhe* first thing, to let Mr. Lawson know. Peter went on board to explain the arrangement, but was back in a minute to ask Da and me to join him. When we went up, we were confronted with the sight of a half-dozen of the crew dancing on the deck. That's what it looked like, at least. Wang was at the front, leading them. And a strange dance it was: turning this way and that, pushing out their arms, kicking up their feet, spinning on their heels, but all of it done slow as molasses in winter. And there was An-Ming and Hu-Lan doing the same thing up on the poop deck. I think Mr. Lawson might have been doing it, too. He was back in his Chinese clothes and seemed a bit sweaty, though how you could work up a sweat moving so slowly was a mystery to me.

It turned out that Mr. Lawson wanted to ask Da if he could go speak to the chandler that morning with Captain Li and the cook. Mr. Lawson said he was willing to pay, of course, and just wanted to be sure neither of us minded me taking the boat with Peter on my own. Da gave me a look up and down, then studied the clear sky and calm water and allowed that I could probably handle it, as long as I kept on eye on the weather and left the sail alone. It made me mad he had to sound off like a schoolmarm with a dunce, as if I'd never been in the boat alone before. I knew the wind would pick up later in the day. Anyway, Peter and I set out into the harbor, leaving Da to ferry Captain Li and the others in the junk's little scow.

The morning turned out grand. The breeze came on soon enough, and I put up the mast and the spritsail, Da be damned, and Peter and I made a swooping run over the chop from ship to ship. He found a taker, and I waited as patient as I could while he went on board to clean and adjust their chronometer. We went farther out after that, through the narrows into President Roads. Just below the Deer Island beacon, we came on an in-bound brig loaded with fruit from the Mediterranean. The captain headed her up and luffed barely long enough for me to set Peter on the ladder, then filled away for the inner harbor. I followed the sweet scent of limes all the way back in. By the time I caught up with them, they were moored off Rowe's Wharf waiting for a gap, and Peter was almost ready to go. We were back at the *Hang-Jinhe* just as Peter's watch showed noon, and the church towers began to chime.

But the ladder was blocked by the handsome canoe that belonged to the new Harbor Police. The deputy mayor was there, speaking with Mr. Lawson and An-Ming. It turned out he'd come out the day before, when we'd all been at the bank. No one on board could understand him then, so he'd left a note for Mr. Lawson. Now he was back to bring the official greeting and gawk at everything.

I pushed us in beside the police boat and Peter hurried up, anxious not to be late his first day of work. I stowed the sail and followed, just in time to hear the deputy mayor invite Mr. Lawson and the whole crew to the Town Hall to meet the mayor and "receive the honors rightly due to a native son long thought lost yet here resurrected after so long an absence." He did lay it on. Mr. Lawson tried to play it all down and said he didn't mean to cause such a fuss, but the deputy mayor was not to be put off. They had to arrange a date for the ceremony before the fellow would leave. Mr. Lawson waved him off, then quickly shut himself up with Peter in the clock room, with Wang guarding the door. Wang knew enough English to let me know I wasn't welcome. Da, it turned out, had taken his pay and stayed in Boston, so there I was left kicking my heels. I went back on deck, wondering what I might do to pass the time. Captain Li had the crew at work, scraping and painting, and I was about to offer to help, when An-Ming hurried out of the stern cabin.

"Come," she said. "Quick." She just about pulled me to the ladder.

"What's all the hurry?" I asked.

"No time for questions. Quick quick!" And she skipped down the ladder into the boat. She was wearing her Chinese outfit again, the one with trousers instead of a dress.

"Row to wharf," she told me, untying the painter before I was even off the ladder.

"Which one?" I asked, pushing off and fitting my oars into the locks.

She put a broad straw hat on her head and took the tiller. "One I haven't seen. I want to visit city without Hu-Lan and Father telling me what to do."

That was something I could understand. "Right, then. Steer us straight toward the tall steeple on the height of the North End. That's Old North, where Paul Revere showed the lanterns to warn the Colonial Army the British were coming."

"Who is Paul Revere?"

I told her as I rowed to Lewis Wharf. She'd heard about the Revolutionary War at least. She was just a bit weak on the details.

"Well, you don't need to know all that," I said as we climbed onto the wharf. "It was all way back when. This is now."

I swung my arm in an arc that took in the crowded wharf, the carts and wagons, the longshoremen and teamsters, the stacks of crates and barrels, the hundreds of people working the busy stores and bays in the great granite block of a building that towered five stories high to the eaves. And the line of ships whose masts towered even higher.

"We keep our boat here," I said. "It's the wharfinger's really; we just rent it. He's the wharf manager and handles everything, rents out the stores and lofts, takes the wharf fees and all. And look here," I said, leading her to the *Flying Fish*. "Isn't she a beauty? She'll be leaving for California any day now. Did you come that way? Did you stop in San Francisco?" I don't know why it hadn't occurred to me before, but now the thought had me jumping.

"No," she said. "Valparaiso, in Chile."

"Oh. Oh, well."

"That disappoints you. You want to go to California?"

"I do," I admitted. "Someday. If I can."

"Then you should."

"I couldn't leave Ma and Bridget," I said, "even if I could

pay the fare."

"Yes, family duty must not be forgotten."

I could have forgotten it, if Da had been well, but I didn't tell her that.

"Where do you live?" she asked. "Show me."

"Oh, you don't want to see that," I said. "There's far more interesting sights."

"No, show me. I can see buildings any day. Show me a home."

I was going to argue with her, but I noticed we were gathering stares. After all, here was An-Ming in her Chinese hat and clothes, with her big fat braid all the way down to her backside.

"All right then," I said, "follow me. And could you maybe try to walk like a boy?"

"What? Why?"

"I'll tell you when we're moving," I said. "Come on, quick quick." She frowned at my teasing, but she came. "A few months back, a woman named Snodgrass walked out in men's clothes and upset half the town," I explained, leading her as quickly as I could through the workers and wagons and all. "She was trying to make a point about petticoats and women's suffrage. You're just wanting to get out on your own in secret, I know that, but sure you're father is going to hear about it if we stand still for any length of time. Folks are going to notice you no matter what, and best they think you're a boy. Pretend you're Hu-Lan's son."

"Hu-Lan's son?" She would've stopped if I hadn't grabbed her hand and pulled.

"Wang's then. Captain Li's. Whoever. Just not a girl."

I didn't take her to the house, not right off. I was embarrassed. Her cousins were Brahmins and bankers who lived on the rich side of Beacon Hill. Her da could afford to hire his own sea-going junk, crew and all. She had her own servant. I imagined they lived in a pretty fine house back in China. She didn't need to see our two tiny rooms.

Instead, I took her along the curve of Commercial Street, past all the wharves. The street itself was a wharf wherever it bordered the water, and the bowsprits of the innermost ships hung over our heads as we made our way between piles of cargo. I took her out on Constitution Wharf to watch the Mystic Ferry come in, and out on Gray's Wharf, for the view of Charlestown and the Bunker Hill Monument and the shipyards on Border Street in East Boston. I pointed out the *Great Republic*, on the ways at MacKay's shipyard, the biggest clipper ever to be built. And then I took her around to Ingersoll's Wharf, for a favorite treat.

Running all the way down the middle of the wharf was a tremendous stack of barrels, five high and four deep, filled with molasses from the West Indies. It was always there, new ones added as fast as the old ones could be carted off. There were always a few that leaked, and the cobbles around the stack were brown and sticky. Flies loved it, and at night you could always spot a big rat or two sampling the stuff. An-Ming and I ran our fingers along the leaking seams, scooping up a free taste of the dark, musky sweet, then ran off, laughing, when a longshoreman chased us away.

I would have gone farther along the waterfront then, but she'd seen enough of wharves.

"Show me where you live, Finn," she said again. "I want to see a real home."

"You'll be going to the Sands' place for supper soon," I pointed out.

"*Wa!* He is rich as a Mandarin. 'He fills his house with potted limes, yet cannot see the blossoms beyond his gate.'"

I wondered where she'd gotten that. "If you say so."

She laughed. "Another said it first. Come, show me your home."

So I took her up over Copp's Hill, past the boarding houses for the sailors and into the crowded warren that had once been fine homes. We walked past shacks crammed into the alleys right beside stinking privies, where wet wash hung out the windows, getting dirty with coal soot as it dried. Where men and women who couldn't find work that day sat on the door stoops, trying to find some hope in a shaft of sunlight, or a little gossip, or a bottle of home-made gin. Where little children in the same tattered clothes they'd worn on the boat from Ireland trudged up from the wharves with rotten fruit or a few broken slats to burn in the stove that night.

"*Zaogao!*" An-Ming muttered. "Why aren't they working?"

"There's not enough jobs."

"Why don't they leave and find jobs. America is huge."

"They don't have the money for a ferry ride, let alone train fare. It's not the same America for the Irish."

"But you and your father don't . . ." She waved her hand, letting the scene speak for itself.

"We got here early," I said, "a year before the famine came to Ireland. Ma and Da already had jobs when the flood of immigrants started arriving. We already had a place to live. Though that didn't stop the landlord from taking half of it away to make into more rooms, and then charging twice the rent every year."

"You live near this?"

"We live in it. You'll see soon enough."

Snowhill Place was a jog off the main streets, hardly more than an alley, with a sliver of sky you could sometimes glimpse between the lines of laundry. We lived on the third floor, so we got some light in the windows. That day the light showed every crack in the plaster.

"*Aiyo*," An-Ming said as I let her in. She turned a circle, surveying the small main room, then peeked into the side room. "It is small. But clean," she added quickly, "and bright, with large windows. Very good for fresh air."

"The winters can be blessed cold," I said. "That's when

you want to have one of the cellar rooms. But sure, this is fine most of the year."

She did another turn. "Where is your room?" she asked.

"Right there," I said, pointing to my corner. "Bridget sleeps on the other side."

"You have a sister?"

"I have three. Molly and Grace moved out when they got jobs. Molly works in a glove factory out in Waltham. That's hard because we don't get to see her much. Grace is maid for a family on Beacon Hill. One of the – what did you call 'em? Mandarins? We call them Brahmins. The girls used to sleep in the side room there, and Tim and I slept out here, with Ma and Da."

"Seven people?" Her eyes darted around the room, remeasuring.

"We've had as many as twenty-five," I said. "Ma's cousins. We put 'em up for a few months, until they found their own place over by Fort Hill. There've been others, too, but that was the most."

"And now only four, much better. Where is Tim? Does he have work, too?"

"He died. Four years ago." I didn't mention that he'd have had my job if he'd lived.

"*Wa!* What happened?"

"Cholera. Seven hundred or so died, mostly Irish. Half of Ma's cousins. It was worse on Fort Hill. Tim went over in the morning to help and was dead by nightfall."

Da and I had gone over to get his body the next morning. It had already half rotted, cholera did that to you. I still dream about it sometimes. None of us talked about it then, not at home. Da wouldn't let us. Ma, she lit a candle every week at church.

"I'm sorry," An-Ming said. "You miss him."

"I do."

"What was he like?"

"The spitting image of Da, but not so quick with his fists.

He liked to laugh, Tim did. He got that from Da, too. The two of them, they used to go on like . . . Da doesn't laugh so much anymore." I couldn't think of anything else to say after that. I remembered Tim, how he used to fill up the room with his smile. How he seemed so much older, but still treated me as much like a friend as a brother. How he would take me out in the boat and let me row. "Maybe we should be getting back."

"Not yet. Take me some place to make you happy."

"California?"

She laughed. "A long row. Some place closer."

"All right, then, I know the place. Come on."

Chapter 6

I LED AN-MING out Margaret Street and down to the corner of Prince and Salem to Hurley's bar. Its real name was *Ma Maire Ban* – My Fair Mary – and it was run by James Hurley, who also owned a little grocery shop next door. Everyone in the neighborhood just called it Hurley's. It opened at noon, served meals, took credit, and was a clean place where the wife and family were welcome. The best thing was the music. Hurley himself played the fiddle, when he wasn't too busy to join in. His wife, Mary, played the flute even better, and there was often another fiddler on hand – I can remember at least six neighbors who played, and one or two who could play the whistle, and more than enough who could tap out a rhythm on the big, round *bodhran* drum Hurley kept hung behind the bar. An-Ming and I could hear the drumbeats and the music as we came near. And there was singing, too.

An-Ming made a face.

"What's the matter?" I asked. "Don't you like it?"

"It is very different from music at home," she said. We listened a minute longer. "Very hard to understand."

"It's Irish," I told her.

"You speak Irish?"

"What's in the songs. I was born in Dublin. They speak English there mostly, and I was only three when we moved. But a lot of the old folk and the newcomers, that's all they speak."

"Will I be able to understand inside?"

"You can understand me, can't you?" I asked.

"Usually. When you speak English."

"I don't speak English," I said, "I speak American. You'll get used to it." I had my hand on the door when I recognized one of the voices that chimed in on the chorus. I dropped my hand. Da was in there, and he was in his cups, I could tell from the way he was singing. I tried to make an excuse for not going in. "It's my da. He'll recognize you right off."

"He has seen me in these clothes," she said. "He will understand. Come."

Before I could say another word, she pulled open the door and went in.

There were still some hours in the workday, but there were a dozen or so people inside, plus the musicians. Mary Hurley was there with her flute, and Hurley himself on the fiddle, and a third fellow I didn't know beating out the rhythm on Hurley's big *bodhran*. They had a space cleared by the side wall, opposite the long bar that stretched three-quarters of the narrow room. The rest of the place was taken by trestle tables arranged to face the music. Hurley hadn't lit the lamps yet, but the light from the front windows showed a happy group. You should have seen their faces when An-Ming came in.

"Hello, Mr. Hurley," I said, before Da could speak up. "This is Li Wang-Hu. He's one of the fellows from the *Hang-Jinhe*, Mr. Lawson's junk. I'm showing him around."

"Well don't just stand there, Finn, bring him right in!" Hurley exclaimed. He set down his fiddle and hurried to the bar. "And a good welcome to you, Mr. Hu. Or is it Wang-Hu?" An-Ming was too busy glaring at me to answer. "I'm sorry, Finn, does he speak the language?"

"I daresay he does," Da put in, giving me a wink over the top of a pint. "I've been telling you, Jimmy, they're a civilized bunch out there."

I breathed a sigh of relief. Da was in a good mood.

"It's Mr. Li, sir," I told Hurley. "They put the family name first in China. But you can call him Wang-Hu. "

"Family name first, eh? How about that. Well, we've been reading all about you folks in the newspapers, Wang-Hu, and Mike here, Finn's da, he's been telling us the rest. Welcome to Boston. Would you like a drink? How about yourself, Finn? It's on the house, for bringing in such a special guest."

"Don't be giving them any of your rotten *poitín*, Jimmy," Da said. "His mother would kill me, and you, too. It'd be wasted on 'em anyway."

"I'll waste the poteen on you then, Mike. How about some cider, lads?"

"That'd be fine, thank you, sir," I said. "It's made from apples," I told An-Ming. "You'll like it." Poteen was whiskey, home-made at that, and I wasn't about to let An-Ming try it.

"I know cider," she said. "Thank you, Mr. Hurley."

"Well, listen to that," Hurley said, drawing two full cups of cider from a keg behind the bar. "You speak English very well."

"Thank you," she said, speaking carefully again. "Finn tries to teach me American, but I think he makes up words. Someday I will have to teach him manners."

"Good luck with that, lass," Da muttered.

"I'm sure you will someday, Wang-Hu," I said quickly, hoping to cover Da's slip. I took the cups from Hurley, gave her the fullest, and lifted mine in a toast. "*Slaínte*."

"Is that American? Or Finn-ish?"

Hurley laughed. "Now that's a good one. He can even joke in the language. And it's Irish he was just speaking to you, Wang-Hu. It means 'good health.' Now sit, and here's some potatoes and fish cakes. You can't drink without eating in Boston," he added, when she started to protest. "It's the law. We'll play you a song while you eat. What do you fancy, Finn?"

"*Nell Flaherty's Drake*," I said. It was my favorite.

"Good choice!" Hurley replied, crossing the room to take up his fiddle. "Start us off, Tommy."

The drummer tapped a quick flourish on the *bodhran*, the Hurleys joined in for a measure, and then the drummer started singing:

"Oh, my name it is Nell and the truth for to tell,
I come from Cootehill, which I'll never deny,
I had a fine drake, and I'd die for his sake,
That my grandmother left me and she going to die.
The dear little fellow, his legs they were yellow;
He could fly like a swallow and swim like a hake,
Till some dirty savage, to grease his white cabbage,
Most wantonly murdered my beautiful drake."

It goes on for another verse about how big and beautiful the old drake was, then launches into the good part, the cursing of the robber that murdered Nell Flaherty's drake:

"May his pig never grunt, may his cat never hunt,
May a ghost ever haunt him in dark of the night,
May his hen never lay, may his ass never bray,
May his goat fly away like an old paper kite.
May every old fairy from Cork to Dunleary
Dip him, song and airey, in some pond or lake,
That the eel and the trout, they may slime in the snout
Of the monster that murdered Nell Flaherty's drake."

And that was just the start of it. Tommy the drummer sang us all eight verses: the lice and the fleas, the monkeys and man-apes and weasels, the four-year-old bug in the murderer's ear – even the scurvy and itch in his britches. It's a fast song, and more than one person was joining in on their favorite parts. By the end of it, An-Ming was looking a bit confused.

"It's about a woman whose duck is stolen and eaten, so she calls down a long line of curses on the head of the thief," I explained.

"But what it's really about," Da said, "is Robert Emmet, an Irish rebel and hero, who was murdered by the English for trying to make his country free. And the curses in the song don't go nearly far enough."

An-Ming looked even more confused.

"Don't mind him, Wang-Hu," Mary Hurley said. "It's old history."

"Not to some," Da replied.

"You're here in America now, Mike O'Neill," Mary said.

"And what do I find when I get here?" Da demanded. "A pack of so-called Brahmins, trying to out-British the English, that's what."

Da had a look on his face, a look that was spoiling for a fight. But before he could get in another word, An-Ming held up her cup and said very loudly, "Very good cider, Mr. Hurley. More please?"

"With pleasure," Hurley replied, a look of relief on his face. "Mary, Tom, play something sweet for us while I pour."

So they started in on "The Sick Young Lover," which was half in Irish and half in English, about a young man who had lost his love, or never won her in the first place – I wasn't sure on that part. Hurley was pouring out a cup for each of us, when An-Ming slipped a small purse from inside her sleeve and pulled out some coins.

"Let me pay you," she said, but Hurley wouldn't have it. "Then this is for the music," she insisted, putting a dollar on the counter. It was Spanish, and it was gold.

Hurley quickly covered the coin with his big hand, glancing around to see who else had noticed. "That's mighty generous of you, young Mr. Li," he said quietly, "but you'd best be keeping such a fat purse out of sight, if you see what I mean. Now you drink up, and I'll make sure this goes to the right place."

He rejoined the musicians in time for the last verse, where the young lover says:

"I'm drunk today and I'm rarely sober,
A handsome rover, from town to town.
Oh, but I am sick now, and my days are numbered,
Come all ye young men and lay me down."

"Now, how about the *The Minstrel Boy*?" Hurley said.

"She doesn't want to hear that," Da objected. "She'll think the only songs we know are about dying."

"*He* won't mind, Da," I said. "I'm sure *he* won't. It's a fine song."

"I've got a new one," Tommy put in. "I just learned it in New York, at the music hall. It's got some dying in it, but it all comes right in the end. And there's a chorus. I'll teach it to you." He set down the drum and pulled a penny whistle from his coat pocket. "It's called *Finnegan's Wake*, and here's the tune."

So he played it through twice and then taught us all the chorus, which went something like *"Whack fol the dah doh, dance to your partner, around the floor your trotters shake. Wasn't it the truth I told you, lots of fun at Finnegan's wake."*

But the start of the song went, *"Tim Finnegan lived in Watkin Street . . ."* Tim was a common enough name, but there was only one Tim in our family. I looked over at Da in time to see him hide his face behind a swig from his pint, and when he came back up at the end of the verse, he stayed quiet on the chorus. I don't remember all of the song, but Tim Finnegan takes a fall and cracks his skull, dead as a post. His friends take him home and lay him out for a proper wake, and then the poteen begins to flow. Before you know it, they're fighting tooth and nail, women and men both, and the pints of whiskey go flying across the room. Some of it splashes on Time, and the song goes:

"Tim revives! See how he rises
Tim he rises from the dead,

Says, 'Whirl your whiskey around like blazes!
Name of the de'il, do you think I'm dead!'"

In the silence after the applause, I heard Da mutter, "Drink doesn't cure a blessed thing."

Mary Hurley heard him, too. "No, Mike, it doesn't," she said. "It's time that cures all ills, if you'd let it."

Da looked up at her. "There's nothing cures the fact of death, Mary. Time just gives you longer to feel it. Come on, Finn. It's time we were getting the young miss . . . the young Mis*ter* Li back to the junk."

That seemed like a good idea. Da was going to call her 'Miss Lawson' any minute.

As soon as we were outside, he gave me a cuff on the back of the head.

"What do you mean, bringing the young lady round here?"

"I told him to, Mr. O'Neill," An-Ming said.

"He should have stopped you."

"He tried, but I am his employer."

"Then he should have warned you to change your clothes, Miss. Only a fool would believe you're a boy."

"That *was* his idea," she said, slipping me an 'I told you so' smile.

"Not a blessed soul noticed, Da," I protested. "Until you spilled the beans."

"Oh, it was me, was it?"

"I'm sure all saw only my Chinese face," An-Ming put in. "They excuse my different clothing for that."

"Here maybe," Da grumbled, "but don't try passing it off on Beacon Hill. You get her right back to the junk, Finn."

"It is time we return to be ready for supper with Lawson and Sands," An-Ming said, in a tone that didn't so much agree with Da as make it her plan all along. She picked up her pace, so I had to hurry to keep up and show the way. Da fell behind. "Walk like boy now?" she murmured.

We came out of Lewis Street and crossed Commercial,

dodging around a press of wagons and carts hauling cargo to the *Flying Fish*. Lewis Wharf was as crowded as I'd ever seen it, men and carts and wagons covering up every cobble. Down past the *Flying Fish*, a line of longshoremen were feeding the coils of a fat hawser out of a huge hogshead, across the wharf, up the gangway, and down into the forechains of one of the Liverpool packet ships. An-Ming ducked right under the thick rope, but one of the men got in my way. I dodged around and ducked under just in time to run smack dab into a rough-looking teamster dragging a fat crate off the back end of a donkey cart. I swear he hadn't been there a moment before.

I skipped sidewise, hardly able to keep my feet, but the teamster staggered back as if I'd been an oak piling. He rounded on me and threw down the crate, barely missing my toes.

"Watch where you're going, you dumb little mick!" he yelled. He peered at me, fists clenched. "What you think, you own this wharf? Get out of my way before I knock you back to Ireland where you belong!"

Chapter 7

The teamster was a thick-necked thug. He was aching for a fight, and he deserved one for the insults. But I had An-Ming to worry about. I glanced down the wharf to make sure she was all right.

The thug grabbed my shoulder and swung me face-to. "Don't turn your back on me, Mick, not when I'm talking to you!"

"I'm just try—" I started to say, but he shook me.

"Are you talking back to me?"

I clenched me fists, trying to keep my temper down. "I said I'm just trying to catch up to my friend. I'll be happy to get out of your way, as soon as you let go of me."

He tightened his grip, shouting all the while. "Oh, it's my fault now, eh? I've a good mind to—"

Suddenly Da was there, one big hand wrapped around the teamster's wrist. "You've got no mind at all, near as I can see," he said. His voice was low, almost quiet, which wasn't a good thing. Now I had to worry about calming him down, too.

I pulled out of the thug's grip. "It's all right, Da," I said. "I just bumped into him is all, and now I'll be getting along, no harm done."

"That's not what I saw," Da said, still clamped hard on the fellow's wrist. "It seems to me this clumsy loud-mouth owes you an apology." The thug glared and tried to jerk his hand free. He might as well have been yanking at an anchor.

"There's no need for one," I said, "and no time. I need to row An-Ming back to the junk."

I looked for her again, and realized we were closed in by a ring of men. More like two half rings. The half behind Da was all Irish stevedores. The other half was teamsters, lined up behind the thug. Everyone of them, on both sides, had an ugly frown pasted on his mug.

"Let him go, Da, please. These men don't need to be losing their jobs over one bump." I turned to the teamster. "I didn't mean to bother you," I said. "I'm sor—"

"No!" Da growled. "Get along! I won't have you apologizing to one like this." He threw the fellow's wrist free and stood facing him, ready for any false move. I could see the man swallow, but he stood his ground.

At that moment, An-Ming pushed her way through the gap in the two lines. "What is this?" she asked. "A problem?"

Da and I both looked her way, and the thug struck.

It was a hard right, but Da seemed to sense it coming. Maybe he knew the man would try it, maybe he wanted him to. Either way he was ready for it. A dip to the left, a slight turn. The thug's swing missed Da's jaw and just barely clipped his ear. Da was back at him in a flash, with a jab to the face that rocked the man back on his heels.

Then all Hell broke loose. The teamsters and the stevedores went at each other yelling like a flock of furies. I almost got knocked down in the rush. I ducked a fist thrown by one of the teamsters, and a stevedore went at him before I could even think to try it myself. All I could think about was An-Ming.

"Anie!" I cried, but I doubt anyone heard it over the hubbub. Someone stumbled against me. Another man went sprawling and almost tripped me. Fists were flying right, left, and sideways. The poor carthorse shrieked with fear and reared, dumping crates into the melee. More men went flat, then grabbed the broken staves and leaped up, flailing at any head in sight.

I stumbled out of the press, almost to the edge of the wharf before I got clear.

"Anie!" I yelled again. And I saw her, farther down the wharf. Someone tumbled out of the mob and made a grab at her, but she dodged him easily, slipping sideways slick as an eel and catching his foot with hers as she did it. He went flat on his face. She'd lost her hat, and her long braid had sprung free, whipping round her every time she moved.

I ran to her, reached for her arm. She twirled, braid and arms flying. Her fingernails stopped a hair from my eyes.

"*Wa!*" she cried. "Do not sneak up!"

"I think I'll remember that," I gasped.

A shrill whistle cut through the clamor of the brawl. I grabbed An-Ming's arm and pulled her down the wharf toward the ladder. "Police! Let's get out of here!"

She set her heels. "Wait! Your father, he is still in the fight!"

"Right where he wants to be," I muttered, "and there's no way we're going to get to him."

She came with me. She didn't want to, but she came.

More whistles shrilled, coming closer. A glance back showed me dark blue uniforms and polished top hats pushing through the spectators massed at the street. The fight began to break up, the brawlers fleeing up and down the wharf and into the stalls. But storekeepers barred their doors, and the ships' crews blocked their gangways. The police came on, laying about with their sticks, collaring as many as they could.

We reached the ladder just as a press of fleeing men caught up. Most ran by, aiming to get around the end of the granite warehouse to the lane on the other side of the wharf. One man came right at us.

"There you are," he growled. He shoved me aside and grabbed An-Ming just as she started down the ladder. He was a tall man, brawny, his face half hidden by a broad flop-brimmed hat. He plucked An-Ming off the top rung like she weighed no more than a kitten. She yowled like a grown cat, twisting about, kicking and clawing, trying to break free. He clamped her arms tight with one long arm and fought to subdue her legs with the other.

I went at him with both fists. I was too short to get at his face right, so I aimed for the kidneys. I hardly dented him; he was built like a brick privy. He caught me on the side of the head with his free arm and sent me sprawling again. But it loosened his hold on An-Ming. She prized an arm free and raked her hand across his cheek, leaving a trail of bloody streaks. He yelled.

"Rake him again, Anie!" I cried, scrambling to my feet. I climbed his back like a ladder and pummeled his ears. "Put her down!" I yelled.

He did, but not like I meant. He took one step to the edge of the wharf and threw her out over the ten-foot drop to the water. Down she went, arms and legs flailing.

I didn't see her hit, because he went after me next, reaching back with his long arms to peel me off his shoulders. And he would have thrown me in, too, or worse, if Da hadn't showed up. He gave the thug a roundhouse right that snapped his head sidewise and made him stagger. I dropped to the cobbles with a thud that rattled my teeth. By the time I was back on my pins, the thug had disappeared around the end of the warehouse, Da was rubbing his sore knuckles, and An-Ming was in the water, blowing out a stream of Chinese curses.

"Can you swim?" I cried.

"Get into the boat, you lump," Da growled, "and be quick about it! The watch is almost on us." He shoved me toward the ladder, and I half fell into the boat. He came down after me in a rush, jerked the painter free, and shoved us off. I already had my oars set and pulled out toward An-Ming.

"Can you swim?" I yelled again, craning around for a look-see.

She gave me a disgusted glare. "Yes!"

"Do you need a hand?" someone called. Billy Adams was sitting in his canoe just outside the Liverpool packet.

"Not from you," Da replied.

"Why, it's Mickey O'Neill," Adams drawled. "Been fighting again? Or just drinking?"

"That's no business of yours, Adams," Da replied. "Get on with you."

"Suit yourself, Mick. You enjoy your swim, miss."

Adams rowed away, leaving An-Ming to tread water. We reached her in just a couple of strokes, and I pulled her over the side, streaming sea water.

"Now what was that all about?" Da demanded when she was safe on the stern thwart.

"That thug tried to kidnap her," I told him.

"What are you talking about?" he growled. "In broad daylight? More likely he was fooled by her clothes and just wanted to rough her up for being foreign. He looked dumb enough."

"He came at her on purpose! All the others were running away already, from the police!"

"Then he's even dumber than he looked. Now let's row her back where she belongs before you come to any more trouble. She'll catch her death in those wet clothes."

"I will survive, Mr. O'Neill," An-Ming said. "Thank you for helping."

Da rubbed his right fist. "It was my pleasure, miss. I apologize for the boy, though. He needs more time to grow up. Then he might make a better bodyguard."

The words burned.

Da jumped off at Long Wharf, leaving me to ferry An-

Ming the rest of the way. I set out for the *Hang-Jinhe* with quick, angry jabs on the oars. She shivered on the thwart, dripping pints of dirty water between the ribs. Her hair was starting to come undone and hung about her face in soggy hanks.

Halfway there, she said, "Finn, do not tell Father, please."

"Mum's the word," I muttered.

Then she added, "We would have bested him in another minute."

It helped a bit. She'd bloodied the bastard at least, and I could hope he'd gone deaf.

Back at the junk, she hurried to her cabin before anyone noticed. I swabbed out the boat as best I could, then pulled myself up the ladder to wait for Peter in the sun on deck. The cook offered me some of their Chinese tea and a sweet cake made with nuts and seeds. I have to admit, what they ate was strange but mostly good.

The steeple clocks were arguing over how close it was to six before Peter and Mr. Lawson came out of the clock room. They'd been hunched over their clocks and plans the whole time and were muzzy as old men. Then An-Ming came out, and Peter perked right up. She had on another silk dress, this one printed with dragonflies and flowers, but she wasn't any happier about it than she had been the day before. She was carrying her bonnet, demanding to know who had designed such a useless piece of headgear. I noticed her hair was still damp, but there was no other sign of her dunking. Hu-Lan argued with her, and she finally jammed the bonnet over the thick coil on the crown of her head. She outright refused to tie it. Mr. Lawson sighed but kept silent.

There were five of us going ashore in the boat: me, Peter, Mr. Lawson, An-Ming, and Wang. Hu-Lan was staying on the junk in case Captain Li needed more translating. I rowed us in to Central Wharf, with An-Ming at the tiller again. Peter offered her the place, and even wiped off the thwart before she sat. She gave him a smile so big he was dazzled, and stayed with us as far as Congress Street. He had a room there in the top floor above Mr. Bonds's shop and usually had his supper at a boarding house up the street. An-Ming invited him to join us, but he gallantly bowed out, saying it was a family reunion and all. Just as he was tipping his hat to her, a woman stuck her head out of a second-floor window half a block down Congress Street, calling for help. Peter, true to form, clapped on his topper and loped down the street to see what the matter was. An-Ming didn't hesitate either. She said something Chinese to Wang and ran after as fast as she could. In that long, wide dress, it looked like she was gliding on ice.

"Go, Wang," Mr. Lawson said. "I'll follow." So we all went.

It turned out there were two women up there, milliners. They had been working past closing time in the room above the store to make a few more hats and a little more money, but the last person out had accidentally locked them in. Some other fellows gathered to answer the call, and they began debating with Peter what to do. I spotted a ladder in the alley beside the store. A great cheer went up from the men, but the women didn't look so happy. The ladder didn't reach high enough anyway, falling just about four feet shy of the window ledge. That led to some more discussion among the growing crowd of on-lookers. Finally An-Ming broke in.

"You," she called, pointing to a teamster at the edge of the crowd. "Bring wagon here, under window. You, Finn, put ladder on wagon." She said "laddah" and her grammar got lost in the excitement, but I could understand her well enough. The men just stood there, regarding the novelty of being ordered about by a Chinese girl.

Peter stepped in. "Good idea! Thank you, An-Ming. Let's go there, my good fellow, lead your horse right in here. Make room everyone, the women on high are waiting."

It was like herding geese, but soon enough Peter and An-Ming had the wagon under the window and the ladder stepped in its bed, and now the top rung was right where it needed to be. The women, however, would have none of it.

"We can't climb down that," the first one said.

"It's quite sturdy," said Peter, who was in the wagon, bracing the ladder.

"You're all under us!" the other woman exclaimed, as if to an idiot. "You'll see everything!"

Peter's whole face went red.

"It's all right, missy," the teamster shouted. "We won't look, will we lads?"

Of course all the men shouted no.

"A likely story!" the first woman yelled, grinning in spite of it.

"It wouldn't be proper," the other one added. "We wouldn't be able to show our faces on the street again." She was the older of the two.

"*Hao ben!*" An-Ming muttered. "They are silly as Hu-Lan! Peter, go help them climb out. Hold their skirts so sinful petticoats and ankles do not show."

Peter stared at her. "Ah . . . Their skirts?"

"Of course. We must get them out."

Peter smiled through his blush. "If you say so."

So Peter went up the ladder, but even that wasn't enough for the women. The first one did try to climb out, but when Peter made a grab at her skirts, he almost tipped her backward into the room.

"*Wa!*" An-Ming exclaimed, stifling a laugh. "Go in and wrap skirts tight. Lift women out window. Finn, hold ladder." Peter saluted and obeyed, and An-Ming fired off a round of Chinese at Wang. He nodded and made his way through the men to clamber onto the wagon and start up the ladder after Peter. Peter figured out how to clinch his arms around the bottom of the skirts and hand the younger woman out to Wang. She shrieked when she saw who it was, then giggled as he carried her down all rolled up in a neat bundle. There was still a bit of ankle and lace peaking out, just enough to brighten up the men, but not enough to soil the lady's honor. There was another great cheer when Wang set her down, and a third when the second was safely on her pins.

Then the teamster cried, "Three cheers for our Chinese boss lady!" and they gave An-Ming a rousing hurrah. She nodded to them, all serious, then slipped a smile at Peter. He grinned back like an idiot.

Mr. Lawson smiled. "In some ways she is just like her mother," he said. "Let's hope she doesn't try to run tonight's meal." His eyes were a bit damp I believe. Then he took another look at An-Ming and frowned. "Where is your bonnet, my dear?" he demanded.

She put on a look of surprise and felt all over the top of her head. "Must have blown off by wind." Her voice was so innocent that none of us were fooled.

Chapter 8

I SHOWED THE WAY to the Sands's place, up over Beacon Hill and down Pickney Street, to one of the bowfront row houses right near Louisburg Square. This was Brahmin country, and the brick bowfronts flowing along on both sides of the street all had little flower gardens out front, and polished brass name plates, and doubled curtains in the windows, lace over deep velvet. Even the cobbles on the street seemed smoother than you found in other neighborhoods. Mr. Lawson kept going on again about how different it all looked: Beacon Hill had been taller, with a tall statue on top, there had been pastures and orchards, the new State House hadn't been built, and not one of the row houses. Not even Louisburg Square. I had to wonder how good his memory was. It didn't seem possible that so much could have changed.

A maid servant answered Mr. Lawson's knock and ran to fetch Mr. and Mrs. Sands. I wished them a good appetite and was leaving to wait in the boat when Mr. Lawson insisted that I stay. Mr. Sands arrived just in time to hear that, and what little smile he'd managed went all straight and thin. But Robert Lawson came toddling out on his daughter's arm, and he was full of greetings.

"Bridget," Mr. Sands said to the maid, who was hovering in the hallway, gawking at An-Ming and Wang, "please show Mr. Lawson's man and this . . . boy to the kitchen." He said "this" and "boy" like he wanted to stick a word between them, a word like "filthy."

The maid led us to the back stairs, but I caught a glimpse of the front room, just filled with dark furniture, paintings, a tile fireplace with a mirror over it, ceramic statues, lace on the stuffed chairs, lamps hung with long crystal jewels, Turkey rugs – it was enough to furnish half the rooms in the house I lived in, with the best stuff still left over to sell.

"I'm Mary," the maid said to Wang, pointing at herself and repeating it.

He looked puzzled. "Bridget-Meili?" he asked.

She laughed and shook her head. "No, just Mary. They call all the Irish girls Bridget."

"This is Wang," I said. "And I'm Finn O'Neill. My sister Grace works for a family on Mount Vernon Street, name of Barton. Do you know her?"

"I do. I met her down at the market," Mary replied. "Here's the kitchen. This is Mrs. Jaeger, the cook. This is Wang, ma'am. He's the manservant for the guests, would you believe? And this is Finn, their boatman. They're eating down here tonight."

Mrs. Jaeger was carrying a roasting pan from the work table to the stove but managed a quick smile. "Welcome," she said. "Please call me Hedi. Now sit down out of the way." She had dark, damp curly hair and a square face, and wore a stained apron from her neck to her knees. And she spoke with a German accent, all vees and dees. I wondered if Wang would be able to understand her at all.

The kitchen was low and steamy and ruled by a huge black cookstove with bright nickel trim. The long, narrow room filled half of the basement, and had a pantry off to one side as well. There was the work table, cupboards, and another sturdy table where the help ate. As soon as she had the pan in the oven, Hedi started asking questions, without stopping a moment. She stirred a pot, checked a sweet-smelling ham in the other oven, and went to chop a carrot. She had a girl helping her feed the fire in the stove, a daughter from the way Hedi ordered her about. Mary polished the silver and ran the trays up and downstairs. A man-servant and Mrs. Sands's lady-maid served.

Right off Mary had to tell Hedi all about An-Ming and what she was wearing. "And her hair! She has it all in the thickest braid you ever saw, coiled round and round and held with long sticks of ivory, and no bonnet!"

"No bonnet?" Hedi asked, looking up from her stove. She was checking the sweet-smelling roast in the other oven again. "What is she wearing, then?"

"Nothing! Not a bonnet or a hat. Nothing at all!"

"She had one," I said, "but she let it blow off while we were rowing in."

The women loved that. So I told them all about what An-Ming wore on the junk, the trousers and tunic, like what Wang was wearing, only longer.

"A Bloomer suit!" Mary exclaimed.

Hedi shook her head. "Even that Mrs. Bloomer knew to wear a bonnet."

"I thought Chinese women always wore long robes," Mary said.

"Not these women." I started telling them about Hu-Lan's dress, when a little bell by the stove gave a ring.

"Time for the fish," Hedi said, cutting me off and handing Mary a long, silver platter covered with a carved dome lid. "Up with you, Mary."

That started the eating. And what they ate! There was oysters and fish cooked in wine sauce, then broiled doves, then a choice of mutton or ham, both roasted in apples, with potatoes and leeks and boiled corn and cold beans in a sweet pickle and fresh baked biscuits. And Wang and I both got to choose from the trays after they came back down. Hedi and Mary kept telling me to take more, but then they'd ask another question about the Lawsons and the junk and the Chinese. I had to eat fast and talk faster, and repeat half of it because Mary was always having to run upstairs to bring more food or haul down the dirty plates and silverware for the girl to wash. They had clean dishes and new forks for every serving!

And Mary would come down with some bit of news for Hedi. "The missus is saying the baby's room is going to be all painted blue."

"I thought it was going to be yellow!" Hedi remarked. "Blue is too dark."

"It'll be yellow again in a week. Or pink."

After the fish, she told us, "The uncle was attacked by pirates on the Canton River! Everyone thought he was killed!"

"He almost was," I said. "A fellow named Wu saved him and nursed him back to health."

"Must have been very good nursing," Hedi remarked. "A hundred years old, they say!"

"Near enough," I told her. "Ninety-one."

"Well, he doesn't look a day past fifty," Mary said.

Hedi snorted. "Cannot be natural. Some Chinese hocus-pocus. No offense, Mr. Wang." Wang smiled and nodded. He understood a little bit, but I never could tell how much, German accents or not.

"How old are you, Ma?" the girl asked.

Hedi flicked the end of her apron at her. "Too old to be asked. You keep washing."

Then Mary went up with the bean pickle to go with the doves, and Wang and I got to work on the leftover fish, while Hedi kept cooking and asking questions. She kept trying to ask Wang about China – food and clothes and such – and he would fumble out a few words, or look completely lost and just smile and shake his head and say, "Sorry, don't know how say." Only it sounded like "soddy." And she would reply, "Vell, dat is all right."

After the doves, Mary told us, "The boss has started on about politics."

"What now?" Hedi asked.

"The usual, do you believe it? With that pretty Chinese girl sitting right next to him?"

"Only half Chinese," Hedi reminded her, "and a cousin-in-law, also."

"Still and all! He's going on about the plague of foreigners and immigrants! The missus is mortified, but she can't shift him. He's telling the uncle about how the Irish and Germans will be ruining Boston and the whole country if we aren't kept down and sent back with the rest of the foreign invaders, mostly the Irish, of course, of course."

"Is Sands a Know-Nothing, then?" I asked.

"He is! American Party, through and through," Hedi replied, jabbing a fork deep into the mutton and giving it a little shake to make sure it was done. "He is quiet about it in public, but we hear it often in this house."

"Too often, if you ask me," Mary said. "He spouts off like we're not even there."

"He knows very well who hears him," Hedi muttered, arranging potatoes on the platter with the mutton. "He knows it right now. Here, up with you."

I looked at Wang then, wondering how much of this he was getting. The American Party – the Know-Nothings, they were called, because that's how they answered whenever anyone else asked about it – they had stirred up trouble for as long as I could remember. Sometimes nobody seemed to pay them much mind, and you'd be thinking they were done and gone. Then a brawl would break out between the teamsters and the stevedores, like today, or there'd be economic trouble, or there'd be sickness, and every time they'd blame the foreigners. The Irish mostly. Like they did with the cholera in '49. Then they'd get someone elected to a bigwig office to protect the so-called true Americans from the rabble. The important ones, the rich ones like Sands, they kept their hands clean in public and spread their foul rumors on the sly. They let the poor ones do the brawling and get hurt.

But Wang was just putting more pickle on his dove. He glanced up at me and smiled in a questioning way. I smiled back and tucked into my own little bird. Mr. Lawson could worry about Sands. And if I were Sands, I thought, I'd worry about An-Ming.

And wasn't I right, because the very next time Mary came down she said An-Ming had finally cut him off.

"'Tell me more about the bank, Mr. Sands,' she says. 'What do you invest in besides railroads and watches?'" Mary looked at us like she'd announced a flying pig. "And you know how the missus hates to talk about business? Well, out she comes with, 'Yes, Jacob, tell Cousin Ann more about the bank.' She was that relieved to shut up the politics."

"Did Sands tell her?" Hedi asked.

"He didn't get the chance. Old Lawson jumped right in, started going on about the water power company on Back Bay and the East Boston ferry and the Eastern Railroad and a tight money market, whatever that is. And the missus was smiling and nodding like she understood a word of it. But that An-Ming, she kept asking questions like she really did understand. And then old Lawson, he says to the uncle, 'Heavens, Matthew, you're right! I should have Ann look at the books if you won't, ha-ha.'" Mary did a fine job imitating Robert Lawson's cackle. "And what does the uncle say but, 'I told you, Robert, she has a far better head for money than I do.' Old Lawson laughs all the harder. "Ha-ha, it's settled then. Ann shall be the new partner, ha-ha! That should tickle Stone and Bloomer and all the rest of the suffragists, eh, Jacob?'"

"I can imagine what Sands said to that," Hedi remarked.

"He had a lemon in his gob all right, lips screwed up

tight as a bum."

"Mary!" Hedi exclaimed. "Watch your own mouth! And you shut your ears," she said to her daughter, who was giggling into the sink. "You will not repeat that."

"What did Sands say?" I asked.

"Well, he just about had his smile working again, when An-Ming speaks up. 'We must keep it very secret, yes, Cousin Jacob?' she says. 'A foreigner *and* a woman. Only worse if I am Irish, yes?'"

"She did not say that!" Hedi stopped moving for the first time that evening.

"She did! Threw it right back in his face. And then she laughed like it was all a joke, and said as how the household back in China was more than enough for her to be running, and how the missus could understand that, she was sure."

"That one has spunk," Hedi said, "but we are the ones who will feel it when she leaves."

"It'll be worth it," Mary said.

Hedi snorted and went back to preparing the desert. It was a trifle: little cakes and sliced melon and oranges smothered in sweet whipped cream, with vanilla bean grated on top. She put the tureen on a silver tray. I was stuffed and still shoveling in bits of ham and mutton, but I stared at that trifle like it was the first food I'd seen in a week. I prayed there'd be some left.

Hedi fetched a square, green bottle from the pantry. She put a bit of whipped cream into a small bowl, added a spoonful of thick yellow liquid from the bottle, and mixed it all up. Then she ladled it over a small portion of cake and fruit on a silver plate.

"That's it," she said, putting the plate beside the tureen.

Wang grabbed the edge of the tray just as Mary started to lift it. "Excuse. Who for?"

Hedi looked at me. I could only shrug. "It's for old Lawson," she said.

"Lawson?" Wang frowned and half rose from his chair,

leaning over to sniff at the plate.

"For Robert Lawson," I told him. "That's who they mean by 'old Lawson'. That's right, isn't it, ma'am?"

"Yes. Robert Lawson." Hedi gave Wang a worried smile. "It is his medicine. Medicine. From a doctor. For his heart." She patted her chest and said heart again.

"It tastes terrible," her daughter put in.

Hedi flashed her a frown. "Of course it tastes terrible. It is medicine, yes? He should drink it plain, but won't. Then Mr. Sands gets angry at us. So I mix it into the dessert."

"Doctor," Wang said. "Robert Old Lawson. I see." He sat back down.

"All right, is it?" Mary asked, and hurried out at Hedi's nod.

I made a note not to touch any leftovers in that bowl.

Chapter 9

I WOKE UP WITH a stomach-ache the next morning, and Bridget teased me no end.

"You'll need to say at least three Hail Marys and an Our Father for being such a glutton."

Ma shushed her, but got in her own digs. "At least I won't have to be feeding him today." Then she made up a lunch for Da and me, as usual. And as we were leaving, she gave me her hug, as always, whether I wanted it or not, and reminded me to ask Peter everything I could about clocks, just in case.

"Now he's working on that special Chinese clock for Mr. Lawson, you'll have even more excuse to show your interest." I could never bring myself to tell her I didn't have any.

Da made his own feelings clear. "Waste of time," he growled, "and that's no joke. All that work and money for nothing more than a big show. A real waterman don't need a gussied-up time piece to know the set of the tide. It's not even good for navigating."

"Don't you listen to him, Finn," Ma said, giving Da a cuff on the arm. "You go your own path here in America. Go where you can get ahead."

Da didn't say another word all the way to the wharf and out to the *Hang-Jinhe*. I couldn't tell if he was angry, sick, hung over, or wishing Tim was there. We split up, like the day before, me going with Peter, and he with the cook and Hu-Lan and a pair of the crew to the markets. When Peter and I came back to the junk at noon, Da had stayed ashore again. And that's how it went from then on.

Over the next few days, the Lawsons were in demand by all manner of people who wanted to meet them and show them this building or that or come on board the *Hang-Jinhe*. Mr. Lawson was very choosey about who he went to see and even choosier about who he let on board. There was a visit from the senior pilots of the Boston Marine Society, who seemed to be most interested in how the *Hang-Jinhe* had managed to sneak in under their noses in the fog and avoid having to pay the pilot's fee. Mr. Lawson had been a ship's captain before most of them had been born. He invited a few other captains on board, too, I think more out of courtesy to Captain Li. Then there was the commodore of the Navy Yard and the commander from Fort Warren, who were most interested in the junk's gun deck. And a delegation from the custom house and another from the Merchant's Exchange. Folks like that were too important to turn away. And the Bonds, too, who came to see the Chinese clocks. Peter and Mr. Lawson were both downright nervous when they arrived, but it was all handshakes and smiles when they left.

The only invitations Mr. Lawson accepted ashore were for the crew's sake. They had been on board for a long voyage. If a benevolent society or auxiliary wanted to treat them to a tour of the city and a meal, that was all right. Letting a sailor loose in town is never a wise thing, even if they are Chinese, so Captain Li sent only a half-dozen ashore at a time, with the host waiting on the wharf and Hu-Lan and An-Ming along to translate and keep them on their manners. An-Ming hated putting on her American dresses and answering the same questions in front of what seemed like the same gawking crowd, but she knew she had a duty to the crew. Either Da or I would row, depending on what time of the day it was.

Mr. Lawson didn't go along on those parties. He spent all his afternoons with Peter. And each evening on the row home, Peter would talk to me about the clock, as if it were all he could think about. The first time he said, "I'm still trying to understand it."

"What's to understand?" I asked. "After all, you can fix chronometers, the best clocks there is."

He didn't answer for such a long time I thought he wasn't going to, and that did prick my interest. When he did answer, it was real careful like. "This isn't that type of clock."

"What other type is there?" Now I was determined to pry it out of him.

He took his time again. "The clocks you've seen . . . the clocks we're all used to, they count the seconds and minutes and hours. Others . . . This one . . . Well, have you ever seen a clock that shows the phases of the moon?"

"I have," I replied. "The moon peeks out through a window in the face of the clock."

"That's right. As the moon face circles behind the clock face, you see what phase it's in."

"Mr. Lawson's clock is a moon clock then?"

"Oh, much more than that! It has a face for the moon, another for the sun, a third for the stars, and a fourth for the major planets, and, even odder, a fifth for . . ." He drifted to a stop, his eyes fixed on something inside his head.

"A fifth face? I only saw four, along with the panel to get at the innards."

"Ah. It's hidden inside."

"That is odd," I said. "What did you say it was for?"

"Actually, that's what's odd. Mr. Lawson calls it *chi*. And before you ask, I'll answer right off that I don't quite understand what it is. I don't believe we have an exact word for it.

It's nothing you can see, like a sun or a moon. To make matters worse, today he just told me that it's not exactly *chi* either, not as the Taoists think of it."

"The who?"

"Taoists. Tao is something like a religion, only it's more a way of life, I suppose. It means *the way*. And *chi* is . . . Well, it's the energy within life. That's one way Mr. Lawson describes it."

"Do you mean the soul?"

"Ah, no. It's not quite . . . It's not about . . . You see, *soul* is too religious. *Chi* isn't about God and man. It's a life force inside everything."

"Faith, you don't want to be saying that to your parson, Peter. If he was Father McMahon, he'd have you saying Hail Marys for a month of Sundays."

Peter wiped his face wearily. "I don't claim to believe it, or to understand it, Finn. Luckily, I don't have to, really. I just have to reproduce the five gear trains and make them run off a proper mainspring and chronometer escapement, using what I can of the Bond clockworks to make everything smaller, sturdier, and more precise."

"That's *all* you have to do? It seems like a lot to me."

Peter laughed. "No, it's quite straightforward, compared to understanding *chi*. I'll leave that part to Mr. Lawson."

The next day, Friday it was, I followed Peter into the clock room for a closer look at Mr. Lawson's clock. He showed me the plans he was making of the clockworks. All the gears were drawn in and all their teeth counted, and there was a string of arithmetic that he said would tell him how strong the clock spring would need to be. It was something to be looking at, but it didn't tell me any more about *chi* or what the clock really did. And Mr. Lawson, polite as he was, made it plain that he didn't want Peter distracted from the work.

That afternoon, I ferried An-Ming and a group of the crew to a gathering where there was a minstrel show and a brass band. An-Ming didn't like the sound of the band, and she couldn't understand why the singers had their faces painted black. I told her people just liked to hear those southern songs sung that way.

"Why paint? Why not have black people sing them?" she demanded.

"Because that would be as bad as having a bunch of the Irish do it," I said.

When we got back I waited on deck, watching the sun drop closer and closer to the city, till it perched on the tips of the steeples, as though the prayers of the faithful could hold back the night. It was a daily match of push and shove, and the sun always won. I went looking for Peter.

I walked softly as I made my way toward the clock room, just in case there happened to be another conversation going on. I heard Peter's voice and moved closer. It wasn't Mr. Lawson who answered, it was An-Ming.

"Yes, Wu was my grandfather, but this was Mother's clock. Wu's was destroyed."

"Ah," Peter said. "And then he died?"

"Yes."

"When was that?"

"Before I was born. I believe his death caused my birth."

"Really? Why do you think that?"

"Mother missed him greatly. She wanted more family. An only child is rare, no children is very unlucky."

"Ah. Well, lucky for the rest of us that you were born." There was an awkward pause, and I could almost see the red light from Peter's ears. "Unlucky for him to have died, of course, but imagine, to have lived so long. To have seen so much history. No, I can't imagine it. Three hundred years? It boggles the mind."

Sure it boggled my mind. Three hundred years? Because of a clock? I shifted another step closer. Before they said another word, two strong hands grabbed me, one by the hair, the other by the seat of the pants, and hauled me into the clock room. It was Wang. He set me down with a thump in front of An-Ming and said some Chinese at her.

She was sitting at the end of the table, right beside Peter, wearing a long robe with what looked like a hundred pearl buttons running down one side from her neck to the floor. It was embroidered all over with pale flowers and edged with sea-blue loops. Her hair was unbraided, piled all up on top of her head and held by long wooden pins tipped with ivory. She looked more like a woman than I'd ever seen her. But the scowl she gave me could have come straight from a Malay pirate.

She said some Chinese back to Wang and he left us. Then she got to me. "How long did you listen?" she demanded.

"Not long," I said.

"Finn—" Peter began, but An-Ming cut him off.

"What did you hear?"

I could tell it would take more than a fib to get me out of this. "Your grandfather Wu lived to be three hundred years old."

"What else?"

"You were born because an only child is unlucky."

"And?" She just wouldn't let me stop.

I could hear Mr. Lawson's clock, ticking steadily on its shelf. And then there was the one beside it, dead still. "He had a clock like those two, and he died when something happened to it."

"*Zaogoa!*" she muttered.

Peter's scowl was almost as ugly. "I was afraid he'd guess," he told her, "though I hardly expected him to spy on us."

"I was just coming to see if you were near ready to leave," I said.

"But you decided to hide in the shadows and eavesdrop instead." He sounded like a school teacher.

"Faith, when I realized you and An-Ming were in here

alone together, I didn't want to come barging in without knowing I wouldn't be interrupting something important between you."

Peter's whole face turned red. He knew what I meant. "Ah, ah, there was nothing to interrupt! We were merely—"

"Do not change subject!" An-Ming said. She was upset enough to be forgetting her grammar, but I couldn't help notice she was also fighting back a smile.

"Well, I did wonder if you might be telling him about that thug who attacked you the other day," I said.

"What's this?" Peter exclaimed. "Someone attacked you, An-Ming? When? Where?"

"Three days ago," I said. "That brawl on Lewis Wharf, the one in the papers. The fellow was trying to abduct her, I think."

"Abduct—?"

"But he dropped her into the harbor."

"Dropped her—!"

"Was nothing!" An-Ming snapped. "We chase him off. Finn is trying to—"

"Who was this fellow? And what were you doing on Lewis Wharf?"

"Visiting! No more about it!" She was glaring at Peter now. "Finn wants to distract."

Peter shut his mouth, but I could see he wasn't worrying about me anymore.

An-Ming still was. "You heard something you shouldn't, Finn."

"About the clock? Don't worry, I won't tell anyone."

"Can I trust you?" she asked. "You weren't 'mum' now."

"Peter's not your father," I pointed out. "I thought—"

"You thought wrong. No more about that. And nothing about what you just heard. It would create great problems."

"No one would believe me anyway," I said. "I'm not sure I believe it myself."

"No matter. Don't even joke. Not to anyone: not father,

mother, sister, closest friend – no one. Understand?"

"I don't. I mean I won't tell, but I'm thinking you don't have to be so worried."

"Finn," Peter said. "What do you think your Father McMahon would say about it?" He let me chew on that a moment, then added, "What do you think old Robert Lawson would say? Do you understand now? Half the city would call it the work of Satan, and the other half would want their own clock. The Lawsons would be torn to bits."

I did understand, though I still thought there'd be a good third that would just laugh at the notion. "What do the Bonds think about it?" I asked.

Peter looked very unhappy. "They don't know," he admitted. "I told them . . . Let's just say I didn't tell them everything. They think it's an astrological time piece."

"They could not know," An-Ming said. "You should not know."

Peter and An-Ming were both so serious, I realized it had to be true: The clock could make you live forever. The strange thing is, I wasn't sure how I felt about it. I couldn't bring myself to think it was Satan's work. But I still couldn't imagine living for three hundred years. And maybe even longer, if nothing happened to the clock. And even if something did, you could get it repaired, or have a new one made, like Peter was doing.

I pointed to Mr. Lawson's clock. "So this really is why your da's so old but doesn't act like it?"

"Yes," An-Ming replied.

"And the other was your ma's, but she died anyway. What happened?"

An-Ming looked down. "A terrible, stupid thing." She took a breath and spoke more carefully, but I think it was more to keep calm than to help her grammar. "There is civil war in my country now. Not at our little town yet, but Mother had to travel. She went in a large group, with hired guards. They were mistaken for rebels and attacked. Mother's driver was wounded, the horses bolted. Wagon rolled over. She struck her head. Never woke up."

Tears dropped on the lap of her robe. Peter reached for her shoulder, hesitated, and then touched her gently, gave her a little bit of a pat. She lifted her head and gave him back a smile, then shrugged and wiped her eyes.

"The clock can't protect you from injury, Finn," Peter said.

"How old was your ma?" I asked.

"One hundred and thirty-seven years," An-Ming replied. "But she looked twenty. She was seventeen when Wu had the clock made."

"So she only grew three years older in all that time?"

"No no. She grew older when she and Father decided to have me. She had to stop clock in order to conceive, so baby could grow inside her."

"Wouldn't that only take nine months?"

"Conception took time. And she wanted to nurse me. Afraid clock would stop her milk." An-Ming frowned. "It stopped anyway after a year. When the clock stops, body's schedule is not normal. Hu-Lan says I was born early and small, but looked and ate and slept like a year old."

"Do you have a clock?" I asked, thinking she was still mighty small for her age.

"No no! To be fifteen for all my life? To be looked at as a child? No!"

She sure didn't act like a child, but I knew what she meant. It's not what you did, it's how the adults treated you.

"Funny, isn't it? I've heard more than one adult wish to be a child again."

"They forget what childhood is like," she replied.

"One of these clocks wouldn't help them anyway," Peter said. "They can't make you younger. They just stop your age, wherever you happen to be."

"How?"

"Don't ask, because I still can't tell you."

"Something to do with that *chi* stuff?" An-Ming looked at me in surprise, then scowled at Peter. "He didn't tell me anything about living for hundreds of years," I said quickly. "Just about how much he didn't understand."

"And still don't," he said. "Mr. Lawson takes each piece I finish and does something with it in his cabin. Then I add it to the clock. All I know is the mechanics. He knows the science . . . or whatever it is."

"Even that only by rote," An-Ming said. "Wu loved Father very much, because Mother did, but he guarded his secrets. They discussed philosophies, but not practice, not application. Father reads Wu's diaries again and again. I help him. There are steps to perform just so, at just such time, but we don't know why. This clock—" She gestured at the half-empty brass framework on the table beside Peter's diagram. "—we can only hope it will work when done."

"Faith!" I said. "You've come all this way and you don't even know it'll work?"

"We believe it will," Peter said. "Ah, that is, Mr. Lawson does. And I'm certain the clockworks will. It will undoubtedly take some adjustment, but he seems very optimistic about his part of it. I'm sure it will be all right," he said to An-Ming. "He'll be all right."

She sighed. "I wonder. Ever since Mother died, he worries so much about it."

"And well he might," Peter said. "She was the second wife he lost, after all, and he loved them both dearly. Such tragedy would make some men despair. He wants even more to live."

An-Ming looked terribly sad, thinking about her mother, I suppose.

"How did your father wind up living with your grandfather?" I asked. "I keep hearing something about pirates."

She told me the tale then, and it brightened her up. Mr. Lawson had been traveling from Canton toward Hong Kong when river pirates attacked his small boat. He dove into the water and escaped because none of them could swim – I was amazed when she told me most Chinese never learned to swim, even the sailors – but he'd been wounded and he almost died before Wu found him. Wu had been returning home from Macao, after returning a Portuguese clockworker to the compound there. His boatman heard the commotion and ducked into an estuary to hide, then snuck out when night fell. They were feeling their way up the shoreline when they heard Mr. Lawson's moans. They took him on home, way up a long branch of the Pearl River. And when they got there, An-Ming's mother nursed him back to health. Wu took a liking to him and he stayed, and soon enough he and An-Ming's mother fell in love, even though he was already close to fifty and she looked seventeen. Once he realized how old she really was, he asked her to marry him. That was when Wu had a clock made for him.

"Is this the same clock?" I asked.

"No no," An-Ming said. "This is the third. They wear out."

"What happened to Wu's clock?"

"He destroyed it," she said.

"*He* destroyed it?" Peter echoed. "Your father never told me that. What on Earth for?"

"We don't know," An-Ming replied. "He kept it in his room, only he allowed to touch it. One day, he smashed it with an ax. By the time we realized, it was too late."

We all thought about that for a minute.

"Finn," An-Ming said. "You still haven't promised not to tell."

"I do promise," I said.

"Swear. Give your strongest oath."

"All right. I swear by the Blessed Virgin and the grave of my grandfather."

She looked at Peter and he nodded.

"Thank you," she said. "We must keep this secret."

"Nobody will hear it from me," I said.

Of course, nobody had to.

Chapter 10

SUNDAY CAME, AND IT was hard to believe that less than a week had passed since the arrival of the *Hang-Jinhe*. I went to early mass with Ma and Bridget, and we all lit candles for Tim. Then I went down to walk the wharves, on the off chance I might spot the thug who'd dunked An-Ming.

You might think it would be quiet on the wharves on a Sunday, but there were church bells ringing in every ward of the city. And after the masses and meetings and services, people came down to be by the water. Captains and owners decked out their ships in signal flags and bunting, and brought their families aboard for picnics. Always some ships arrived and some set sail, with music and cheering and the beautiful flash and slap of canvas catching the wind.

Some Sundays I could make a little money by rowing well-wishers out into the harbor to wave their ships off. This day I just went from wharf to wharf, looking. I didn't see the tall fellow anywhere, but I did run into Pat Delany.

"Finn!" he called, hurrying to catch up. "I noticed you're still working for the Lawsons."

"Not directly," I said. "I'm rowing Peter Jenkins, for Bond and Sons."

"Good! What can you tell about this great, fine clock

he's making?"

"Where'd you hear about a clock, Pat?" I demanded.

"It's all over town, Finn. Why else would Mr. Jenkins be out there every day and into the night?" Pat came close and lowered his voice. "Is it the truth, Finn? It'd mean a lot if I could take the story to the editor. If you gave me the details, I'd write it out myself first, see?"

Pat had gone through the last two years of school with me, and I knew he could write well. He'd tried hard to get a job as a reporter, but had to settle for selling the papers on the street corner and passing news tips to the editor. "They'd print what you write?" I asked.

He nodded. "I think they would, Finn. They don't have to use my own name on it, see? I could use a pseudonym."

"A what?" I think Pat read Mr. Webster's dictionary just for the fun of it.

"A pen name, so the readers wouldn't know I'm Irish."

"And they'd pay you for it?"

He nodded again, eyes bright. "But it's having the story printed that counts for me."

I thought, An-Ming will have my guts for chowder, or whatever kind of soup they eat. But Pat was the one who needed feeding.

"I'll give you a story," I said. "And if it doesn't get printed, nothing you ever write will."

The next day started like any Monday, with Bridget half asleep through breakfast and Da coughing the Sunday mess out of his chest, pretending it was nothing. Still, we managed to meet Peter on time. He had one of the morning papers, the *Post*. Pat worked for the *Herald*. I wondered if the editor really would print his version of the story.

The morning went quickly enough, and we were back at the *Hang-Jinhe* by noon. Peter fair flew up the ladder, then hauled himself to a slow walk when he didn't see An-Ming on deck. She still hadn't appeared by the time he reached the companionway, and he went to his clocks a disappointed man.

The junk was quiet. Da had taken Hu-Lan, the cook, and a couple of crewmen to the markets. Captain Li had the rest of the crew at work paying the seams on the main deck, pouring hot tar onto the fresh laid caulking. There's always fixing to do on a ship. I sat in the sun, watching and eating my dinner. An-Ming came out on deck as I was finishing up. To my surprise, she was wearing one of her American dresses, and she didn't look all that happy.

"Peter's in the clock room," I said.

"Where else?" she replied, as if she couldn't care less. "I wish to have dress made. Your mother sews, yes?"

"She's a seamstress, she is, for Mr. Tierney on Pearl Street. They're the best in town, anyone will tell you."

"No doubt. Can they make new dress by Thursday? We have to meet the mayor Friday." I think she'd have said, "We have to shovel the privy," with a kinder voice.

"Thursday will be easy," I told her, grabbing the dinner pail. "Let's go."

"Wait. Wang must come with us. Always." She was back to that privy voice. "Hu-Lan told Father I had fallen into harbor. He asked Peter why."

"Peter's not too good at fibbing," I remarked.

"No." And there was Peter, at the bottom of the privy.

So Wang came with us, carrying two long bolts of silk fabric wrapped in muslin. I rowed us into Liverpool Wharf and led them up Pearl Street, where we were greeted with even more stares than usual, and bouts of whispering. I wondered if the *Herald* had come out yet.

Mr. Tierney was delighted to see us, greeting An-Ming like she was one of his best customers. He was a spry gentleman, from Irish grandparents, but a tailor in Boston all his life, like his father. And he had a son learning the trade. Ma was one of five women working for him, not counting Bridget. He polished his specs over and over, going on with

An-Ming about the style and the pattern she wanted for the dress. He polished them some more when Wang unwrapped the silk and handed it over. They dickered over the price a little, though it seemed to me An-Ming did it more for the practice than to save a dollar, and she threw in whatever remained on the bolts. Mr. Tierney's little eyes were shining by the time he called Ma down to get her started on the measuring.

Ma was even more delighted than he was. She flashed me a big thank-you of a smile, as if it was all my idea. And she took to An-Ming right off. An-Ming was acting the perfect lady, and she treated Ma like one. She told Ma what a great help I'd been, and Ma said, yes, I was a good boy, which gave me a case of Peter's Ears. Luckily, they got through that bit quickly and moved on to the dress. They went over the style and pattern and all that again, and then Ma started to lead An-Ming back to the fitting room. That was when Bridget came in. School had finally woken her up, and now she was bright and brisk as a bee. She buzzed at An-Ming, going on about how wonderful it was to finally meet her and how I'd been having all the fun and hadn't hardly told them anything about it.

So An-Ming invited her and Ma out to the *Hang-Jinhe*. You should have heard Bridget squeak. Of course, Ma said they couldn't think of it.

"We couldn't be bothering you like that, Miss Lawson," she said.

"Is no bother," An-Ming insisted. "I welcome a quiet visit. Speeches are tiring."

"Oh, you wouldn't notice us at all," Bridget said.

"Well, I don't know when we could come," Ma countered.

"Next Sunday after church service?" An-Ming offered. "Please."

"Oh, yes, Ma!" Bridget pleaded.

Ma laughed. I knew she wanted to go but was just being

polite. "It would be a great honor, Miss Lawson," she said. "Thank you."

"Yes, thank you!" Bridget exclaimed, beaming like a bright star. "And you must come to our place for supper some night."

Ma went pale, then flushed with embarrassment. Of course, she didn't know An-Ming had already seen our place. All she could imagine was bringing this daughter of a Boston Brahmin and a Chinese Lady into our tiny kitchen to eat turnips and cabbage and maybe a bit of corned beef or a fish cake that was mostly potato. I felt a little weak about it myself.

"Now I am honored," An-Ming said. "May I bring Father? He thinks most highly of Finn and Mr. O'Neill. He would delight to meet you."

Ma went white again, but she managed a smile. "Sure, he'd be welcome, too. Our home is small, but it's open to everyone."

"The wealth of home is measured by worth of family, not size," An-Ming said. I don't think she made that one up on her own either.

"We do our best," Ma replied. "And now we'd best be getting you measured. Bridget, come along and help."

I think Bridget had realized her mistake by then, but An-Ming's answer had her glowing again. She flashed me a great smile and followed them into the fitting room. Wang took up a post by the door, and I found a stool. There was quiet talk from inside the room and the rustle of cloth, and then another big squeal from Bridget.

"Will you look at that? Trousers! It's like a Bloomer suit!"

Wang and I cooled our heels for over an hour by the chime of the Old South clock, but everyone was in a fine mood, particularly Bridget and An-Ming, who were close as sisters. We took our leave and were making our way back down Pearl Street toward the wharf when a newsboy's cry cut through the chatter and rattle of the crowded street.

"Hoy, hoy, hoy! Adventure in the Far East! The ancient astronomical instrument of the Orient! Read about the Chinese clock being built in Boston Harbor! Only in the *Herald!* Hoy, hoy, hoy!"

An-Ming stopped dead, listened to the fellow repeat his cry, and turned to me with her Malay Pirate look.

"Now don't jump to conclu—" I began.

Her scowl grew darker. "No? Where should I jump? Your throat?"

"You'll want to read it first. Then you can kill me."

"Do not think I won't," she muttered.

She marched up to the newsboy and demanded a paper. He was so surprised to see her and Wang he almost dropped his bundle. Then he got his wind back and tried to shortchange her. She hit him with a stream of Chinese so hot it nearly wilted his ears. He wound up giving her the paper for free. She clenched it in her fist all the way to the boat, unrolling it only when I was rowing us away from the wharf and didn't have a hand free to defend myself.

The evening *Herald* was a single four-page sheet, and the front page was all ads. She snapped it open and found the story right on page two. I watched her eyes skim down the text.

"*Zaogoa*," she muttered. Then she read on. Her glare softened a bit, but I didn't dare break the silence. She reached the end and shook the paper. "Ridiculous."

"What's it say?" I asked, dying to hear. "Read it for us."

Wouldn't you know, she read it to Wang, in Chinese. He looked surprised and puzzled in turns, and almost laughed out loud once. He swallowed his smile quick enough when she glared at him. They had a bit of a conversation when she was done, and it seemed to me he was trying to say it wasn't all that bad. She didn't agree with him.

"Who's it by?" I asked

"You don't know?"

"I might," I admitted.

She looked back at the story. "'Our correspondent.'"

Poor Pat didn't even get a pen name. "Take the oars and I'll give it a read," I said, with a big enough grin to make it a joke. An-Ming didn't crack a smile. She closed the paper, tucked it under her arm, and tended the tiller in silence. When we reached the junk, she told me to come, one sharp word, then led me to the clock room. Mr. Lawson and Peter looked up in surprise when she stormed in, me trailing like a bad dog.

"Whatever is the matter, my dear?" Mr. Lawson asked.

"Listen," she said, and she read the headlines: "Boston Firm Builds Mysterious Clock for Chinese Sage. Marvelous Chronometer to Reveal Riddles of the Firmament."

"Rumors have flown up and down our fair streets this past week regarding the unexpected arrival in our gracious harbor of the exotic Chinese junk, the *Hang-Jinhe*, or *Flying Golden Crane*," she continued. "Even more startling than the appearance of this exotic craft was the presence on board of a Son of Boston's Finest, long thought lost: Mr. Matthew Lawson, and his charming half-Chinese daughter, Ann. Mr. Lawson disappeared in exciting circumstances many years ago while traveling on the Pearl River near the trading enclave in Canton. It was feared – nay! Believed in all certainty! – that he had been murdered by blood-thirsty river pirates. Not so, good Readers. Our Correspondent has discovered the precise nature of his rescue, and of the quest which has brought him back to his Home Port after all these many years.

"According to very reliable persons who have been on board the junk and have spoken in direct confidence with both father and daughter, Mr. Lawson's rescue was affected by personal bravery and the intercession of an unforeseen Oriental Samaritan. When his small boat was attacked by the large party of pirates, Mr. Lawson defended it with pistol and sword until all but he were overwhelmed. Gravely wounded, he dove into the river, more willing to risk the mercies of shark and crocodile than the vicious cruelty of the barbarians who had slaughtered his companions. Faint and bleeding, he managed to hide himself deep within the thick greenery of the marshy riverside. There he lay, adrift like Moses in the reeds, as night fell, and the pirates gave up their fruitless search for his body.

"He knew not how long he languished there, but sometime before dawn, his moans were heard on board a small *sampan* creeping upriver in the marshes to avoid the very same cutthroats who had so ravaged Mr. Lawson's craft. On board was an aged and highly respected Chinese sage, by name of Wu, and his young daughter, Wu Jian-Ming. Pulling the now unconscious Lawson from the tender embrace of the water fronds, they dressed his grievous wounds and continued upriver to their distant home. There, the daughter nursed him day and night, through pain and fever, from sickness to convalescence, until our fellow Bostonian could once again resume the normal activity of a well man.

"In the meantime, kept abed by his frail state, Mr. Lawson spent long hours in discussion with Mr. Wu, comparing the philosophies of their two dissimilar cultures. In time, he became proficient in the Chinese dialect and more and more a scholar of the Chinese sciences. In that time, too, he and his nurse developed the special affection that sometimes arises between man and woman thrown by chance into such close company. They were married by Chinese priests in a ceremony few Westerners have been privileged to witness (a rite which was later properly confirmed by a Christian minister of the Canton congregation), and later she bore him a daughter.

"Among the knowledge acquired from Mr. Wu was the art of astronomical prediction, much valued by the Chinese court, where the position and movements of the celestial objects has long directed the daily decisions of the Mandarins who serve as court officials, and even of the Emperor himself. Mr. Wu had developed a number of ingenious clocks to count the complicated turning of the heavens and was sought after from far and wide for his prognostications.

"But trouble brews in China, as Our Readers are well aware. The civil war now wreaking havoc from Shanghai to the very walls of Peking has sent its tendrils of destruction even as far as the small, isolated town in which Mr. Lawson had found refuge. Mrs. Lawson was struck down, and the aging Wu died of grief. His clocks were destroyed. Himself beset by grief and the advance of age, Mr. Lawson determined to return to the City of his Birth, bringing with him his young daughter, that she might be acquainted with whomever of her American relatives might still survive here. Hoping, too, to combine his knowledge with the resources of his family's successful business ventures (he is directly related to the founders of the Harbor Bank, State Street, and once a partner in the mercantile firm of Lawson and Sands). It was mere serendipity that he also found here the expertise in clockwork and chronometric construction found only in Boston in the firm of Wm. Bond & Son, Congress Street, enabling him to re-create in more modern form Mr. Wu's magnificent astronomical clock.

"The clock itself will have five faces, one each to measure the movements of the Sun, the Moon, the Planets, the Tides, and the Hours, driven by the most modern chronometer escapement and mounted with many priceless clockwork jewels to assure its precision and longevity. Space prohibits a more complete description of its workings, but Our Readers can be assured that we will print details as they become available. With the rumors now laid to rest, we can all wish Messrs. Lawson and Bond a quick and successful completion of their Project."

"*Phew!* Sure, that Pat can blow a tale, can't he," I said.

"Pat?" An-Ming asked, the glint returning to her eyes.

"A friend of mine," I said.

"And you told him all about clock, after swearing oath of secrecy!"

"Hold on," I said. "The whole city already knows there's a clock, because of Peter here."

"Wait a minute!" Peter exclaimed. "I haven't told a single soul what this clock will d—!"

"Of course you haven't," I said. "And neither have I. Read it again. Where does it say anything real about what it does?"

"It does mention the five faces," Peter replied. "I didn't even tell Mr. Bond about that."

"And what are they? Sun, Moon, Planets, Tides, and Hours. Not a word about that *chi* stuff, or centuries of life. Don't you see? I didn't tell them about *your* clock. I told them about a different clock, a clock to stop the rumoring, so they wouldn't come asking, or maybe figure it out on their own."

"How did you figure it out, Finn?" Mr. Lawson asked, scowling.

I should have blushed, I suppose, but I was thinking I'd done pretty well by them with that article. "The only way anyone would ever learn, sir. I overheard a few chance comments."

"You eavesdropped," Peter corrected.

"You spied!" An-Ming snapped.

"And there you have it," I said. "Only a spy could learn. As long as we don't say a word about it anywhere else but here on board, we're all right."

Mr. Lawson *hmphed.* "You've inherited your people's gift with words, Master O'Neill."

"Oh, it wasn't all me, sir. I didn't say anything to Pat about crocodiles or Moses or Protestant weddings or prognosticrucians."

"The bit about the pistols and swords was yours then?"

"Well, I figured you to be at least that brave, sir."

"Ha! I wish I could say it was true. You realize Peter will now have to come up with some story for Mr. Bond as to why the article doesn't match what we told him. And as to drawing on the family's resources . . . By Heavens, surely you and your friend could have left that part out! It will not win us any regard from Jacob Sands. I suppose it's just as well Robert has decided to come out here for a visit tomorrow. Perhaps I can pour oil on the waters."

Chapter 11

WHEN PETER AND I arrived at the *Hang-Jinhe* the next afternoon, we found Da in a foul humor at the top of the ladder. He answered Peter's cheery hello with no more than a grunt and nearly pushed me back down the ladder ahead of him.

"It took you long enough," he growled.

"It's just gone on noon," I protested.

"And that's longer than any man should have to spend in the company of that Sands bastard. Come on, get to your oars, before I leave you here to swim home tonight!"

I could see there was no reasoning with him. He went on and on about Jacob Sands. I gathered that Sands had come out with his wife and old Robert Lawson about midmorning on the *Peabody*. Da had rowed over to fetch them all in the *Hang-Jinhe's* boat, with one of the Chinese crew to help. Sands had made some remark to old Robert about remembering Da's dark face, then told Da outright to "let the Chinaman do the rowing because I'll be damned if I'll let my wife be soaked and abused by an Irish thug." And then he had the nerve to tell Mr. Lawson and An-Ming that they should hire a different boatman.

"'An American, who'd know how to row without being retaught every time he was made to pick up an oar,'" Da repeated, in a poor imitation of Sands' sour voice. "His blessed lordship even offered to hire one for 'em! What does he know about rowing? Or being American, for that matter? I didn't come to America to be that kind of American, I can tell you that!"

"I hope you didn't tell him," I muttered.

"And what if I did?" he shouted, turning around. "What if I did? Do you think it'd make a half-penny difference to the likes of him? Or are you more worried about your blessed Mr. Lawson and his bossy little girl, about what they'd think? Is that what you—?"

Da's shout turned into a sharp cough that didn't stop for half a minute, and when it did, he was red-faced and sweating.

"Do you want some water?" I asked carefully.

He glared at me. When he could finally catch his breath, he said, "I'll get a drink soon enough. Get back to rowing."

He fought the cough the rest of the way to the wharf.

I wasn't worried about Mr. Lawson or An-Ming. I knew they wouldn't listen to Sands. But Da could still get himself into trouble talking back to someone like that. The *Hang-Jinhe* wouldn't be staying here forever. Sands could speak to Mr. Bond and to the wharfingers, and pretty soon Da wouldn't be able to find anyone to row for, nor a boat to row in. That would kill him sure as the coughing. And then what would Ma do? If only Da would keep his blessed mouth shut.

When I got back to the junk, the *Peabody* had returned, and Sands and his wife and old Robert were just getting ready to leave. They'd had a tour of the ship and a long dinner at a table set up on the afterdeck, and apparently a good long chat about the clock and the so-called "family resources."

"We'll see you at the bank tomorrow, eh, Matthew?" old Robert was saying.

"First thing in the morning," Mr. Lawson replied, "but

only because you insist. You must try to forget the exaggerations of that reporter. I'd write to the editor if I thought it would make a difference and not simply stir up the hornets' nest worse than it already has been."

"No, no, he's absolutely correct. It is your due and our duty. You are part of the family."

"You are kind, Cousin Robert," An-Ming said. "I feel most welcome."

"It is simply wonderful to have you here, Ann," Eleanor Sands said. "I hope you won't keep hiding yourself away on this boat in the future. I would love to introduce you to our circle of friends. They are very anxious to meet you, aren't they, Jacob?"

"It seems to be all anyone talks about," Sands replied. "And we can hardly bring them out here *en masse* . . . unless you were to move closer. I could easily arrange a space for you at India or Commercial Wharf. We have interests in both."

"I appreciate the thought, Jacob," Mr. Lawson said, "but it is much easier for Li to keep watch on our crew here, and for Ann and myself to avoid the gawkers and busy-bodies."

"We do not want more exaggerations in newspapers, yes?" An-Ming said, smiling much too brightly. "Please now, the day cools. Take Cousin Robert to your warm home."

"Don't bother about me, my dear," old Robert said, patting her arm. "I shall be fine."

The very saying of it made his daughter cluck and fuss with his scarf and his coat. Warm as it was, he was bundled like a baby, and I had to wonder if his face was pale gray from age or indigestion or simply being smothered. Mr. and Mrs. Sands coaxed him to the rail, where the crew had rigged a bosun's chair to the main boom. They lowered him gently into the ship's boat, and then Mrs. Sands, and then even Mr. Sands, who didn't appear any happier in the chair than he had on the ladder. I made to join the Chinese crew in the boat, but then I remembered Da's foul mood and decided they didn't need me. Sands had more than enough to complain about, and at least the Chinese crew couldn't understand him.

The next morning, Da told me he wasn't going to come any nearer to Sands than he had to. He stayed in our boat with Peter and put me off on the *Hang-Jinhe* to row Mr. Lawson in to visit the bank. So I got in the junk's little scow with him and Wang and brought them up in front of the Custom House. Four boys were waiting for us, just so they could fight over the chance to earn a penny as the day's boat-guard. They were surprised it was us instead of Da and Hu-Lan and the cook, but that didn't stop them from asking. I told Mr. Lawson I didn't mind waiting, but he wouldn't have it. He picked out one of the lads and insisted I come along and keep Wang company. I didn't think Mr. Sands would appreciate it, but I didn't say it out loud.

Sure, when we arrived, I got a grand sour glance from Sands. He showed Mr. Lawson into old Robert's office, to a pile of thick ledgers and sheaves of loose papers and a clerk in a stiff collar who was there to help. Then he put Wang and me on a pair of hard chairs outside the door. Wang settled down like he was used to it. I got the fidgets in half a minute. I tried to start a chat, but the clerks at the desks and the counter all gave me a frown. I shut my mouth and tried to look like Wang, calm as a new moon. That lasted all of two minutes. The bank men scratched with their pens, or spoke quietly with the few customers who came in, or carried papers back and forth from Sands' office. I could see the doors to a big vault safe on his back wall, and I tried to imagine the piles of money and stocks and all. That took up another minute or two. Spending it took a few more.

I shifted in my seat, which made it squeak, and all the clerks looked up at me. So I thought about the clock some. When I'd been little, Da had told me and Bridget stories of the old Irish heros. One of them, Ossian – the son of the great Finn McCool – had been lured to the land of *Tir na nÓg*, the Land of the Young, by a fairy maiden who he loved. What he didn't know was that each year in that land was a hundred years in ours. When he went back home, he found the land all changed, his old companions dead and gone. A lot like what happened to Mr. Lawson. But when Ossian got down from his fairy horse and touched the soil of Ireland, all the years caught up with him at once. He grew old and died on the spot. I didn't like that thought. It sounded like what had happened when An-Ming's grandfather stopped his own clock. Like what would have happened to Mr. Lawson if Peter hadn't spotted the little pin stuck in the gears. Even the best chronometer could break.

I tried to think of something else. There wasn't much in that bank to spark the imagination. I yawned, maybe a bit louder than was polite. All the clerks frowned at me. I frowned back. Their frowns got darker. I shrugged and looked at my hands. They *hmphed* and went back to their work. I gave it a moment, then shifted my chair so it squeaked. When they all looked up, I was studying a fly buzzing up in the chandelier. Leaning the chair way back, on two legs. Quiet as a mouse, mind you. I could feel their frowns growing darker by the second. It was a bit like being back in school.

Just at the moment I figured one of them would say something, I let the chair down with a thump, gave a good squeaky wiggle, and yawned again.

You never heard such a chorus of *humphs*. You'd have thought a pack of seals was swimming by in the street.

I looked up, all innocence, and the one with the biggest sideburns, the boss clerk, I guess, started to get up. Wang turned to me and said something long in Chinese. Then he winked.

"You can say that again, Mr. Wang, sir," I replied, and I sat up straight, ankles crossed, hands folded neatly in my lap, like Bridget in church. Of course, I hadn't understood a word he'd said. But it did the trick; the clerk sat back down.

After that, Wang would say something to me every couple of minutes, and I'd reply politely, squeaking my seat while I did. The clerks were just as happy as I was when Mr. Lawson finally came out of the office.

He and Sands said a few words on their way to the door, and we were all about to leave when a carriage drew up to the curb in a rattle of hooves and wheels. Eleanor Sands opened the door and stepped down before the driver had even dropped his reins. She turned and helped old Robert climb out.

Old Robert didn't look any better for a night's sleep; if anything, he looked worse, leaning heavily on his daughter's arm. Mr. Lawson and Sands went over to greet them.

"All through, then, Uncle?" old Robert asked. "Is everything to your liking?"

Mr. Lawson returned his smile with a weak one. "All seems in order, though there is such a great deal in there, Robert, I fear I have just barely touched the surface. I know so little of the nature of commerce here in this day and age. I was a captain and a merchant, accustomed to barter and bargain for solid cargo, at a price I could halfway guess at. 'Long term' meant the length of a voyage. Your investments are quite varied and seem sound. That's the best I can say."

"Then Ann really should review them," old Robert said.

"Good heavens, Father," Sands exclaimed, "think of the impression that would make on our investors! A woman auditing our books? I suppose next you'll suggest hiring some to be clerks and tellers."

"She is family," old Robert insisted.

"So is Eleanor, and you don't see her sitting at a desk poring over ledgers. She has her own place in the household, and is quite content with it, aren't you, my dear?"

Mrs. Sands looked surprised at even being asked. She glanced from her husband to her father and settled on a vague smile and half a nod aimed at neither of them.

Sands kept on, at Mr. Lawson. "Unfortunately, a small,

irritating swarm of women have decided that suffrage is their God-given right. They buzz about the town like wasps, stinging whoever tries to defend the status quo. They'd be at our doorstep in an instant, followed by a dozen nosey reporters. And in my opinion, we've been in the newspapers more than enough."

"I couldn't agree more," Mr. Lawson said. He was speaking calmly enough, but I could tell he wouldn't mind giving Sands a sting or two himself.

"Well, I say we should sleep on it," old Robert said, frowning mulishly at Sands.

"Yes, Father," Mrs. Sands said, relieved. "It's too close to dinner to make such momentous decisions."

"And there is no reason we couldn't keep it quiet," old Robert grumbled. "It's a family matter. This is a family business."

"I'm sure it's not even necessary," Mr. Lawson put in, before Sands could fire off another broadside. "I certainly didn't see any poor addition or spelling errors. Ann will undoubtedly tell me to let you mind your own business."

"Still, she should be offered the chance," old Robert muttered. "It's only right."

"Of course, Father," Mrs. Sands said, in the way you talk to a sulky child, or an adult who's grown back to childhood. "Now, we must let Uncle Matthew get on with his day."

I think everyone was happy to get away from that argument. Sure, I was.

We arrived back at the junk to find Da already gone to the markets with Hu-Lan and the cook. And we found Peter and An-Ming in the clock room, bent over the table. He had turned one end of the table into a workbench, with a little vise and a tiny anvil and a jig for cutting gears. His tool kit now included saws with teeth so fine it was hard to believe they'd cut butter, let alone brass. And he had a set of bright files and rifflers, as sharp as knives, and some of them narrow as toothpicks. There was some work he had to do at Mr.

Bond's shop, with help from the master clockmakers, but Mr. Lawson liked having him close at hand, for secrecy and for company. And there was no doubt Peter preferred being close to An-Ming. Right then, she was handling one of the tiny files as easy as she did a pair of chopsticks, smoothing the teeth on a gear. Peter was fitting a set of gears into some arrangement, so close beside her their heads were near to touching. Nothing wrong in that, of course, but they did jump apart when we surprised them. Peter blushed. An-Ming looked calm as Wang in the midst of his slow morning exercise.

"How was bank, Father?" she asked, pulling out a chair for him.

He started pacing instead. He didn't even correct her grammar. "Unsettling. The books appear to be all in order, and I must say Robert and Sands have stacked up an impressive list of investments. But I have no idea how sound they are . . ." He trailed off, still pacing. "It's all too orderly," he said finally. "There wasn't a single correction in those ledgers. Not one. Everything lined up, all the names properly spelled, all the figures summed to a point the first time. My bookkeeping never looked like that. Not even your mother's did."

"Perhaps this was a copy they show to their shareholders," Peter said.

"Yes, and that's the problem. I should have seen the originals." He turned to An-Ming. "You should study them, if only to soothe Robert. He is determined to make us part of the firm."

"*Hoa ben,*" An-Ming grumbled.

"It may seem silly to you," Mr. Lawson told her, "but it is very important to Robert."

"He does seem rather fixated on the notion," Peter remarked.

"He has been disappointed in that respect," Mr. Lawson explained. "He has a son, Simon, who wants nothing to do with the business. Sands is his son-in-law, but that's not the same to Robert. Let us hope Eleanor gives birth to a healthy grandson"

An-Ming snorted. "Hope that Cousin Robert lives to see it."

"What's the son do, this Simon?" I asked. I could well imagine not wanting to work in a bank, but I couldn't imagine giving up the money.

"He's in the Navy," Mr. Lawson replied. "Captain of his own ship and quite happy at it, according to Eleanor. She also admitted that Simon and Sands don't get along."

"It is not difficult to dislike Sands," An-Ming said.

"A diplomatic way to phrase it, my dear. Peter must be having a good influence on you."

Peter's ears flared, but An-Ming just smiled.

"Ah, I have this for the clock," Peter said, gesturing at the table.

Mr. Lawson forgot about the bank and hurried over. Peter held up a set of four or five gears mounted in a framework of small brass plates and rods. He set it on top of the diagram, lining it up with itself in the sketch. They started talking about how it would fit in and what had to be made next, then Mr. Lawson made for the doorway, clockwork in hand.

"I will prepare this," he said.

"First eat dinner, Father," An-Ming said.

"The timing—"

"Can wait. This is not the heart stone. You have been all morning with your head full of numbers. You need a clear mind for invocations."

"Yes, of course." He hovered by the door, obviously wishing he could get right on with it, whatever it was. I decided to eat quickly, and keep an eye on where Mr. Lawson went after he had cleaned his plate.

Chapter 12

WITH THE COOK AND Hu-Lan both ashore, Wang put together a small meal for the Lawsons. Peter sometimes joined them, but this day he stayed in the clock room, too excited by the gears to eat, I guess. I ate alone, sitting on deck. A fine breeze had come up to ease the summer heat. The *Hang-Jinhe* tugged gently at her anchor. The harbor was busy as ever and always fun to watch, but I kept a close eye on Mr. Lawson and An-Ming, who were at the table on the stern deck. As quick as I was to down my dinner, Mr. Lawson was with me, bite for bite. An-Ming tried to make conversation, but he was letting her do all the work of finding words. The bit of clockwork sat beside him on the table, and he touched it now and again, patted it like, as if it were a living thing that he wanted to keep content. As soon as he was done, he started to rise, but An-Ming pointed out that she was still eating, and a gentleman in China wouldn't be so impolite. He grimaced, but he stayed.

Finally she was finished, and they came down to the main deck and went into the stern house through the starboard companionway. Wang started to clean up the dinner table. I made as if to go into the port companionway, to the clock room, then skipped back out and scurried along close to the bulkhead, where Wang couldn't see me. The crew had already eaten and were caulking the seams up on the foredeck. No one noticed me slip after the Lawsons.

I'd been that way once, when An-Ming had showed me around. The mate's cabin was first in. Wang had a little box of a cabin past the mate's, and Hu-Lan had one past Wang's. An-Ming's cabin was next, tucked into the stern quarter. Mr. Lawson's cabin was across the companionway from An-Ming's and ran across the stern of the junk to the portside companionway, where it had another door right opposite the clock room. The rest of the space between the companionways was a wardroom, where they could take their meals.

An-Ming hadn't shown me Mr. Lawson's cabin, and the door was closed now. But I could hear them talking quietly inside. I put my ear to the door.

"Best to wait for the moon," An-Ming said.

"That shouldn't matter," Mr. Lawson replied. "This part of the gear train will move the sun. Sunlight will probably help. Here, please light the incense."

"Probably? You will take that chance?"

"Wu said—" and he slipped into speaking Chinese.

She argued back, also in Chinese. The sweet-spicey smell of incense started to fill the companionway. My nose began to tickle, and I squeezed it hard to keep from sneezing. They kept arguing. The smell got thicker than the fog in a high mass, more like the markets at the end of the day, when the unsold fruit and meat begin to go by and swarm with flies and wasps. My eyes were watering. The arguing stopped, and a chime rang inside the cabin, three times. Mr. Lawson began speaking again, only his voice was slow and heavy, chanting. The chime rang again, and An-Ming joined him, high pitched, whining. The hairs rose on the back of my neck.

I'd like to tell you there was some kind of sign, some flash of light or movement of the seas, but what happened was I heard footsteps on deck, coming closer. Then a shadow fell across the companionway. And there I was, kneeling on the deck with my ear pressed to Mr. Lawson's door. I scooted across the companionway and slid into An-Ming's cabin.

I caught a glimpse of a green silk robe lying over the end of her narrow bed, a pair of green slippers beneath it. A shelf with books. A small, carved chest. It was tempting to look inside the chest, but I turned and pressed my ear to the inside of the door. The footsteps came into the companionway and hesitated. I heard a door latch rattle, then a door close. It was either Wang or the mate. There were more chimes from across the way. I peeked out. The coast was clear, so I tip-toed toward the light on deck.

I got as far as the mate's cabin when the latch rattled again. It was Wang's door. Sure, I skipped fast then! I shot out on deck and scooted as fast as I could for the rail. When Wang came out, I was looking over the harbor, cool as you please. I took a deep breath, like I was just enjoying the day. And sneezed so hard I almost shot my brains out through my nose. All I could smell was that blessed incense. And I still didn't know what Mr. Lawson did to the clockworks.

I did find out one thing later that afternoon. Peter left the junk early.

"You won't need to wait for me, Finn," he said, steering us across the channel toward the city. "I'll be going directly home."

"From where?" I asked.

"Brattle Street. I'm going to see E. Feinmann, the jeweler."

"A jeweler is it? Are you buying a ring for her then?"

"A ring? Why would I buy—?" His ears burned. "No, I am not buying a ring, Finn, for anyone!"

"No need to get all riled, Mr. Jenkins," I said, fighting a grin. "It was an honest mistake after seeing your two heads so close together over your set of gears."

"She was merely helping me!" Now his whole face was red.

"Well, that's good. I suppose she is a bit young for you. More my age."

"She's not that young. And that's not the point! The point is we are . . . ah, we are merely . . . interested in many of the same things. The clock for one thing, but there are others. For example, cultures. Yesterday, she showed me a book with some scenes of her country."

"I suppose China would be a fine place to live, wouldn't it? Settle down there, like Mr. Lawson. Raise a family."

"That wasn't even part of the discussion. And I will not discuss it any further!"

Peter was so easy to tease, but I could see he'd reached his limit. "What is it about the jeweler, then, if it isn't a ring you're after?"

"It isn't, and no more about that."

"Yes, sir."

Peter took a breath and tried to settle himself. "I am going to see Mr. Feinmann about having some jewels made for the clock."

"What sort of jewels?" I remembered only too well the great blood-red stone set in the middle of Mr. Lawson's old clock.

"The new clock will need close to a dozen, cut from sapphire," Peter said.

"Not ruby?"

"Sapphires come in several colors," Peter said. "Ruby is one of them, but rubies are more rare and also more costly. I expect most of these will be clear stones. It will depend on what Feinmann can obtain."

"What are they all for?" I could imagine a dozen sapphires would cost quite a bit, even if they weren't red.

"Wear points in the clock work," Peter replied. "There are a number of places where metal would wear down too quickly from the constant friction and the action of the escapement. That's the part that stops the gears, then lets them free at a fixed rate to count the time. The tick-tock part. Each tick and tock represents the strike of a small catch, or hook, on the scape wheel, from which all the other gears are driven. They keep the spring from winding down all at once. Imagine two tiny hammers striking constantly on a ring of tiny anvils. After a while, something will begin to wear, and the action will slow down or speed up. That's bad enough, of course, but eventually something will break. The clock will stop. By using tiny jewels at the striking points, we can hold off that time for quite a while. Sapphire is very, very hard."

"Like diamond?"

"Not that hard, Finn, but as close as matters."

"This new clock, I've noticed it's not much bigger than one of your marine chronometers; certainly not as big as Mr. Lawson's old one. Are these jewels going to be smaller?"

"Oh, by quite a bit," Peter said. "And there will be more than twice as many. The old clock has only three: two in the escapement and one for the main bearing."

"The big one in the middle," I said.

"That's right. That will be the hardest to make. Most of the others will be standard sizes that Mr. Bond orders regularly. The two on the escapement will be a little larger than normal, but of much the same design. The main bearing will be nothing Mr. Feinmann has even tried before, I'm sure."

"The heart stone," I muttered.

"What?"

"That's what it is, isn't it? The heart stone? I heard An-Ming call it that."

"Yes, it is the heart stone." Peter touched the front of his coat, right over his heart. "I have the plan for it in my pocket. I can't wait to hear what Mr. Feinmann says when he sees it."

I would've liked to hear that myself. Even more, I

would've liked to see the raw stone, and him cutting it. I'd have been happy to collect the slivers that fell off.

Da had settled down by the next day and sent me off with Peter again, while he ferried Hu-Lan and the cook. As usual, he stayed ashore when they were done and let the Chinese crew row the others back. The only advantage to it was that Hu-Lan only paid him for the morning. Mr. Lawson always paid me the balance at the end of the day, and I collected the wage from Peter, too. So most of the money made it home to Ma.

An-Ming needed to go to Mr. Tierney's that day for a second fitting. so right after dinner, the crew hoisted a big wooden tub from the hold, and set it on deck with four wooden screens around it. The cook already had a fire going on the hearth, which was just outside the forward deck house. Water was heating in a big pot, and soon a line of crewmen were passing buckets behind the screen to fill the tub. I had no idea what they were planning to cook.

Then An-Ming appeared from the stern house, all wrapped in a flowing silk robe, green with bright gold cranes embroidered on it, like on their big flag. Hu-Lan came out behind her, carrying a rag and a brush and a big fluffy cloth. I was beginning to get the idea when the mate shouted something, and the crewmen all turned and looked everywhere but at the screens. I pretended I didn't understand.

An-Ming and Hu-Lan went behind the screens and pulled the corners tight, but there was a gap at the bottom. I caught a glimpse of An-Ming's ankles as she dropped the beautiful robe on the deck and stepped into the tub. She gasped and muttered some Chinese curse that made half the crew laugh. Hu-Lan scolded her and hung the robe over the screen, and then there was a bunch of splashing and scrubbing. Water slopped onto the deck and ran out the scuppers.

I was leaning on the rail, more or less looking at Boston while I watched from the corner of my eye for another glimpse of ankle, when Peter came out. He stretched and rubbed his eyes and wandered over to me. I could tell his mind was still on the clock.

"All done already?" I asked.

"Ah, just for now," he replied. "I needed a break. What are you doing? I thought you were taking An-Ming to see your mother at Tierney's."

"An-Ming's getting ready," I remarked, all casual.

"Is she?" he murmured, gazing at something invisible about two feet in front of his nose.

"She is. Right behind you, in fact."

"What?" Peter blinked, turned, and stared for a moment, slow as a sot. Then his ears became a wonderful sight. I had never seen 'em so red.

"Finn!" he exclaimed. "Good heavens, don't look! That's An-Ming in there! A young woman! Have you no morals at all?"

"I don't see you turning away."

He spun back to the rail. "Well, I have now."

"You don't have to on my account."

"Will you please look away! You'll embarrass her! She'll think we're all heathens!"

"And how do you know she's not?" I said it as a joke, but it did occur to me that I had no idea what faith the Chinese held to. Pat's article in the *Herald* had said Mr. Lawson was a Protestant, like all the rest of the old Boston folk, but he had married a Chinese woman. And he almost seemed to worship that clock. Had he converted?

I got to thinking about it so hard, I missed when An-Ming stepped out of the tub. Then I realized that Peter wasn't looking at me any more. Oh, his face was turned my way, but his eyeballs were slid so sideways he could just about look out through his own ear.

She did have pretty ankles. Feet, too. And if she'd stood

there getting dried off any longer, I think Peter and I both could have written poems about her toes. But the robe went back on, and the slippers, and she emerged all covered, with her wet hair wrapped in the towel. Hu-Lan, all spattered and flushed, shoed her across the deck and back into the stern house, but not before An-Ming had noticed Peter and somehow flashed him a smile, all the while pretending he didn't exist. It was quite a performance. And he pretended he wasn't looking, but his ears gave him away. I wondered if he might be buying a ring for her someday after all.

Chapter 13

MAYOR SEAVER'S PARTY FOR the Lawsons was a big to-do. The Boston Band played, and Ordway's Aeoleans put on their minstrel show, with *Old Folks at Home* and *Sawanee River* and some jokes I couldn't hear because I was too far away. I managed to get close enough to the food to fill a plate. There were heaps of oysters and broiled hams and pitchers of beer and cider and lemonade, and hundreds of people it seemed, all done up in their finest. An-Ming out-shone them all in her new dress, as pretty a girl as I'd ever seen. But she still wouldn't wear a bonnet, no matter how much Hu-Lan and her father might argue. He wanted her to look as American as she could, but she would only go so far.

The whole crew came along, scrubbed and dressed in their spare kit. Even Peter was invited. Ever since the article had come out in the *Herald*, he'd been something of a celebrity, whether he liked it or not. The mayor hired one of the East Boston ferries to haul everyone. Mr. Lawson asked Da and Me to stand watch on the *Hang-Jinhe*, at full wages plus a bonus for not getting to join in. I was disappointed, but we couldn't turn down an offer like that, even Da had to agree. I half expected him to head off to Hurley's as soon as the ferry left, leaving me on my own. Instead, he offered me the chance.

"You'll be wanting to see all the hullaballoo, I'm guessing," he said. "Go ahead, take the boat. It don't need the two of us here. Just make sure you're back before they are."

I was so surprised, I gaped at him like the town idiot.

He gave me a light cuff on the ear. "Get on with you then," he growled, "before your brains fall out of your mouth."

"Are you sure, Da?"

"I just said it, didn't I? Go on, before I change my mind."

"Yes sir!" And I was down the ladder in a trice. He watched me go, even gave a nod as I rowed off. I never really could understand him.

Two days later, Sunday, when the whole family was invited to have dinner with the Lawsons on the *Hang-Jinhe*, he wouldn't come. Ma had reminded him that morning, and you should have heard him.

"I told you to beg off when the girl came for her fitting!" he shouted.

"I tried," Ma replied, "but you know what the young lady is like. She wouldn't listen."

"Then you didn't tell her loud enough! Sweet Jesus, Kate! We can't be having dinner with the likes of them!"

"I don't see why not," Ma replied. "You and Finn are out on that junk with them every day, and I know they've fed you. Finn's told me."

Da glared at me. "We eat with the Chinese crew, for God's sake, not with the bloody Brahmins!"

"You watch your language, Mike O'Neill! Bridget and I have been invited, and I will not insult those good people by saying no."

"You'll make fools of the lot of us."

"I know which fork is for fish and which for meat," Ma told him.

"And what'll you say to them? 'Good die, yer ladyship. A foine day for the races, innit?'"

"They don't talk like that, Michael, and you know it. They're Americans, not the British. This isn't Dublin. It's different here."

"There are days I wonder," Da muttered.

"An-Ming likes us, Da," Bridget said. "Truly she does. She won't be putting on airs."

"Everyone likes you, *cailin*. The rest of us aren't so blessed."

"She likes all of us. What was it she said, Ma? 'The wealth of a house is judged by the worth of the family.'"

"Did she say that now? Well, let me warn you, girl, there's a big chink between saying and doing."

And you're proof enough of that, Da, I thought. But I kept quiet, because I knew Bridget just might turn him around. If anyone could do it, she could. He calmed down at least. He seemed to agree. But when the time came after mass on Sunday, he was nowhere to be seen.

I rowed Ma and Bridget out, and we had a fine visit. There was no row of forks to choose from, though they did offer us chopsticks to try. An-Ming was dressed like Hu-Lan, only brighter, in a long skirt topped by an embroidered shirt and a tunic with wide sleeves, and they talked about clothing a lot. Bridget even tried on one of An-Ming's Chinese outfits. Not the pants, of course – Ma wouldn't let her – just the skirt and shirt and tunic, and she looked as pretty as ever. Mr. Lawson asked Ma about Ireland and her family, and answered her questions about China. She asked about the clock, of course, and he showed her. He didn't go into the workings of it, but just seeing it was enough for her. I knew it would make her the talk of the neighbors for some days to come.

I was the one who felt awkward. I'd been used to my place there as boatman. Being a dinner guest, freshly washed, hair combed, clothes brushed, I didn't feel quite like me. I stayed quiet, thinking about Da mostly. Where he was, and why he wouldn't come. And what he'd say when he learned the Lawsons would be coming to visit us in another week.

In the midst of it all, the Cunard steamer *Britannia* set out from her pier on East Boston. Everyone rushed to the rail to wave her off. Two thick plumes of black smoke billowed from her stacks as she steamed by, churning up a great wake with her wheels. The tugs and the other steamers in the harbor blew their whistles, and she answered with loud blasts from her own. She pushed her way out whatever the wind and tide, bound for Liverpool by way of Halifax, keeping the tight schedule promised by Mr. Cunard.

"Oh, wouldn't it be exciting to be on her?" Bridget exclaimed.

I shook my head. It was clipper ships for me, heading the other direction. Now, two days later, when the *Flying Fish* made sail for California, that was something to exclaim about. There was an offshore breeze and an ebb tide, and the captain sailed her right off from Lewis Wharf. Her topsails bellied out as she pulled free, and then her topgallants and royals, soaring high above the sails of every other ship on the water. She came out steadily, gaining speed, her headsails drawing well. A mob of small craft flitted in her wake, well-wishers waving and cheering. The wind carried the sound of band music and singing. She had flags flying on every stay, it seemed, and the captain had the crew setting sail after sail. The big lower courses took the wind with a whoosh and crack that echoed over the water. And just as she passed the *Hang-Jinhe*, the skysails went loose of the yards and snapped open, tiny and white and a mile high. Sure, she looked fine. I'd have jumped aboard in an instant, had someone offered. But they didn't, and I had Peter to row and the *Hang-Jinhe* to look forward to, so life wasn't all bad.

Aside from that, it was a quiet week. There was always Peter to row out in the morning, to find new custom for Mr. Bond. There was always the market trip for Da, with the cook and Hu-Lan. But the invitations had slowed down, so there was less ferrying to do. Mr. Lawson and An-Ming went to see old Robert at home one day. He wasn't getting any better, but he loved chatting about old times and trying to talk Chinese, so they spent a good bit of the afternoon with him. And Friday, Eleanor Sands took An-Ming to the theater to see the afternoon show. Two of her lady friends came along, and all their maids, Hu-Lan included.

That same day, Mr. Sands took Mr. Lawson to the race track. Mr. Lawson wasn't too keen on it, but he went. He was still trying to get on Mr. Sands' good side, careful not to mention the books or the business. Wang went with them, so Mr. Lawson gave Da the two bits for the theater and told him to keep a close eye on An-Ming. I could understand why he'd want a grown man like Da for a bodyguard, but I sure wished it was me going. They went to the Boston Museum, which was the only theater that had an afternoon show. It was a real museum, too, with wax works and strange creatures; even Mr. Barnum's Fiji Mermaid, the ugliest thing you ever saw, Da said. He also said it looked to be sewn together from a monkey and a fish. Da didn't trust anyone, not even a genuine museum.

They saw three short plays featuring Miss Eliza Logan, back by popular demand, according to the program Da brought back for Ma and Bridget. Da said Bridget was prettier and could sing better, too. He said Miss Logan did play the lover well, pining for the peasant boy like she meant it, but later, when she was supposed to be frightened during *The Phantom Breakfast*, he didn't believe her.

"I've seen you frightened near to death," he told Ma. "It's not something you want to make believe about."

It was Friday evening. The fine weather had been holding, and Da's cough seemed to be easing up. The play had put him in such good temper, and dinner had made him sleepy, so Ma picked that time to be telling him about the visit from the Lawsons.

"Mike," she said, "what do you think we ought to have for dinner Sunday? The Lawsons will be coming, and I want to treat them to something they'd like."

"The Lawsons will be coming." He said it very quietly, which wasn't a good thing. He looked Ma in the face, eyes half closed, as if he couldn't give a tinker's dam.

"That's right," Ma replied, looking right back at him. "They asked us, and we asked them. I know they're not our class, and we can't possibly treat them the way they're used to, but I'm going to feed them a good meal just the same. I'm sure it'll never happen again, but at least they'll have one chance to see the Irish know how to honor a kindness and show proper thanks."

Da didn't say anything for at least a minute. Then he got to his feet. His hands wer clenched at his sides. "I'm sure you will show them, Kate. You're just like your father. No sense of who's who in this world."

"And it's a good thing, isn't it?" she said. "Else he never would have let you court me, and then where would we be? Now, what should we have for dinner on Sunday?"

"I don't know and I don't care. I'm sure you'll do yourself proud. Just don't set a place for me."

He walked out, slammed the door, and stamped down the stairs. He slammed the front door, too. And we didn't see him till Sunday night.

Saturday I rowed Peter and ran the market trip, too. Luckily there was no party for the crew that day. Ma and Bridget made a special trip to the Haymarket on their way home and bought a good-sized hen and a fresh cabbage and potatoes, and I brought home a pound of cod from T Wharf. That night we boiled the potatoes and the cod and tidied the place and brushed our clothes again. We had enough dishes, what with the girls gone, but Ma borrowed two more glasses from the Flanagans and enough spare forks and knives from a few other neighbors to make up a full set for everyone. Even Da. She didn't say anything, but she listened close every time someone came up the stairs. Me, I thought we were better off without him.

Sunday we went to early mass, then Ma and Bridget went home to start cooking. I searched the wharves for scrap wood for the fire, just to be sure we had enough to cook everything, and also made sure the kettle and bucket were full. Then I ran down the street to bang on Hurley's door to get a jug of fresh cider. It was the Sabbath, and he couldn't take money from me. I left it on the counter, so he could put it in the box first thing in the morning. We were spending a lot on this meal, but Ma wasn't about to serve plain water to guests like these.

Then I got the boat and went out to the *Hang-Jinhe* to fetch the Lawsons. And Wang. Mr. Lawson wouldn't go anywhere without him, which turned out to be a good thing. Hu-Lan was left behind, in case Captain Li needed an interpreter.

There was a fine breeze blowing, and I put up the mast and sail. That got us back to Lewis Wharf sooner than Ma was expecting, so I offered to show Mr. Lawson around.

"Thank you, Finn," he said. "I used to live here in the North End, with my first family. I meant to visit earlier, but I was afraid it might bring back sad memories. That doesn't seem so likely now. It is so changed, I hardly recognize it. As with all the rest of Boston. Please, do show me around. I would particularly like to visit Copp's Hill."

"The burial ground, sir?" I blurted.

"Yes. My wife and son are there."

Well, that was a thought. The Copp's Hill burying ground hadn't been used since before I could remember – it had gotten filled up with all the old colonials – yet Mr. Lawson's first family was there. It reminded me how old he really was. It's one thing to say ninety-one; it's another to think how much happens in that stretch of years. How many people are born, live, and die! He was a walking history book, even if he didn't look old enough.

We made our way to the top of the hill. He saw houses he recognized, though not a one of them was still home to the families he'd known. Almost all the North End was Irish. His own home was gone, replaced by a crowded boarding house in need of paint. Worse, when we got to the burial ground, he couldn't find the graves of his wife and child. Sometime in the fifty-odd years he'd been gone, the cemetery had been changed. Trees planted, lanes moved, headstones fallen. Graves had been moved, too, or covered over. Even reused.

"They would have been here," he said, and it wasn't memory that made him sad. It was the loss of the thing he remembered. We were down on the northern edge, with a view toward Charleston and the tall spike of the Bunker Hill Monument. Which I guess wouldn't have been there when his wife and son were buried.

"It has all changed," he said. "Still, I have fond memories. And it remains a lovely view. What more could one ask?"

"I'm sorry, Father," An-Ming said, taking his hand.

He gave her a smile. "Thank you, Dear, but don't be too sad. Had they lived, I would not have gone to China and met your mother. We cannot change the past, nor predict the future. We can only try our best and hope the outcome makes the world a little better. I think I have been lucky in that respect." He stared across the river again. "I do wish Nathanial had lived to see all that I've seen. I suppose that's what every parent wishes who has lost a child."

He took a breath and forced the smile back on his face. "Come, I'm making us all gloomy. Show me more of *your* North End, Master O'Neill."

"I know," An-Ming said. "To sweeten the mood. Come, Father."

She meant the molasses, of course, and I let her lead us down the north side of the hill to Ingersoll's Wharf.

Despite being overcast, the day was warm where we

were, shielded from a southerly breeze by the hill behind us. The sweet-and-sour burnt-flower smell of molasses mixed powerfully with the mud-and-salt stench of low tide. The flies were out in force. Still, Mr. Lawson laughed when he saw the stack of barrels. He strolled out along the wharf, gazing at them like they were old friends.

"Here is something I do remember!" he exclaimed. "Boston has always had molasses. Now let's see how well the taste stands up to memory."

He swiped the tip of his finger along a leaking seam, and stuck it right in his mouth. His smile grew, and he nodded. "Yes," he said, "every bit as good. Come, join me. I'm sure the distillery won't miss a lick or two."

An-Ming and I didn't wait for a second invitation, and then we got Wang to try it.

"Good!" he agreed. "Vely good," a sticky tongue mixing up his L and his R even worse than usual.

We all enjoyed a few more licks as we walked to the far end of the wharf to look across at the shipyards in East Boston. The *Great Republic,* on the ways at McKay's shipyard, dwarfed all the other hulls nearby, and the buildings, too. We marveled at the size of her, wondering if she'd be finished in time for her scheduled launch, now just a couple of weeks away. Then Mr. Lawson checked his pocket watch and said we should be getting along. He pulled out his kerchief, dabbed his lips, wiped a streak from An-Ming's chin, and we all turned to go.

The tall thug who had knocked An-Ming into the harbor was standing halfway down the wharf, blocking the way to the street, and he had two ugly friends with him.

Chapter 14

It's one thing to scoop up a smallish girl in the midst of a brawl; it's another when she has three men beside her. Even when one of them is ninety-one and another is a small-sized boy. But it was the dinner hour, and Ingersoll's Wharf went off at an angle, with a warehouse on one side and the stack of barrels on the other. The view was blocked. No one could see our predicament. We might have made a run for it around the end of the stack, but An-Ming was in a dress, and I wasn't sure Mr. Lawson would be able to run very fast for very long. He didn't seem all that worried, though. Serious, but not worried.

"Are these friends of yours, Finn?" he asked.

"The one in the middle's the ruffian who attacked your daughter, sir."

His face grew hard. "Is that so, Ann?"

"Yes." She was sporting her Malay pirate look. I didn't think she'd've run even if she'd had her pants on.

Mr. Lawson said something in Chinese to Wang, who nodded calmly and began walking right toward the three thugs. An-Ming started to follow.

Mr. Lawson grabbed her arm. "You will only get in the way, Ann," he snapped. He tried to push her behind him, but she wouldn't have it. The best he could do was keep her by his side.

Well, he hadn't said anything to me, and I was ready for another try at the tall fellow.

Wang reached the men before I could catch up. The tall thug started to say something like, "Take care of this one, Sam. I'll get the gir—," but Wang made a quick move toward him. It was just a feint. The fellow on the left – a broad, ugly tough with a broken nose – went to grab him. Wang leaned back, turned just a little, and the fellow stumbled right into his arms. Before you could blink, the ugly thug went sailing over Wang's shoulder and smashed upside down into the wall of the warehouse. He bounced head first onto the cobbled wharf and lay there.

Wang had already turned back to the other two. They took a second to think about what had just happened to their mate, and I guess decided he must have tripped over his own feet. I'd have been more careful, myself. The tall one moved first, stepping in with a roundhouse swing at Wang's head, followed by a hard jab at his gut. Wang blocked them both. It was like the slow dance he did every morning, only so fast and smooth he didn't seem to move at all. Then he kicked upward. I didn't see what happened next. I went for the third tough, who was coming around at Wang's back side.

He wasn't expecting me, and I landed a solid right on his jaw. It was like hitting a sack of bricks, angles and all. I put a left into his belly, and his gut was hard as his jaw. He aimed a backhand at me, like swatting a pesky fly, but I ducked it and crossed with a poke to his nose. No bricks there. I felt it crack. He cursed a blue one and struck out blindly, faster than I expected. His big fist hit my shoulder hard enough to send me sprawling toward the barrels. I caught my balance and was just about to go back at him when he grabbed Wang's arm. That wasn't a good idea. In less time than it takes to tell, Wang spun around, twisted the man's arm so far back that I could hear the joints pop, and sent him flying. Right at me.

I threw myself to the cobbles and the thug crashed into the stack of barrels behind me. It was a solid stack, three barrels wide and half glued to the ground by the sticky seep of molasses, but the man was hard and he hit heavy right in the middle of the bottom barrel. A couple of staves cracked. The barrel sagged. The stack began to sway.

"Finn! Look out!" An-Ming cried.

I was looking, sure. But Wang was still dealing with the tall fellow, who didn't seem to know when to fall down. So Wang threw him at the same place.

His flailing legs knocked me flat again. Then he smashed into the cracked barrel.

The barrel gave way completely and molasses poured out in a gluey wave. The barrels above it tipped and tumbled, knocking down more on either side. The low ones bounced and rolled. The tall ones hit the cobbled wharf and split. It was a torrent of wood and molasses. And I was pinned face-down by the smashed barrel and the groaning body of the tall thug.

I was trying to pull myself loose when another barrel rolled across my back and forced my face down into the mess. The molasses glued my arms and chest to the cobbles. I lifted my head back as high as I could, but the molasses was at least six inches deep, and it stretched out in a brown sheet that covered my nose. A gob of molasses filled my mouth. I couldn't breathe!

I tried to swallow, but the gob was too big and too thick. I began to choke. I tried to pull free, fighting the weight on my legs and the tarry mess that seized me to the cobbles.

"Finn!" An-Ming's voice was muted by the sheet of molasses that coated my head and oozed into my ears. I couldn't reply. I could only cough and spit and choke whenever I tried to breathe in. She yelled something in Chinese, and I remember thinking that was a stupid way to help when she knew I couldn't understand a word of it. I sank back onto my elbows, but I kept wriggling, head as high as I could hold it, blindly trying to snake my way out of the mess.

Then the weight on my legs shifted and was gone. The broken staves pulled away, dragging at the tails of my coat.

"Hold on, Finn!" Mr. Lawson's voice.

Hands took hold of my shoulders and heaved.

"Pull gently!" And more Chinese.

Slowly, painfully, they peeled me from the ground like they were stripping the skin off a raw chicken. My arms came free, then my chest, then my stomach, thighs, shins. They kept lifting till I teetered on my feet in the muck. Then another heave and they lifted me right out of my old boots, walked me forward, and set me down on the cobbles in my stockings.

I jerked my arms free of their grip and scrubbed at my face and mouth, trying to clear out the molasses.

"Let me, Finn." An-Ming. She pushed my hands away and wiped my face with a cloth. My nose cleared and I could finally take a full breath. I took another, and coughed out sticky balls of spit. It didn't seem sweet any more. I almost threw up, which would have been an awful thing. I still couldn't open my mouth all the way.

"Easy, lad, you're all right now," Mr. Lawson said. "Here, Ann, take my kerchief, too."

An-Ming managed to wipe off enough that I could open my eyes and mouth, but what a mess I was. We all were. They'd smeared themselves pretty badly dragging me out. And I was covered enough for the four of us anyway, sticky as one of their Chinese seed cakes.

"I'm all right," I gasped. "What about the thugs?" I peered through the dirty brown film that hung from my brows and lashes, fogging my sight. Wang was watching the two by the stack. The tall one was groaning. The other was prying himself up, his nose oozing blood and molasses. I flexed my sore, sticky hands, satisfied with the hurt now.

"One of them ran off," Mr. Lawson remarked, "and those two—"

An-Ming cut him off with a sharp string of Chinese.

"No, Ann, Not into the harbor. We'll send for the police."

He said it loudly enough for the thugs to hear. The tall one tried to heave himself up. His partner grabbed an arm to help, and the two of them tried to run away through the molasses. It was funny to watch, but the sticky mess also slowed down Wang. Before he could reach them, they reached dry cobbles, stumbled to the edge, and threw themselves into the water. We heard a splash and the sound of them swimming toward the next wharf.

"Damn!" Mr. Lawson said. "It appears they can swim."

"Wang and I can run around and meet them," I said.

"Without your boots? No, we'll tell the police and let them deal with it. And we'll be doubly watchful, now that we know who we're dealing with."

I was more of a mind to take care of it then and there, but Mr. Lawson was in charge. Wang pried my boots free, and we went as fast as our sticky feet would carry us over the hill to Snowhill Place and home, trailed by brown footprints and a cloud of flies.

Ma and Bridget were struck dumb when they saw us. Mr. Lawson immediately explained what had happened and assured them I was fine. Then Wang tried to say it was all his fault and spent some time apologizing, mostly in Chinese, which An-Ming tried to translate. Ma got her breath and said it wasn't anybody's fault except the ruffians who'd attacked us, and I should have watched where I was walking. Didn't I feel like a fool then. But An-Ming spoke up for me and said if I hadn't jumped in to help, it would have been three to one.

"Well, that's better then," Ma said. "He's got a bit of his father's fight in him, I daresay. At least I've got the kettle on already. Bridget, fetch the basin down – no, Finn, don't you touch a thing! Go right down to the wash house with her and clean yourself up." She sighed. "I don't know what we'll do about those clothes."

"Sure, we could serve them for dessert," Bridget whispered to me, with a huge grin.

Ma heard. "You can if you wish, missy, but I think you'll find them a tough chew. I guess you'll have to wash them, too, Finn, and wear them damp."

"I fear he'd have to boil them for hours," Mr. Lawson said. "I'll find a new set for him."

"No, you can't do that, sir" Ma said. "You've been more than kind to us as it is."

"I insist. He was protecting my daughter. I owe him at least a clean change of clothing."

And nothing Ma could say would change his mind. He and Wang set off in search of new clothes, on a Sunday, mind you, while I followed Bridget down to the shed to take a bath. The second one that month, too, and this one one needed a great deal more scrubbing and two changes of water. Bridget teased me through the door the whole time, when she wasn't complaining about hauling the water. It took so long, Mr. Lawson and Wang were back before I was done. They'd managed to find a set of ready-mades by banging loudly on a shop door all the way over on Winter Street. There was a shirt, trousers, a jacket, stockings, and even a wool waistcoat and a pair of white cotton britches. I'd never had underclothes before. I'd never had new clothing, for that matter, only hand-me-downs. The only thing I still needed was a new cap. My own was stuck to the cobbles on Ingersoll's wharf at the bottom of a pool of molasses.

Mr. Lawson and Wang had managed to clean themselves up a bit, and Ma had scrubbed off the worst parts of An-Ming's dress, along with my boots. Finally we were ready to eat, near two hours past the time. Ma showed Mr. Lawson to the head of the table.

"Won't Mr. O'Neill be joining us?" he asked.

We'd known the question would come. I held my breath, waiting to see what Ma would say. She didn't miss a beat. "I'm afraid he's out helping a sick friend."

"Nothing serious, I hope," Mr. Lawson said.

"Nothing time won't heal, I'm sure," she replied. "You're not to worry about it, please. Now sit before anything can cook a moment longer."

Ma had done herself proud on the table, with a clean cloth and the borrowed tableware filling the gaps in the service, and Bridget had found a spray of fall daisies in someone's garden. The chicken smelled delicious, and the codfish cakes were starting to add to the perfume as she gave them a final browning in the skillet. There was cabbage and carrots stewed with the chicken, and there was colcannon made from the rest of the potatoes and cabbage.

Ma and Bridget were just starting to serve the fish cakes when Da barged in, leading a man and a woman and six young children.

"Kate!" he called, "put on the kettle. We've got—" He noticed the group of us at the table. "Oh. It's you, then, is it? Still here?"

You knew blessed well they'd be here, I thought.

"Yes, they're still here, Michael," Ma said. Her voice was polite as could be, but she never called him Michael in a good mood. "We're just sitting down to eat, in fact."

"A bit late, isn't it?" He sounded like he'd had one drink at least. But he was wet from the waist down, and his coat was flecked with damp, like he'd been out on the water, not in a bar.

Mr. Lawson rose. "It's our fault, I'm afraid, Mr. O'Neill. We were delayed."

"Someone attacked them, Da!" Bridget put in. "Mr. Wang fought them off, all three of them. And Finn almost drowned in molasses!" Sure, she couldn't leave that part out.

Da looked from her to Wang to me, a bit confused. He

frowned, shrugged. "We'll hear more about that later, I'm sure. I hope you'll excuse me for barging into your dinner, Mr. Lawson, but we've a few more to squeeze around the table."

"Michael!" Ma exclaimed.

And I thought it was just like him to horn in on the meal that Ma had made especially for the Lawsons.

"Well, what do you expect me to do, Kate? Put them out on the street?"

"You might tell us who they are!"

"Devil take it, wife, give me a minute and I will!"

The family was hanging in the doorway, looking as lost and flogged as I'd ever seen. Da pulled the man forward. "Kate, this is Sean Dwyer, O'Neill on his mother's side, from County Clare. And here's his wife, Mary Ellen. She's an O'Connell."

Da grew up in County Clare, so they were second cousins or closer on both sides. Right off the boat, too, I guessed, from the style and stench of their clothes, and I could tell from the look on the woman's face that she didn't speak much English. Da proved it by switching to the Irish when he introduced us.

"They're family," Da added.

"And just arrived, I see," Mr. Lawson replied.

"No. They've been held on Deer Island for almost a month now. I only found out today."

Deer Island was a big jail, but it also had two hospitals and was made to serve as a quarantine. Most Irish immigrants were held there for a week or two at least, though the English and French and Germans never were, unless they clearly had a foot and half through Death's door.

"I'm glad you were finally given a clean bill of health and cleared for the mainland," Mr. Lawson said to Dwyer.

Dwyer just smiled in reply. I realized then they hadn't been cleared. All of the family were as damp as Da, as if they'd waded through waves to get into a small boat. The ferry from Deer Island left from a pier. And it didn't run on Sundays.

"Well, here they are," Da said, "off that Devil's island at last and ready for a good meal."

"We will leave now," An-Ming said, rising beside her father.

"You can't do that!" Bridget said. "You haven't eaten a bite!"

"No, Ann is right," Mr. Lawson said. "We will just be in the way."

"You will not," Ma said firmly. She stepped in front of the door, as if she could block them in. "You are our guests today." She turned on Da. "Michael—"

"Katie *grá mo chroí,*" Da said. *Love of my heart.* It made me even angrier to hear him play up to her like that. "I can't throw them out. They're family."

"They can come back—"

"They've got no place else to go."

"You knew we had gues—"

"They lost a son on the way over!"

Ma stopped. She turned to Mrs. Dwyer with such a look. Ma grew up in Dublin. She didn't speak more than a few phrases of the Irish – barely more than me, and all I learned came from songs and the fairy tales Da told us – but her face said it all. She took Mrs. Dwyer in her arms and held her.

"*Fáilte,* Mary Ellen. *Fáilte.*" Welcome. She turned to Dwyer and the children. "We'll squeeze round. There's room for all."

"We really should leave," Mr. Lawson said.

"Please stay," Ma insisted. "We've fed more than this on less."

"We will help provide," An-Ming said.

"You can't," Ma replied. "We're already too much in your debt."

"Not for you," An-Ming said. "A welcome gift for

Dwyers."

"Well, that's it then," Da said.

Mr. Lawson was all for going out on his own to buy more food somewhere, but Da said I knew the neighborhood. I would have volunteered anyway. I didn't want to be there when Da started asking about the molasses. Mr. Lawson sent Wang along with me, which was all right. Wang was good company – he hardly ever said anything. Mr. Lawson also gave me a note and a couple of dollars and told me to go to the Tremont House. Well, it was a bit out of the way, but it was a Sunday after all. A hotel was just the sort of place to find food already cooked. Good food it was. A look at the note and the coin was all it took. We were back in less than an hour with a basket full of roast beef, a jar of gravy, a dozen baked potatoes, and another big jar of baked beans. It all smelled wonderful, except for the beans. They'd been cooked with molasses.

So everyone had their fill after all. And the story of the fight had already been told by the time Wang and I got back. Mr. Lawson was telling the Dwyers about China, with Da translating. And over dinner, they told us about Ireland, which wasn't the best of news. So many of Da's old friends and relations had died in the famine or left for New York or Montreal or wherever they could get to. Times were still hard there, and people were leaving in droves. Smaller droves, maybe, but big enough. They made it sound like the country was more than half empty. Mrs. Dwyer started weeping at one point, and the two girls sitting on either side put their arms around her. Dwyer tried to apologize, but Ma said it was all right, we knew how hard it could be.

Da had Bridget sing a song to cheer us all up, and Bridget did have a beautiful voice. Then An-Ming sang a Chinese song, which translated into a love story like you might hear anywhere, though it sure did sound strange to our ears. Ma brought out the dessert – bread pudding baked with molasses. I couldn't touch it. But before long, every bit of it had been eaten and the children were falling asleep at the table, with it hardly gone dark out.

"Now you must let us take our leave, Mrs. O'Neill," Mr. Lawson said. "This has been the most pleasant evening I have spent in a long time. But it has been a full day for all of us. Your houseguests need rest, and so do we."

There was the usual stretch of good-byes, of course, but we were out the door soon enough, Da too, to help row.

"The wind's picked up," he said. "The boy'll be needing the help."

I would have told him to never mind me, stay and help Ma make up beds for the eight extra bodies you've brought in, but Mr. Lawson accepted and thanked him. I knew Da wouldn't listen to me anyway.

The wind had backed around to the northeast, hard on our beam. We all got splashed a bit by the spray. It was colder, too. I was glad for the new wool waistcoat and was wishing for a cap. We were all quiet for the first stretch, talked out during the meal. Mr. Lawson broke the silence as we came within hailing distance of the *Hang-Jinhe*.

"Mr. Dwyer was a farmer, I gathered," he said.

"He was," Da agreed.

"What will he do here?"

"Same as the rest. Try to find work on the wharves or in the digs."

"He has many children to feed," An-Ming remarked.

"One less now," Da said.

"Yes," Mr. Lawson replied. "To lose a child . . ." He trailed off, remembering, I suppose.

"It happens," Da said. "Some have lost three or four, and a wife or husband, too. All on top of starving and being thrown off your farm, then shipped off in a stinking, leaky coffin to a place where they don't speak your language and the only jobs you're offered pay less than a black man just out of chains would stoop to take. They've been through the wars, they have. They're wounded, inside and out. Haunted by it. But you know what? You get over it."

Mr. Lawson sighed and squeezed An-Ming's hand. "Do we ever get over it, Mr. O'Neill? The memory of those lost lives, the shock of a loved-one's death; one way or another, the loss stays with us for the rest of our time."

"Life goes on. We go with it or we go mad. Not much choice."

"A stark philosophy, yet so it would seem," Mr. Lawson said. "We, at least, have found our own ways to endure."

Some in a new country with a new family, I thought, and some in a bottle.

"You put yourself at risk, going to Deer Island like that," Mr. Lawson said then.

"I'm more apt to drown than be arrested," Da replied

"I was thinking of the chance of infection."

Da snorted. "The people there aren't sick. They're just Irish."

We were at the junk then, and the Lawsons took their leave with thanks and another half dollar for each of us for the row. Da tried to refuse – "We can hardly invite you to dinner, then charge you a day's wage to get there," he said – so Mr. Lawson gave both coins to me and told Da he could argue with me about it.

We started back toward the wharves without a word. Now the wind was on our other beam, and it had picked up. The boat was lighter without the Lawsons and Wang, and we had a job of it to stay our course. The temperature was dropping. The spray stung. And Da coughed. I was already mad at him for bringing the Dwyers home, and Mr. Lawson had given me another reason. I couldn't keep my mouth shut.

"He's right, you know," I said. "You shouldn't have gone out there to Deer Island."

"Afraid I'll catch something, boy?"

"More like make it worse."

"What are you talking about?"

"You know what I'm talking about, Da. You've been coughing your guts out every morning since last winter."

"So I get a dry throat from sleeping with my mouth open? So what?"

"Is that what you think? That it's just a dry throat? Then why are you coughing now, after all that cider, with all this blessed spray in our faces?"

"I'm not coughing now."

"You were, and no more than a minute ago!"

"So I coughed! So what? Can't a man clear his own damn throat once in a while? And what about you, then?"

"What about me? I'm not coughing."

"I'm not talking about coughing, boy," Da growled. "I'm talking about fighting. Or should I say falling down. I heard what happened on Ingersoll's. You let him deck you! You let a common street thief knock you flat."

"They were no street thieves! The tall one was the same fellow who tried to grab An-Ming when you were brawling with the teamsters. They're after her, I tell you!"

"You're pissing into the wind! They thought they'd found some easy money is all. And they would have, if Wang hadn't been there. You'd have drowned in a puddle of molasses. What kind of fighting is that?"

"If Wang hadn't thrown those two thugs into the barrels —"

"What then? What would you have done? Roll over and let 'em walk on you?"

"I bloodied his nose! And you're just changing the subject!"

"Am I? Well, let me tell you, boyo, before you start coming at me about a dry throat, you'd better be able to handle yourself in a fight. Because you're going to get your ears boxed well and good complaining at your elders and your betters when you can't even stand up for yourself. Do you understand?"

"You can't—"

He swung around and gave me a backhand box on the ear.

"I can, boy! I can. Now shut up and row."

Chapter 15

Mr. Lawson never did call the police – he said he didn't want the notice – but that didn't stop the rumors from going round. Too many people had seen us walking from Ingersoll's, and everyone in the house had seen the sticky footprints leading up the stairs. Word got out that Mr. Lawson's Chinese bodyguard had single-handedly bested a dozen of the worst thugs and crimps on the wharves, using some type of Chinese boxing nobody had ever heard about.

Straight off, Pat Delany came looking for me to see what I could tell him. I tried to stay mum – Mr.Lawson had asked me to, and, truth is, I didn't want to admit to taking a swim in molasses. I didn't feel good about it, but I told Pat I hadn't been there. He produced a roll of old newspaper with a sticky wad of cloth inside that turned out to be my cap.

"I found this ground into the cobbles down by the stack of barrels on Ingersoll's, Finn," he said. "I couldn't help notice you've been bareheaded the past couple of days."

"It could have belonged to one of the thugs, you know."

"So there were thugs!" he crowed. "And what about your bath Sunday? Jimmy Bailey said you were in it for more than an hour, and still smelled like bread pudding when you got out."

"What he was smelling was my own ma's good cooking," I replied. "Sure, we had the Lawsons to dinner on Sunday, with Mr. Wang and a few others beside."

"And they didn't mention a little run-in on the way over?"

"All right, Pat, there was a run-in. Three thugs went after us, and Mr. Wang set 'em straight, but I'm sworn not to talk about it. It could cost me my job. I almost lost it once already, when I told you about the clock. I've already told you more than I should about this." Sure, Pat looked disappointed. I punched his arm and said, "Whatever I can tell, I'll tell you first. I will."

So Pat went off unhappy, and the rumors stayed rumors. And, as they died down, so did the general interest in the Lawsons. After all, it had been near a month. The welcome parties were over. The *Hang-Jinhe* had been anchored out by the number six buoy long enough it was beginning to look like part of the scenery. People got on with their lives.

But Mr. Lawson didn't forget the cause of the rumors. He went to Sands, told him what had happened, and begged him to keep the story from old Robert, so as not to trouble his failing health any further. Sands offered to hire on a team of bodyguards, but Mr. Lawson said no, it would just cause more talk. Instead, he started carrying a stout walking stick. And he put even more rules about An-Ming going ashore. She had to have two men with her, Wang and one other at least, plus Hu-Lan if she wasn't needed on board to translate. And only in daylight, and never in lonely parts of the city.

Sure, An-Ming was none too happy about all that. It was starting to be dark by six, which put the chop her time ashore. And she hated being coddled.

"Wang is enough!" she railed. "He has shown it!" We were all in the clock room together on the Tuesday after. It was raining to beat the band outside. An-Ming was helping Peter again, when she wasn't complaining. I was just trying to keep dry.

"He took them by surprise," Peter replied, looking up from the clockworks. "Next time they'll be prepared. They could very well come in greater numbers. And armed."

"You are bad as Father," she grumbled.

"I'd certainly like to know who these ruffians are," Peter said, not for the first time. "Are you sure you didn't recognize any of them, Finn?" He'd asked that before, too.

"Just the tall one," I repeated, "and him just from the brawl. I'll guarantee they aren't from the North End. Nor even Irish, not from the way he spoke."

"What could they possibly want?"

"Da thinks they're just street thieves who decided the Lawsons'd be easy marks."

"What do *you* think, Finn?" An-Ming asked.

"I can't say for sure."

She gave me a sharp smile. "But?"

"It seems to me a plain thief wouldn't go to all that trouble, not in broad daylight, not against a group of us. Why'd the tall fellow go after you twice? And what was he starting to say right before Wang stepped in? 'I'll get the girl'!" I shook my head. "It's you they're after. Abduction, plain and simple. They're wanting ransom."

"They can't believe they'd ever get away with it!" Peter exclaimed.

"Your street thief isn't always the sharpest nail in the keg," I noted.

"But this is Boston, not some heathen country like India or China or—" He went red and glanced at An-Ming, horrified at himself. "I didn't mean . . . Ah, that is . . . Not your part of China, of course."

An-Ming was scowling, but not at him. "It happens in my China. Why not here, where so many, many poor share streets with the rich? It is the same wherever there aren't jobs for all, and high wages are hoarded by few. Most hunger quietly, others steal, some do worse."

"So you see, your father's precautions make sense," Peter said.

Now she did scowl at him. "You're no help," she snapped. "I'll go crazy!"

Well, she wasn't tied to the mast or anything like that. She went to the market every day with Hu-Lan and the cook, and Wang and another crewman. Mr. Lawson and Sands took her to the races once, even, where she was made a fuss of by Sands' investor friends. She went to the Mechanics Association Exhibition at the Faneuil Hall markets. And Eleanor Sands asked her to the theater again. Mr. Lawson had a hand in that, I think. He let her go, in any case, even though it meant being out after dark. But only with Wang and Hu-Lan and this time Peter, who she invited to come and was only too pleased to go.

I got to go, too, because Da was spending his days helping the Dwyers get settled in East Boston. Dwyer wound up working regular for James Bliss, the chandler, and I think Mr. Lawson had a hand in that, too. I was happy to have them out of our place, so I could go home. With Da like he was, it'd been too blessed crowded for me. I'd squeezed in with the Ryans the first night, but An-Ming learned about it from Peter and let me stay on the junk. They found me a corner up forward and a spare mat to sleep on. It was damp, but sure better than being at home. I missed Ma and Bridget, though, so I did move back in when the Dwyers left.

The weather stayed cold, and big skeins of geese showed up in the sky one day, heading south. The market gunners had a field day out in the marshes, and there was fresh goose for sale at the Haymarket. We could afford one that year, with the double pay from Mr. Lawson and Bond & Sons. It was tough, but good in a stew.

I took An-Ming sailing once when the sun was out and

the wind fresh from the northwest. Mr. Lawson warned me to stay close by the *Hang-Jinhe*. Wang was with us, of course, but An-Ming took the tiller, I handled the sheet, and we scooted over behind Governor's island almost as far as Point Shirley, ignoring Wang's complaints. He finally grabbed hold of the sheet and spilled the wind, and we drifted with the chop until An-Ming gave in and headed back to the junk, staring daggers at him the whole way.

After that we were only allowed to row, and only with the junk's boat in company, manned by two crewmen. Mr. Lawson just wasn't taking any chances. I rowed us up the Charles as far as the fens, then back out and into the Mystic River, where we had a good look at the *Great Republic* abuilding at Mr. McKay's shipyard. She had all four of her lower masts in and was set for launching on the next spring tide, the fourth of October. That was hardly a week away. They'd had to postpone the original launch date because there hadn't been enough lumber. Now the yard was busy as an ant hill in the rush to meet the new schedule. The whole city was astir over it, another reason for everyone to forget Mr. Lawson's clock. The *Great Republic* was the largest sailing ship ever built before – 325 feet long, with the lower main mast a full 200 feet tall from deck to truck. The betting was high on how many records she'd break. I wondered if maybe some day I'd be on her, flying over the water, around Cape Horn and across the Pacific to Australia to make my fortune. Why not? Today I had work with good people, Ma and Bridget to worry about, Da . . . Well, Da to deal with. But that couldn't last. Maybe someday I'd be free to leave. California, Australia . . . I could still dream.

Meanwhile, Peter was near to finishing the clock. He'd made all the gears that weren't ready-made by Bond and Sons and had fitted most of them into the five sets that made up the separate clockworks. The case had been built by the junk's carpenter from a piece of the finest walnut. It was about fifteen inches on a side, mostly an open frame to hold the four outside faces, which had been cut from brass and coated with enamel, hand-painted by Hu-Lan and fired at the new Boston Watch Company in South Boston. Three of the sides and the top had faces. The fourth side was covered by a carved panel that opened to get at the works. It was a beautiful thing. The faces were just like on the old one: symbols and creatures painted in bright colors. Each corner post was carved with a dragon, and the top frame was carved with vines and flowers, and the back was carved with a turtle, surrounded by five cranes. It took your breath away.

We made a trip into town, Peter and me, to collect the jewels from Mr. Feinmann, but only the little ones were ready. The heart stone was taking longer.

"We've managed to find the stone," Feinmann said, peering at Peter over a pair of magnifying spectacles that made him look like a weepy dog. "The shaping is more difficult. The drills keep breaking, you understand. We have to work very slowly. But better that than breaking the stone, eh?"

"It will be ready by next week?" Peter asked, his face all anxious.

"Tell Mr. Lawson he can depend on it," Feinmann replied, carefully sweeping the twelve smaller jewels into an envelope and handing it to Peter. It looked like a king's ransom to me, a mix of white and yellow gems fit for a crown. But Peter tucked it into his breast pocket as though it were no more than a letter from a distant aunt. He was far more concerned about the one that wasn't there.

"What's so important about getting the heart stone next week?" I asked, when we were back out on the street and making our way down toward the wharves. "His old clock is still ticking away all right, isn't it?"

Peter glanced around nervously at the passersby sharing the sidewalk with us. "Yes, it's all just fine," he muttered, "but let's not talk about it now, all right?"

So I waited until we were back in the boat and away from the wharf. "Now then, why is next week so important?"

"The stars and the moon," Peter said. "They have to be aligned properly. It has to do with the ceremonies, the, ah, blessings that accompany the final assembly of the clock."

Peter wasn't very comfortable talking about it, and it made me feel a mite odd, too. He'd said "ceremony" and "blessing," as if we were talking about a wedding or some such. And I suppose that was the easiest way to think about it, like christening a new ship as she slid down the ways into the water. After all, you wanted the highest tide for that, a spring tide near the full moon. Or the new moon, like we had coming on next week for the launching of the *Great Republic*. But the stars had nothing to do with launching. And the shrill chanting I'd heard the time I'd tried to listen in on one of Mr. Lawson's clock "ceremonies" hadn't sounded much like a blessing to me, Chinese or not.

This was some kind of magic, an enchantment, like a song sung by the *Daoine Sidhe*, the old Irish gods in the stories Da had told us when we were little. Ma hadn't liked those stories, because they were myth and magic and not Christian. Oh, she didn't mind the tales of Leprechans and fairies and Irish heroes like Finn McCool, even the one about Ossian. They were just tales. But the *Sidhe* were gods. And as far as she was concerned, there was only one true God, the one we prayed to at mass. I didn't know if the Chinese gods were like the *Sidhe* or not, but I knew Ma wouldn't like Mr. Lawson nearly so much if she knew he was dealing with them.

I was thinking about all that as we came up to the *Hang-Jinhe*. It had started to rain a bit on the way back, but An-Ming was waiting by the rail, wearing a round straw hat almost as broad as a lady's parasol. She was in her tunic and trousers, and looked very Chinese. Very different. A person I could imagine singing songs to Chinese gods. She greeted

Peter in Chinese, and damn if he didn't answer in Chinese. I stared at Peter, and he went red to the tips of his ears.

"You're talking Chinese together, then?" I said.

"Ah, it was simply 'good evening,'" he replied.

"Is that what it was? Sure, it sounded a bit more tender than that." I made it a tease, but for some reason, An-Ming seemed even more strange when he spoke Chinese to her. The both of them did. Maybe I just felt left out.

"Hurry!" An-Ming called. "It is raining harder! *Women kuai xhang de hao shi le!*"

"Ah, *ni kuai jin fang li qu, wo mashang gen ni zai yiqi.*" he tried.

An-Ming laughed and said something else that made his jaw drop and his face burn.

"I guess that wasn't quite what you meant to say," I remarked. "Try it in American."

Peter nearly fell out of the boat grabbing the ladder.

I made fast and hurried up after him. I still didn't have a cap – the mush Pat had found wouldn't stop stinking of molasses – and the rain was cold.

"Finn, you look like *luo tang ji*," An-Ming said. "Chicken in soup? Ah, drowned rat?" She held out a package, something soft wrapped in paper and string. "For you. Take it."

I unwrapped it, and there was a fine wool cap, just like my old one, only new. I turned it over in my hands. "You've already given me a whole new set of clothes," I said.

"From Father," she said. "This is from me. It fits?"

I put it on. "Like a charm. But I really can't—"

"It is custom here to give presents on birthday, yes? Peter says yours is this month."

"Sure, but weeks ago."

"Forgive this humble soul for lateness," she said, with a smile that was no more humble than Da in a fight. "Now come inside. You will drink tea and watch Peter work. That will be his birthday present to you."

"What's that?" Peter said.

"You sit and watch him row. Now he will sit and watch, and drink tea, while you and I put jewels in the clock."

"But I steer while he's rowing," Peter protested.

"Then Finn can tell you where to put jewels."

"Can I keep any leftovers?" I asked.

"Of course," An-Ming said.

"There'd better not be any left over," Peter said. "Not if we want the clock to run."

"You didn't order extras?" An-Ming exclaimed. "*Hao ben!* What if you drop one into a crack?"

"I'll send Finn to look for it. He's slippery enough."

Laughing and joking, they headed for the companionway, and I was swept along in their wake. They didn't seem so strange after all.

Chapter 16

THE TUESDAY CAME, OCTOBER 4. Most of the shops and stores and factories were closed, so the people could go to see the launch of the *Great Republic*. Bond & Son was closed as well, but I picked Peter up at dawn, as usual, and we pulled out into the harbor as the sun rose over Governor's Island into a crystal clear sky. Ships would still be coming in that day, and Peter was paid by the clock, not by the day. Besides, the launch was set for noon. We'd time beforehand to hail a few inbound craft and hopefully get custom with one.

And we did, a smart brig sailing under the Cunningham flag, in from Fayal with a load of figs and olives and oil. Peter was on board by 8:27 on his watch and done by 9:42, the quickest turn around I'd known him to make. He wasn't half seated in the stern of the canoe before I pulled for the *Hang-Jinhe*.

We came under her stern and rounded for the ladder just as another boat hailed from a few yards off. It was Jacob Sands, gripping the rails of a seventeen-footer that I knew all too well – Billy Adam's boat.

"Hello, the junk!" Sands called. Then he noticed us. "You there! Stand off! Make way!"

I made to pull all the harder – we were first in, after

all – but Peter put a hand on my arm.

"Best wait, Finn," he said. "Mr. Lawson does want to stay on his good side."

So I rested on my oars while Billy Adams cut in front of us. He had a smirk on his face that cried out to be smudged with the sharp end of an elbow.

Mr. Lawson was waiting for Sands and invited him on board. Sands fumbled his way up the ladder without losing his footing or his hat. I could see Adams was all for staying there, so we couldn't get alongside, but Mr. Lawson himself told him to shift. He said it niceways, with a "please" even, but it was still an order. Adams had no choice but to let us in, but he was sneering the whole time. If ever there was a boatman matched to his passenger, it was Adams to Sands.

I made our painter fast to the ladder and skipped up after Peter.

"Hey!" Adams called, but I ignored him.

Sands was there to take the Lawsons to the launching. In fact, he should have been there an hour before. Just as I topped the ladder, I heard him telling Mr. Lawson how every tug and "decent craft" had been commandeered to ferry crowds of people over to East Boston.

"It seems half the city is going," he complained, "and mostly riff-raff. Luckily, we are McKay's invited guests and will be certain of good seats on the ship herself. I was able to commission Mr. Adams to be our personal ferryman. He is a proper American and will get us there in good time, and dry, I might add. Is Miss Lawson ready?"

"I'm afraid Ann is somewhat under the weather," Mr. Lawson replied. "She won't be joining us after all."

"Really?" Sands replied. "Eleanor will be dashed. She has taken quite a fancy to her young cousin. Nothing serious, I hope?"

"No, no," Mr. Lawson assured him. "Merely a bit of dishumor in the stomach. I suspect she enjoyed an overlarge meal last night."

"Ah, well, her loss," Sands said, without a hint of care. "This will be the event of the year. Assuming that great lump of a hull makes it down the ways."

"Is there any doubt of that?" Mr. Lawson asked. "From all I hear, McKay is the premier designer and builder in the country."

"He's gone too far this time," Sands said. "She is, after all, well over three hundred feet long and twice the tonnage of any other ship ever built."

"I take it, then, that the bank has not invested in her."

Sands snorted. "On the contrary! I have bets laid that she won't even earn back the cost of her building. At three-to-one odds. You should consider a wager yourself, Uncle. It would be the easiest money you've ever earned. It's not too late, and I know just the man."

"Speaking of late," Mr. Lawson said, "we'd best be going, hadn't we? Even with your Mr. Adams at the oars, we will be pushing the time."

"Of course, of course," Sands replied.

Mr. Lawson turned to Peter. "Will you join us?" he asked. "With Ann indisposed, there will be an empty space in our party."

Peter was startled to be asked. "Oh, ah, that's very kind, sir, but I do really wish to bring the clock closer to being ready for the heartsto – for the final assembly."

"Well, if you're sure. I shall give a full report. A good morning to you, and you, Finn."

Sands tipped his hat to Peter. Me, he ignored. The hat was a new, shiny model, the tallest beaver I'd ever seen. It made his face seem small. What I noticed most, though, were his coat and trousers. There were spots of water splashed on them. Billy Adams was no better than any other man at the oars.

I went ahead of Sands down the ladder to shift our boat. I didn't trust Billy Adams not to scrape it hard against the *Hang-Jinhe* when he brought his own boat alongside. As I watched Sands come down, I was wishing he'd lose that new topper right into the harbor, but he managed with a hand from Adams. Mr. Lawson didn't have any trouble at all, nor Captain Li, who'd been invited, too, or Wang, who went wherever Mr. Lawson went, invited or not.

Then I stood off while the junk's crew lowered their own boat. The mate was taking as many as would fit to watch from the water. Once they were well away, I climbed back aboard and found Peter staring after them with a wish in his eyes.

"We could go watch, too, if you've a mind to," I told him. "The launch is at noon. You'd be back by one, with plenty of time to fiddle with your gears."

"Well, you could go, Finn," he said. "I really should stay."

Now that was hardly what he'd said earlier that morning. "Sure, someone has to watch after An-Ming if she's not well," I teased.

Peter gave a rueful laugh. "Sure, indeed! What's sure is that Hu-Lan surely won't let me come near her."

"'Tis a cruel fate, Mr. Jenkins, as my ma would say. Cruel, cruel."

"Someday, Finn, when you're old enough, you'll know just how cruel. And I hope I'm there to see it."

"See what?" It was An-Ming, decked out in her Chinese pants and jacket, looking as bright and healthy as ever.

"Me, pining away for my sick lover," I replied, with a grin at Peter.

He rewarded me with a blush, then quickly changed the subject. "Anie, should you be out on deck? Your father said you were ill."

"I told him it was my woman's time," she said. Now, that made us both blush. "*Wa*! Are you both silly? It is a ruse. I cannot stand another day with Sands and his glances."

"What?" Peter exclaimed. "Has he been eyeing you?"

"No! I am foreign. He humors Father, but clearly disdains me."

"The nerve! Who does he think he is?" Peter grumbled.

"The owner of the Harbor Bank," I said, "but we're getting the better side of the deal."

"Yes! Absolutely! Well said, Finn." Peter doffed his hat and held it to his chest, making a bow to An-Ming. "His loss is our gain, for we will have the pleasure of your company today."

An-Ming smiled. Even I was impressed. She was bringing out a gallant side of Peter Jenkins that I never would have thought he had.

"I think to see the launch will be much better from the water." She took Peter's elbow and pulled him toward the ladder. "Come."

Peter fumbled with his hat. "But what about—?"

"Quick quick!" An-Ming said. "Before anyone sees!"

"But Wang is gone."

"You two will guard me." She was near dragging him across the deck.

"Come on, Peter," I said. "We'll be on the water in plain sight of a thousand people. No one's going to try anything."

"Yes! Come, Finn, we'll go without him." She dropped his arm and took mine.

"Well, I suppose . . ." Peter dithered. "But we should tell Hu-Lan at the least."

"*Hao ben,*" An-Ming groaned. "She will waste time with argument. Quick!"

It was too late. Hu-Lan came out of the stern house, took one look at the three of us by the ladder, and hurried over, spouting Chinese the whole way. An-Ming fired back, and it was Chinese broadsides point blank. Peter made the mistake of trying to put in a calm word, but they both turned on him and switched to American, except for the occasional shot of Chinese at each other. I stayed mum by the rail, but I was laying bets with myself on An-Ming. Sure enough, she fired a final salvo, dodged a grab by Hu-Lan, and skipped down the ladder. The Chinese pants gave her the advantage.

"Come, Finn!" she called. "Peter?"

Peter mumbled apologies to Hu-Lan and promised to keep good watch, then followed me down to the boat. An-Ming was already at the tiller, ignoring a steady stream of threats and curses from Hu-Lan. At least, that's what they sounded like. I had the painter untied and was just about to shove off, when Hu-Lan gave a final cry and started down the ladder as fast as she could in her full skirts. An-Ming frowned, shook her head, sighed, nodded, and sat scowling while Peter and I helped Hu-Lan into the bow seat. Hu-Lan scowled back, and at Peter when he sat beside An-Ming. I shoved off, set my oars, and finally we were away.

The inner harbor between Charlestown and East Boston was crowded with all manner of small craft, and some not so small – lighters, yachts, rowboats, ferries, tugboats, even a few of the smaller excursion steamers. Every one of them was packed to the gunwales with people. Every spot on land that gave even a glimpse of McKay's shipyard was packed, too. Even the stacks of lumber were piled with people. The ships along the wharves were crowded with men and boys hanging from the ratlines and yards. The Mystic River bridge was lined end to end with carriages, wagons, and carts, all filled to the brim, with more people squeezed between. I'd said we'd be in plain sight of a thousand people. Well, the papers said later that fifty thousand had turned out to watch, and I believe it.

I rowed carefully through the press of boats, trying not to laugh when Peter and An-Ming began to argue over which was the best course. Peter was thinking to find the straightest path, but she wanted to be sure we weren't spotted by her father or the crew in the junk's boat. And she had the tiller, so round about we went, close to the Charlestown wharves and along the far side of Mystic River bridge, before cutting in toward McKay's behind a screen of boats.

We took up position just outside a little excursion steamer, the *Argo*, from Salem.

And what a view we had. Beyond the *Argo*'s white deck-house and blue-striped stack, the *Great Republic* loomed high on the ways. Her bright yellow-metal sheathing gleamed gold in the clear sunlight. Her black hull seemed too large to be possible. Her five masts soared higher than steeples, and they were only the lower sticks. When she was fully rigged, she'd reach the clouds. She was sporting banners on all her masts, two on her main: a long, coach-whip pennant and a huge white flag sporting the United States coat of arms. Even the bowsprit had a jack-staff rigged with the Union Jack on it. A thick hawser drooped from her bow in a long curve, out over the water to the big propeller tug, *R.B. Forbes*, ready to take charge once she had slipped down the ways. A tall grandstand stood at her bow, but the truly important people were on her deck, along with the Boston Brass Band. That's where Mr. Lawson and Captain Li would be, with the Sands. I hoped, in all that hoopla, they wouldn't notice us lurking behind the *Argo*.

We had hardly arrived when a great clatter arose from the shipyard.

"What's that?" An-Ming asked.

"They're knocking the wedges out," I said. "She's held in the ways by dozens, maybe hundreds of big wedges. They've got to knock them out to set her free. Then she'll slide right into the water."

"If she doesn't stick," Peter added. "Sands said he's betting that she's too big to move."

"Mr. MacKay knows what he's doing," I said. "Besides, you can be sure they've smeared a potful or two of tallow on the ways to grease them up."

"More like a hogshead, I'd imagine," Peter said.

"What do you think?" An-Ming asked. "Will she stick?"

We both cried no.

She laughed. "Maybe I should have made a bet with

Sands."

"Never bet with your in-laws," Peter told her. "It will only end in bad blood."

"I imagine he can afford to lose a little," I said. "He's got a whole bank full of money."

"That money is not his," Peter said. "He'd better not be betting with it."

"Isn't that what bankers do every day?" I asked. "Make bets on railroads and such."

"That is investing," Peter replied. "The careful banker chooses businesses with a good chance of success."

"I imagine the sport at the racetrack thinks he's being pretty careful."

"Enough of Sands!" An-Ming exclaimed. "Here is a great ship launching! Talk of that!"

So we talked about ships, the clippers and the barks and brigs being built in the many shipyards in Boston. I pointed out the ones we could see abuilding on both sides of the harbor, and the one under the shears at Grand Junction wharf, waiting for its spars to be set in. Meanwhile, the band on the *Great Republic* played some songs, the passengers on the *Argo* drank and sang and cheered, and Peter kept checking his watch. The constant din of hammering rang from beneath the *Great Republic* as the wedges fell out by twos and threes.

Just as the first church bells began to chime noon, a cry went up all around.

"She's moving!" I yelled.

"A minute late," Peter remarked, closing his watch.

An-Ming shoved his arm. "A ship so large sets its own time!" she said, laughing. She stood for a better look, leaning on Peter's shoulder, and he carefully put an arm around her waist to brace her, blushing all the while. Hu-Lan frowned, but they weren't paying her any mind.

The *Great Republic* moved slowly at first, as if she couldn't quite believe she was free of the land at last. The band struck up *Hail, Columbia*. The cheers grew and grew as she picked up speed. I saw a fellow on the grandstand smash a bottle on her bow just before she slipped out of reach. He whipped off his hat, swung it round his head, and threw it after her with a great cheer. Many of the young men took it up, littering the harbor with bobbing toppers, like rakes tossing their hats at the feet of a favorite actress.

The *Great Republic* touched the water lightly for so large a thing. Her fine lines cut an entrance, and she slipped in with only a gentle splash and a smooth wave that hardly troubled the small boats clustered right by the shipyard shore. The hawser dipped into the water, shaking a rainbow of spray into the air. The great hull turned slightly, answering the drag of the heavy rope. It wasn't a great change in course, just a gentle curve to the left. While Peter and An-Ming and even Hu-Lan joined their voices to the cheering, I watched the high, sharp stern of that giant hull ease slowly round till it was all I could see.

It was coming right at us.

Chapter 17

I TORE MY EYES from the looming hull and swung out my oars.

"Hold on!" I yelled, digging in. I pulled to port and backed starboard as hard as I could. The boat spun and An-Ming almost toppled into the harbor. Peter made a lunge and caught her, tipping the boat so far they both almost went in. Hu-Lan shrieked. I kept pulling.

The *Argo*'s whistle drowned out Hu-Lan. Her paddle-wheels began to turn, lifting the water into waves of foam. We weren't more than a boat length away, far too near for comfort.

"Tiller, Peter!" I yelled. "Starboard! Starboard!"

But Peter was down on his knees in the bilge, face buried in An-Ming's jacket, one arm round her bottom and the other braced on the wale against the mad rocking. An-Ming's arms were clenched around his head and his hat, but she managed to reach the tiller and throw it over. I pulled again, still backing starboard, pointing the boat into the clear.

And now I was looking right at the *Great Republic*. She towered over us like a falling wall. The *R.B. Forbes* had steam on and was starting to move, but it would be some minutes before she took up the slack in the rope. Even that wouldn't help. You can't stop a ship that size in less than a hundred yards, even with her going so slowly. We had to hope we could slip out of her way in time. We had one advantage: the *Argo* would catch her first and maybe slow her down.

The little steamer was making a tiger's try to get out of the way. Her wheels were turning faster, the hull finally starting to move. Which didn't help me any, fighting against the surge of her wake on our bow. I pulled for all my life.

"Straighten out, Anie!" I yelled. "Straight ahead!" She threw Peter's hat into the bilge and lurched over his shoulder to grab the tiller with both hands.

Hu-Lan kept screaming. I could hear cries from the *Argo*, too. I didn't look. All I could see was the black weight of the *Great Republic*, coming on like a rising tide. Her stern arched over the *Argo's* taffrail. I bent my back and put my heart into the oars.

With a creak and a crack, the *Great Republic* struck the *Argo's* flagstaff, bent it half round, and snapped it off. A section of her taffrail went with it. More screaming. The little steamer's stern lurched sideways and pressed into the water, then lifted on the great hull's wake and slid clear. The *Great Western* brushed her off and came on.

I had time for two more hard strokes. The black hull reached us. Rolled beside us. Gave us a nudge with her wake. The canoe tried to turn, but I held her straight and rowed another couple of strokes. The broken flagstaff knocked on our rudder as it drifted past, followed by bits of the *Argo's* rail. The black hull kept rolling by. You can't know how long three hundred and twenty-five feet really is until you can reach out and touch it as it glides beside you. Finally the bow went by, and the giant carved eagle under her bowsprit glared down on us.

Next time you won't be so lucky, it seemed to say.

I rested on my oars, but my arms started to shake a

little, so I took a few slow strokes to cool down. Peter and An-Ming had sorted themselves out finally and were sitting side by side with the tiller between them. Peter was trying to apologize to her for what he called "my rough handling." She laughed like it was the greatest adventure in the world.

"Quiet! You saved me," she said, and when he kept begging pardon, she kissed him. It was just a peck, but it shut him up. Funny thing was, he didn't blush. He cleared his throat, opened his mouth again, and settled on a big grin. He was happy as a clam at high water.

"*Zao gao!*" Hu-Lan muttered. By then I knew it could mean anything from *Uh-oh* to *Sweet blessed Mary, what a mess!* I could see her point. Peter had missed getting rammed by the *Great Republic*, only to be swamped by An-Ming.

The *Forbes* got the *Great Republic* under control before she reached the bridge, then towed her down to the navy yard to be rigged. I joined the fleet of small boats following behind. The *Argo* came along, too. Luckily, no one had been hurt, and no serious damage done. As she idled near the Navy Yard, a row boat came alongside the *Argo*, and a small figure handed up her flagstaff and dripping ensign, rescued from the water. I recognized Bridget right off. And there was Ma, sitting with Gracie on the stern thwart. And Da at the oars, of course.

"There's your family, Finn," An-Ming said. "Hello, Bridget! Hello, O'Neills!"

Bridget heard her and called back. Ma waved and pointed us out to Gracie.

"Your sister?" An-Ming asked. "I must go meet her."

I wasn't so sure I wanted to find out if Da had seen us almost get drowned.

"Would you mind not mentioning what just happened?" I said. "It'd upset Ma."

An-Ming gave me a look. I think she knew who I didn't want to upset. But no one said anything about us; just the

Argo and the *Great Republic* and all the hullaballoo.

"Did you see Captain Gifford smash the bottle on her bow?" Bridget asked, all excited. "It was Cochituate Water instead of champagne, so the temperance ladies wouldn't be upset."

"Really?" Peter asked. "Where did you hear that?"

"One of the boatmen," Bridget replied. "He was just off the ways when the *Great Republic* started to move. He caught three hats in his boat and heard the swells talking about it when they came to get them back."

Da chuckled. "I never heard the McKay's were tea-totalers. Some rake probably drank up all the champagne last night."

"Father is invited to celebration," An-Ming said. "He'll be surprised if they serve water."

"It takes more than water to soothe the throat after all the cheering's ended," Da agreed. "I imagine Hurley's will be busy this afternoon. We'd best hurry if we hope to find seats."

"You're going to Hurley's?" I asked. It seemed a fine idea, except that I had to ferry An-Ming and the rest back to the junk before we got caught out by Mr. Lawson.

"Not me," Gracie replied. "I have to be back before the missus."

"I do you wish you could come," Ma told her. "I wish we could all be there. Molly, too."

"And Tim," Bridget added.

We were silent a moment, remembering the times we'd all been together at Hurley's. Then Ma came out with, "Would you care to join us, Miss Lawson, Mister Jenkins? I'm sure Finn would. Would you mind, Miss Hu-Lan? You'd be more than welcome."

"If Mr. O'Neill doesn't mind, we would be honored," An-Ming replied.

Hu-Lan said something in Chinese that didn't sound too honored.

"Hu-Lan agrees," An-Ming said, not missing a beat. "Peter? Do you need to return?"

"Me? Oh, no! Work can wait till tomorrow. And if there's no room at a table, I'll be happy to stand."

"We'll have to if we don't move sharp," Da said. "Let's see how fast you can row, boy."

We made a race of it through the crowd of boats back to Lewis Wharf. Da won, but only because he managed to sneak between a tug and a ferry. Ma yelled at him, and so did one of the crewmen on the tug. An-Ming tried to steer us through the same gap, but I decided to back oars and take the safer course. An-Ming grumbled, but the family waited for us at the wharf, so it didn't matter. Except for the losing part.

Gracie came as far as Hurley's, but she wouldn't let Ma drag her inside. It meant her job to be gone when her lady arrived home. She gave us big hugs and hurried off . Ma watched until she had disappeared among the busy crowd.

"Come on, Kate," Da said kindly. "We're blocking the doorway."

She sighed and let him take her hand and pull her inside.

It was a good thing we'd hurried, because we got the last group of seats. Even Peter and I got to sit down, but only just. And people kept coming in after us. Soon there was hardly room for the fiddler to move his bow. Not that you could hear the music well. Everyone was going on about the launching.

Mary Hurley and her young son and daughter were there to help, but Hurley himself came from behind to bar to take our orders.

"Welcome back, Master Wang-Hu," he said to An-Ming. Everyone at the table but Da and me gaped at him. I hid a smile.

"I'm sorry," An-Ming said, smooth as silk. "Wang-Hu could not come today. I am his sister, An-Ming. And this is my *ama*, my chaparone, Hu-Lan."

Hurley looked as startled as the rest of them. "I beg your pardon, young miss," he said. "You're the spitting image of your brother."

"Spitting?" It was An-Ming's turn to be confused.

"That means you look just like him," I explained.

"Ah. Many say so. You are Hurley? Wang-Hu tells me about your wonderful cider. Could we have some?"

"You certainly may, Miss," Hurley looked around the table. "How many for cider?"

All of us but Da said yes; he took a mug of the ale. An-Ming ordered up a big plate of cod and potatoes, too, fried with onions and apples, then insisted that everyone take forks and share it. She insisted on paying for it all, too, with money from Hu-Lan's purse. Ma tried to protest, but An-Ming had her way, as usual.

We had a fine time. Da had more than one ale, but it brought out his good side that day. There was plenty of music and plenty to talk about, what with the launching and the counterfeit money that had been going round and a lecture there'd been the night before at the Melodeon by Patrick O'Donahoe, the Irish patriot and exile. Da had actually met the man once back in Ireland.

"He blamed the latest defeats on our own feuding leaders," Da told Hurley and some others who'd come to the table to listen. "He said we were better off here – our adopted country, the land of Washington and Warren, he called it – and we should put past differences aside."

"Sounds like good advice to me," Hurley said. "It's time to let bygones be bygones." Hurley knew of the troubles and, unlike many of the early comers, he sympathized. Because of where the bar was, I imagine, and because he was Catholic. He'd even bothered to learn a bit of the language, but despite that and the name of his bar, he was far more American than Irish.

"I've said that myself, Hurley," Da replied. "I still say it.

But I can't forget how the filthy British broke O'Connell and drove so many out in forty-three."

"That's enough, now, Mike," Ma said. "We're celebrating today."

"So we are, Kate," Da replied. He lifted his glass. "Here's to the *Great Republic*, both of 'em. May the country sail as well as the ship."

Those who could hear him over the music and chatter raised their glasses and gave a cheer.

The cider was a wee bit gone by. It had a sparkle in it that made us all forget the time, even Peter. His watch stayed in his pocket. And his hand stayed under the table, as did An-Ming's beside him. A smile never left his face. Hu-Lan didn't seem to notice, but then, An-Ming kept the mugs refilled. We were all a bit giddy. It wasn't till we heard the church bells tolling that we realized the hour.

"Good heavens!" Peter said. "Was that seven?" He extracted his hand, red and warm, and pulled out his watch. "It was!"

"*Wa!*" Hu-Lan exclaimed. "We must go!"

"She's right," Peter said, rising. "Your father will be worried sick, Anie."

"He knows I am with you," she protested.

"But not where. And look, it's already dark."

Hidden in the back corner, we hadn't even noticed when the lamps were lit.

Ma got all motherly and took their side. "Sure, you must get along, Miss Lawson. And, Mike, you go with them. Let's not forget what happened the last time."

"Ma, shh!" I hissed. Every ear around us had perked up.

"Well, they all know," she replied, in a half whisper that was louder than her normal voice. "And I'll never forgive myself if something should happen on her way home this evening."

"Don't worry yourself, Kate," Da said. "I'll go along." He downed the last of his ale and rose. "Are we ready, then?"

An-Ming gave in with a good temper and a smile. She and Bridget hugged. Ma thanked Hu-Lan and begged her to come again. We all said our goodbyes to the Hurleys. Then it was out the door and into the night. It was crisp and clear, and smelled of the flats at low tide. The sky was dark as pitch above the yellow glow of the gas lamps on each corner. I could make out a few of the brightest stars in the strip of sky above the street. There would be no moon that night.

We said a final goodbye to Ma and Bridget and started down Prince Street, the five of us. Hu-Lan put herself firmly beside An-Ming, so Peter walked with Da. I brought up the rear, and that was all right. There were still people out and about in twos and threes, coming home from work or dragging out the celebration. One group went by singing. A neighbor greeted Da and me. We were mostly quiet, mostly happy, except maybe Hu-Lan, feeling the weight of the hour. We crossed North Square and tucked into the alley beside the Bethel, our usual route.

Halfway down, a voice hailed us from behind. "Hey! O'Neill!"

We stopped and turned. There was a tall silhouette blocking the mouth of the alley, backlit by the gas lamps on North Square.

Da stepped past Hu-Lan and stood with me."Which O'Neill?"

"Don't matter."

"Who's calling?"

"No one you know."

"Then don't bother me." Da turned to go.

"O'Neill, listen! I've got an offer."

Da turned back. "I don't deal with people I don't know," he said.

"The boy knows me," the man replied.

"It's the filthy thug who tried to grab An-Ming," I said. My jaw was clenched, my fists too. I was ready to go after him then and there. Da put a hand on my shoulder and held me back.

"You've got some explaining to do, Mister," Da told the man.

"In good time." He crossed his arms and leaned against the wall of the alley.

"What's your game? What do you want with the girl?"

"No harm. There's someone who wants to meet her."

Peter pushed his way between us. "Then he can come forward in daylight and make himself known, like an honest gentleman, you ruffian! Get along, before I call the watch!"

The tall man laughed. "Very brave, sport. But I'm afraid Officer Curtis and the rest are busy breaking up a fight on the other side of the hill. How about it, O'Neill? Do you want to hear my offer?"

"I've heard enough already," Da said. "Finn, take the ladies down to the wharf. Peter and I will deal with this dog."

"But—"

"Do it!" He shoved me back.

"Go on, Finn," Peter said. "Take An-Ming to safety. Please."

"I'm not leaving," An-Ming said.

"And I'm staying with her," I added.

Peter turned. "What about Hu-La—?" He cut off, staring past us down the alley. "O'Neill! There's more of them."

An-Ming, Hu-Lan, and I turned. Two more figures were sneaking up the alley toward us. They stopped when they saw they'd been caught out.

"Here, too," Da said.

Three more had joined the tall thug. One of them was Billy Adams.

"Well, well," Da said quietly, "if it ain't the biggest Know-Nothing of 'em all. Peter, you and Finn rush those two. Ladies, you follow them. I'll hold off this litter of curs."

"Right, Da," I said. "Come on, Peter."

"I'm with you. Anie, stay with Hu-Lan. Finn, Go!"

We made a rush toward the two men down the alley, only An-Ming didn't stay back. She darted past us and threw herself feet first at the closest thug. She hit him with a yell that drowned out the thud he made when he hit the cobbles. Quick as a cat, she rolled, crouched, and sprang back up. The other one took a wild swipe at her. He had some kind of club in his hand, a stone or lead tied in a sleeve. It hit her on the side of the head and she went down.

"Anie!" Peter cried. He was one step ahead of me and landed two solid jabs to the thug's gut and an uppercut to the jaw. The man went down in a heap. I dodged past them and knelt by An-Ming. She was out cold.

Peter grabbed her wrist and shook it, rubbing her face. "Anie? Anie?"

"No time no time!" Hu-Lan cried, catching up. "Look!"

Da was right in the midst of it, punching and kicking at the four behind us. The narrow alley had them tangled up, but he was giving ground. Billy Adams broke past him.

Peter and I heaved An-Ming up. She was so slim, she weighed hardly a thing. He grabbed her by the waist and draped her over my shoulder.

"Take her!" He cried. He started running toward the fight.

"But—"

"Go, Finn!" he yelled.

"Quick quick!" Hu-Lan cried, tugging my arm.

The thug Peter had downed was groaning. She gave him a kick and ran down the alley. I followed as fast as could without dropping An-Ming.

Chapter 18

WE MADE IT TO Lewis Street, one short block from the wharf, before I heard footsteps hard on the cobbles behind me. I risked a look back, hoping to see Peter and Da. It was Billy Adams, gaining. Another one came around the corner not ten yards back. I stumbled under An-Ming's weight, light as it was.

"Faster!" I yelled, regaining my stride.

Hu-Lan looked back. "*Wa!*" she gasped. She slowed, letting me catch up.

"Go!" I panted. "Go!"

She pulled the long, ivory-tipped skewers from her hair. Her braid uncoiled down her back almost to her knees.

"You go!" she said, gripping a skewer in each hand. "Go fast!" And she ran back toward the on-coming thugs, screaming a line of Chinese that curdled my blood.

Adams hesitated, then tried to dodge past her. She tripped him and he went sprawling onto the sidewalk. She jumped on his back, stabbing with the skewers. He yelped like stuck pig. The other one was almost on them. I almost set An-Ming down to go help. But then a third man hove into sight. The tall one. I ran.

Windows opened in the upper stories. People were

shouting. Hu-Lan's screams turned into cries. I kept running. Across Commercial Street and onto the wharf. Past the bales and barrels, the shuttered stalls, the gangways. There was no sign of the watchman or even a deck watch on any of the ships. I made it all the way to the ladder. Somehow, I managed to get An-Ming down the whole low-tide height of it, then almost fell into the canoe. I fumbled her onto the stern seat and scrambled to the bow. The boat jerked and tipped under my feet. I grabbed the painter, tore the knot loose.

But there weren't any oars. They were up in the locker, where we always left them. And no time to go back for them. I grabbed at the dripping seaweed that coated the granite blocks of the wharf and pulled. The seaweed slid through my fingers, slippery as fish. I found the crack between two blocks, jammed in my fingers, and pulled. The boat moved. I slid my hands forward along the crack, pulled the boat ahead, and again, and again. Yard by yard, I pulled the boat to the end of the granite wharf. Lewis Wharf, like most of them, had long wooden piers built out from its end, on tarred pilings. The water ran under, with room for a small boat beneath, even at high tide. I rounded the granite corner and pulled us under the pier, into darkness as deep as a grave.

I had no idea how much of a lead I had on Adams and the rest – or even if they were still chasing me – but I wasn't going to wait around to find out. I pulled the boat toward the other side of the wharf. It was hard going. The seaweed tangled my fingers and made them slip. The barnacles on the granite sliced at my palms. The salt stung. And if I pushed out by the least bit, the boat tried to swing away, leaving me stretched over the water, gripping the stone and barnacles with cramped hands.

Lewis Wharf was a wide one. It had three piers jutting off the end, and ships lay in each gaps. I worked around their bows, trying to stay under the pier, trying not to splash. Then I reached the far side and had no choice but to go into the open. There were ships wharfed along the whole length, of course. I slipped between the last two of them, silent as a wraith, and what did I find but a ship's boat, tied alongside the farthest out, hidden from the wharf. I felt inside carefully. There was a pair of oars!

A light was flickering in the stern cabin, but no sound came from the deck. I lifted the oars slowly, one at a time, careful not to knock them on gunnel. I was just fitting them into the oarlocks when I heard a quiet voice in toward the street. Another voice answered, from the water. I couldn't make out the words. Then there was the sound of hands and feet on a ladder, the clunk of a boat against the wharf, the wash of ripples, more voices, angry. I dipped my oars gently and slipped under the gleam of the stern window, into the harbor.

There was glow from the city, but no moon. The water was dark but for the reflection of stars and the dozens of stern lanterns hanging on the ships moored along the channel. The tide was running in, with a faint easterly breeze to help it along. I stayed in the quiet water just off the wharves, trying to find a dark line between the city's lamps and the ships' lanterns. An-Ming was still as a coffin, and I took a moment to try to lay her out more gently on the thwart. She was warm to my touch and still breathing. I said a quick prayer to the Virgin and covered her as best I could with my new wool jacket. Then I took up the oars again and struck out into the maze of moored ships. I had a good mile to row to the *Hang-Jinhe*, all in silence.

An advantage to rowing is you're looking behind. Dark as it was, I was sure I saw another boat pull out from Lewis Wharf. It might have been the harbor police. More likely not. I slipped behind the nearest moored ship and set a course for the next one. I zigged and zagged from ship to ship, always slipping around in the shadow at their bows, avoiding the stern lanterns. I caught glimpses of the boat behind me. It headed across the channel, down toward the *Hang-Jinhe.* I stayed among the ships on the west side, skirting the South Boston flats. The moored ships thinned out. I felt exposed in the long gaps. The breeze picked up, and the waves slapped softly against the canoe. No way I could avoid that. I rowed steadily, past where I knew Governor's Island to be. I made out the lantern hanging from the *Hang-Jinhe*'s stern. There were lights in the cabin windows, too, and lamps on deck. They were awake, watching, worried, I was sure. I kept rowing. Finally, when I could make out the dark bulk of Castle Island topped by the sharp line of Fort Independence, I cut across the channel and made my way back up, coming at the *Hang-Jinhe* from her opposite side.

I had to keep looking over my shoulder now. I paused and searched the dark water for signs of another boat lurking nearby. The lights on the *Hang-Jinhe* made everything else seem twice as dark. I threw caution to the wind and began to pull as hard as I could. I took another look, searching. Something moved beyond her, I was sure of it, something low on the water, splashing against the rising chop.

"Ahoy the *Hang-Jinhe!*" I cried. "Mr. Lawson! Captain Li!"

They heard me. A clamor of Chinese rang across the water. Lamps rushed to the rail on my side.

"Finn? Is that you?" It was Mr. Lawson. His voice was strained.

"It is! And Anie!" I cried. "She's hurt bad! More light! There's a boat chasing me!"

In hardly a moment, I heard Captain Li shouting commands. More lanterns flared into life, and then torches. The junk seemed like to catch fire. I could make out the men on deck now, and some were holding long shapes that could only be guns. I scanned the nearby water, but there was no sight or sound of another boat.

They hoisted An-Ming aboard in the bosun's chair and

carried her to her cabin. Mr. Lawson hovered over her, looking as old as I'd ever seen him be. The mate used some kind of smelling salts to bring her around, and the first thing she did was throw up. After that and a sip of lemon water she was dizzy but able to talk. And the first thing she said was, "What happened?"

I had told Mr. Lawson the guts of it as soon as I was safely alongside, but he'd been too worried over An-Ming. Now I told it again with all the details.

"We've got to go back quick as we can," I ended.

Mr. Lawson was himself again, and he looked angry. "We will, Finn. In force."

We took both boats and ten of the crew, along with Wang and Captain Li. They left the guns, but some carried tarred, knotted ropes and odd jointed clubs. At the last minute, An-Ming stumbled out on deck and tried to follow us down the ladder. Her father held her back. She was too dizzy to put up a fight and almost threw up again. Mr. Lawson took her back to the cabin, talking softly to reassure her. He left the mate in with her, with strict orders to keep her in bed.

He also wouldn't let me row. "You need a rest, Finn," he said, and he put two of the crew at the oars, using a second pair borrowed from the junk. I'd have rather been rowing. It took forever just sitting.

We came into Lewis Wharf and hurried up Lewis Street. There was no sign of Hu-Lan. Then I spotted one of her hair sticks, broken in the gutter. I shouted her name, and all the Chinese crew took up the refrain. Windows flew open and people yelled to shut up. Someone even threw a bottle.

In the silence that brought on, a woman in an upstairs window called, "Are you Mr. Lawson?"

"Yes, I am," he replied.

"She's up here," the woman said.

"Is she all right?" I shouted.

"A bit the worse for wear, no thanks to those plug-uglies. I'm thinking they broke her arm. I sent for a doctor but he ain't come."

"I'll be right up, Ma'am," Mr. Lawson said. "Finn, look for the others." He said something to Wang and Li in Chinese, and we were off.

But the alley beside the Seamen's Bethel was empty. Even the rats seemed to have deserted it. Then I spotted Peter's hat in a corner by an ash bin. It was half stove in.

"Peter!" I called. "Da! Are you near?"

There was no answer. I went out into North Square and called again. The door to the Bethel opened and a man came out with a lantern.

"What outcry is this?" he demanded. "What new tempest breaks the calm sea of the night?"

"I'm sorry, Reverend Taylor," I replied. "I'm trying to find my father and my friend. We were set on by a gang of toughs, trying to kidnap Miss Lawson, from the Chinese junk, sir. Did you see what happened?"

"I heard the dogs fighting," he said, "and sailed out to fire a godly word across their bows, but the curs backed wind and tacked off before I came in range."

"They all went? All together?"

"Aye, though they were worse for the weather, and towing two that couldn't stand on their own." He held the lantern high and cast a sharp eye on Wang, Captain Li, and the others. "You'll not find them now, lad. Take your Mongol army back to their ship and let the rising peace of God be a tide of forgiveness to wash your weary soul."

I stared at him. I just stared at him, thinking *Tide of forgiveness? When the thugs had dragged off two men who couldn't walk on their own?*

Wang broke me out of the shock. He bowed to the Reverend.

"Tank you, sir," he said. "We go." He took my arm and walked me toward Prince Street. "Home," he said. "Maybe home."

I seized the meager hope. "Yes. That's where they'd go if they were hurt." I pulled free and ran up the street.

The hope died as soon as I went through our door. The place was dark.

Bridget jerked upright in her bed, blanket clenched at her neck. "Who is it?"

"It's me. Did Da come home?"

"Mike? Is that you?" It was Ma, calling from their room, with the answer I'd feared.

"It's me, Ma," I replied.

"What is it? Where's your father?"

"Da's gone. The thugs took him." To Wang I said, "Go tell Mr. Lawson. All right?"

Before he even reached the door, Ma was out of bed, lighting a lamp and asking questions. I told what had happened.

"Sweet blessed Mary," she said. "Why'd they haul them away, your Da and Peter?"

"I don't know, Ma. It was An-Ming they wanted."

"The poor girl. And poor Miss Hu-Lan." She hurried back to her room. "Bridget, get dressed. We're going to the police. Finn, you get back to Mr. Lawson. Look for your father and Mr. Jenkins. Ask at Hurley's, he hears more than most. Check the alleys and all the wharves. Everywhere you can think of they might have dumped them. Try to find that tall man. Ask at the boarding houses, but don't go alone. And tell Mr. Lawson he can bring Hu-Lan here if she'd like."

So we started searching. We woke Hurley first, on the way back to Lewis Street, but he hadn't heard anything. Nor the police. They'd had more than enough fights to deal with once the celebrating picked up. They weren't too interested in this one now it was over. Mr. Lawson himself had to go to the station to make them take notice, and it was only when he told them who Peter was that they stirred their shanks and sent out a man to make inquiries.

By then it was almost dawn and people were stirring. We told the neighbors and started in on the boarding houses. But no one there would admit to seeing Billy Adams around, or even to knowing the tall man. Mr. Lawson offered to pay for the information, but it didn't work. They took the money and told us the same. MacLean, who Billy Adams worked for, just laughed. I went down to the wharves after that, to try to find as many of the boatman as I could. Da had made a lot of enemies when he was a runner for MacLean, but he had friends, too. No one had seen him, but they all said they'd keep an eye out and an ear to the wind.

The sun was up by the time we got back home. Hu-Lan was there now, her arm in splints and a plaster on her face where the thugs had hit her more than once. The doctor had given her a draught of something to help with the pain, and she was dozing in Bridget's cot. Ma was there, waiting for news. She'd sent word to Mr. Tierney that Da was missing and she'd be in late. He was a good man, Tierney, and wouldn't mind if she missed a day or two. But it was hard on us to miss the pay. Bridget was missing school, too, scouring the North End alleys again with Captain Li and two of the crewmen. They came back soon after we did, with nothing to report.

"We will widen the search to East Boston and Fort Hill," Mr. Lawson said, trying to sound assured. I don't know how he managed. I was dead beat and gloomy as a ghost. "First, I'll let Jacob Sands know. His friends have influence. And we must tell Mr. Bond about Peter. Then I must go see to my daughter."

Hu-Lan pushed herself up with her good hand. "I go," she said.

Ma and Mr. Lawson both tried to talk her out of moving, but she wouldn't be stayed.

"I must go," she stated. "An-Ming need me."

Mr. Lawson gave in. "Perhaps you need her. It seems the only way to get you to rest."

"I'll row her back," I said, forcing my tired legs to stand.

"No, I'll send her in the junk's boat. You can row me out later."

So Captain Li and two of the crew went off half-carrying Hu-Lan. Ma poured tea into the rest of us and made us eat a quick bite. Then Mr. Lawson and three others headed for the bank and Mr. Bond's shop, and then to Fort Hill and the South End. Ma went with them, because we had family and friends over there. Bridget stayed at the house, in case someone brought word. Wang and the rest went with me down to Lewis Wharf, to row over to East Boston. We were crossing the street to Lewis Wharf when Pat Delany came running up, so excited he forgot his grammar.

"Finn!" he cried. "It's word I've got, word of your Da!"

I grabbed his arm. "What is it, Pat?"

"He's been crimped! He and the clockmaker, Jenkins!"

"What? Where'd you hear that?"

"A stallkeeper I know on Commercial Wharf. He'd slept in his shop last night, too drunk to go home. End of the night, he says, near dawn, he gets up to relieve himself off the side of the wharf. He sees a knot of men come out of Lewis Street, dragging two others. They dump the two bodies into a boat and head out."

"Bodies? What do you mean, bodies? Dead?"

"No, no! Only that they were out cold. One of them came to enough to struggle when they were lowering him into the boat. He fell into the water, but they conked him again and hauled him on board."

"How do you know it was Da? It could have been some drunk sailors."

"They called him O'Neill when they hit him. They were laughing."

I almost shook Pat, like he was the one laughing. "You're sure they were going to crimp them? They weren't going to just dump them?"

"I'm sure, Finn, I'm sure. Calm down. You're near to breaking my arm." He loosened my hand. "The boatman said, 'We'll see how he likes the warm water in Africa.'"

"Africa?"

"That's what my friend heard."

Africa. It might as well have been China. "Did your friend recognize any of them, Pat?"

"He wasn't sure, but he thought the boatman sounded a bit like Billy Adams."

"Damn him!" I looked at the mass of shipping crammed to the wharves in front of me, the forest of masts stretching along the waterfront for as far as I could see. How was I going to find Da and Peter in all that?

Pat knew just what I was thinking. "I checked at the Exchange," he said. "There's a British brig clearing today for the Guinea Coast, by way of Bermuda. She's the *Lady Devon*, Captain Tyler. Back hull, blue stripe, no figurehead, just a scroll, and a line of roses carved on the name boards."

"Which wharf?"

"She's lying out in President Roads already, waiting for the tide."

"God bless, you, Pat," I said. "Do one thing more for me, will you? Find Mr. Lawson and tell him everything you just told me. He's on his way to the Harbor Bank and then to Bond & Son. Can you do that?"

"I can, Finn. I will." He started off.

"Wait, Pat!" I called. "Take these fellows with you." I turned to Wang and Captain Li. "Did you understand that?" I asked. "Da and Peter are on a boat leaving for Africa. Africa. They're being kidnapped." Wang nodded. "Good! Go with Pat here. Find Mr. Lawson!"

I ran down the wharf. The wind was light, from the southeast. There was no worse wind for clearing the main channel through the Narrows. If it held, there was a small chance I could catch the *Lady Devon* before she sailed.

Chapter 19

I WASN'T THINKING STRAIGHT. I ran to the locker, grabbed the oars for our boat, scrambled down the ladder, and almost fell into the boat. Untied in such a hurry I almost dipped the bow under. Then pushed off right into the path of one of the packet ships, working in toward the head of the wharf. I just managed to row out of the way, while half a dozen sailors cursed me for the idiot I was. My heart was pounding.

"Slow down," I told myself. "Slow down and go faster."

It was something Da always preached. "Flailing the oars ain't going to help, boy. You need a long reach and a steady pace. I took a breath, blew it out slow, and began to row.

President Roads lay two and a half miles from the wharves, beyond Governor's island and the tight spot at Lower Middle rocks. Past all that, the outer harbor opened up. Ships would anchor there to wait for for the tide to turn so they could make the passage out the main channel through the Narrows. Two and a half miles isn't a long way to row, but I had the tide and the breeze against me. I lined up the New North steeple with the end of Lewis Wharf and put my back into it.

I made good time, as good as I'd ever rowed by myself.

I knew that, but the little boat seemed to crawl through the water. I passed India Wharf and adjusted my marks to steer as straight a course as I could. Every four strokes, I looked over my shoulder to check the incoming traffic. It slowed me, but a collision would slow me a lot more.

I worried about the tide and the wind. You have to understand something about Boston Harbor to know what I was up against, and why I had any hope at all. The flood tide, as it neared high, would actually set to eastward, out through the main channel at the Narrows, enough to help a ship ease her way through. My hope was the breeze. The southeaster that was slowing me down also made it blessed hard for a square-rigger to tack out through that narrow channel at any tide. If that wind backed just a few degrees either way, and the pilot knew his stuff, the *Lady Devon* could do it. I prayed for the wind to hold.

I passed outside the number 11 buoy and adjusted my marks again. The wind freshened but he tide began to slack. It was a mixed blessing: easier to row against, but it meant the flow at the Narrows would soon swing eastward.

I passed the number 9 buoy, and now I could see the *Hang-Jinhe* moored across the channel. I wondered how An-Ming was. And Hu-Lan. If anyone could see me. If they would know it was me and would guess what I was doing there. My mind jumped to the *Lady Devon*. Where were they anchored? How close to the Narrows? Would they even try the Narrows? It was the only deep channel, sure, but if she was a small brig she just might slip out to the northeast on the high tide, through the Broad Sound Channel. If the pilot was willing to try it. She was a foreign ship; she'd be using a Boston pilot, who'd know the channel. The wind was better that way. And if the wind backed even a little more to the south, she could slip out Hypocrite Channel, a better heading for Bermuda and Africa. If—

"If, if, if, O'Neill!" I chided myself. "You don't even know if she's there. Pat could be wrong. She could be lying past South Boston in Nantasket Roads. She could have sailed at dawn. She could have hired a tug. You won't know till you get there. Just keep rowing and worry later."

I passed close by the tip of Castle Island and into the broad reach of President Roads. It was almost four miles from here to the outer islands and the channels that led to the open ocean. The feel of the sea changed, the waves lengthened. The wind took on a chill but held from the southeast. I looked over my right shoulder, where the bulk of the shipping lay. There were five dozen anchored there at least, a mess of schooners, a few barks and ships, a fair number of brigs and brigantines, in no particular order. My eyes jumped from brig to brig, square-rigged vessels with two masts. It was hard to pick them out among all the others. I was looking for a blue line on a black hull. A scroll under the bowsprit. I started to row again. New ships came into view from behind the others. I kept rowing, kept searching.

I only spotted her because she started to put on sail. The flood was setting strongly to eastward, out through the Narrows. A pilot had decided to try it. And, yes, there was the blue line and the scroll. Those red dots on the nameboards could only be roses.

I hailed them, but the wind was in my face and I was much too far away, a hundred yards at least. They eased up to their anchor under staysails and jib, slipped backward as the anchor pulled free, then began to move slowly, close hauled on a starboard tack toward the Long Island light. Right across my path. I veered to cut her off.

It was a long, slow race, and I might have won it right then if she'd kept her heading. But just as I was about to hail her again, she came about and headed off on the opposite tack. Now she set her spanker and the rest of her staysails, all the fore-and-aft rig she could fly. She was pulling away from me, toward Broad Sound. My heart sank. She might be trying for the other channels. Or she might simply be beating her way down to a better approach to the Narrows. I had to hope that was it. The brig and I would both have to round the shoals at Nix's Mate before we could enter the Narrows. I just might get there first.

But the *Lady Devon* had the wind on her quarter now, and she drew away from me faster and faster. She would have to tack soon and sail back to the Narrows, but she was making good speed. If I'd had taken the time to grab the canoe's sail, I'd have had a better chance to beat her. Another blessed *if.* I kept rowing, despair filling my heart.

I was right in the shipping channel, but I held to my course, the straightest line out. There was a pair of schooners tacking down behind me. I wasn't too worried about them, but something else was coming – the white tugboat, the *Quincy*. She was lashed alongside a big barkentine, towing her toward the channel. No need to tack when you've got a steam engine and paddle wheels to push you through. She was coming straight down the channel toward me.

Here was my chance. I stopped rowing long enough to pull our little anchor from under the bow seat and bend its long rope onto the painter. I coiled the line neatly behind the rowing thwart. When I looked up, the *Quincy* and her tow were almost on me. I sat down, set the anchor in my lap, and took up my oars.

The *Quincy* sounded her horn. I waved and began to pull to the side. She swung the other way just a bit, so as to pass about three yards to my right as I sat facing her. That was too far. I pulled hard on my left, swinging closer to her. She sounded her horn again but came on straight as an arrow. She wasn't moving more than three or four knots, but she was throwing up a three-foot bow wave against that southeasterly breeze. I pulled till she was almost on me.

The *Quincy* swept by so close the bow wave almost flipped me. Then it was past and I was turning in the wash. I stood, like a circus rider standing on a bareback stallion, and threw the anchor underhanded as hard as I could. I fell backward onto the thwart, watching the metal hook spin slowly, trailing an arc of line. It dropped behind the *Quincy's* rail. I grabbed the rope and took a quick, short tug. It slipped, snagged, slipped again. I saw the shank of the anchor lift into sight at the taffrail. Then the hook caught firm, the rope jerked, and I almost tumbled into the water. I let the line pay out, scrambling over the thwarts to the bow. I gave the line a quick turn around the cleat on the breasthook and slowly, carefully took up the strain. The bow of the canoe swung to follow the *Quincy*. She started to move forward. I leaned back against the pull and squeezed the rope hard, stopping the slide. The canoe picked up speed. The *Quincy* was towing me down the harbor like a whaler on a Nantucket sleigh ride!

I held fast to the line, feet braced on the boat's ribs, leaning back to keep the pull in my arms and legs. I had let out about half the rope, so I was trailing the tug but not the ship it was towing. The canoe bounced and yawed in their mixed-up wake. It seemed we were hopping over the water. I craned my neck for a glimpse of the *Lady Devon*, but the tug and the ship blocked my view. I just had to hope the *Lady Devon* would tack again and head back toward the Narrows.

We churned past the headland at the end of Long Island and started to cross the gap to Nix's Mate. That's when a deckhand on the *Quincy* noticed me. He came back to the taffrail and shouted something I couldn't hear. I suspect it included a deal of cursing. I loosed one hand long enough to wave. He took it all wrong. With a shake of his fist, he hurried forward and come right back with an axe. One swing was all it took – my line parted like a thread, and the *Quincy* left me wallowing in her wake.

But there she was the *Lady Devon*, bearing down toward the Narrows. She had tacked after all! I hauled in my cut line, grabbed the oars, and pulled for all I was worth.

Nix's Mate was a gravel shoal at the mouth of the Narrows, marked by a tall black pyramid. A ship with any draft at all had to stay well clear, but little boat could slip past with room and to spare. I angled my bow to cut off the *Lady Devon*. It was a hard pull against the freshening breeze. I kept looking over my shoulder to see how I stood against the *Lady Devon*. I couldn't bear not to – it was going to be that close. She was on a tack that would bring her near the head of Gallop's Island. I'd be there to meet her, if I could keep up the pace.

The waves were steep right over the shallows of Nix's Mate, and fighting through them slowed me. The next time I looked over my shoulder, the *Lady Devon* wasn't more than twenty yards away. She started to come about.

I stood and shouted. I waved my cap. I did everything but dance for them. But the crew were handling the sails, the pilot and captain were at the wheel. An idler at the stern saw me and waved back. I cursed him. I prayed she'd catch in stays. Run aground. Be struck by lightning. She wasn't. She came about neat as you please and headed away on the opposite tack.

I shook my fist at her transom, but I wasn't done yet, no sir. The channel was about a quarter-mile wide at most. The *Lady Devon* would have to pick her way through in short tacks. Once beyond the Narrows, she'd have to swing wide around the shoals at the Brewster Bar, and then heave to, if only for a moment, to put off the pilot. I could row a straight line. I could cut right over the Brewster Bar. I could still catch her.

I was fooling myself, but I couldn't quit, not this far out. I put my back into rowing.

Twice, I almost caught them in the channel, but the inbound shipping almost ran me down. My only safe course lay close to the islands, where the waves were steeper and harder to fight. I cut across the channel as soon as I could and set out for the beacon marking the Brewster Bar. Two tacks later, The *Lady Devon* cleared the end of the Narrows. One more long tack and she made her final turn to clear the shoals. She was sailing as close to the wind as she could, kicking up a spray from her bow as she met the growing waves. Ahead lay Little Brewster Island, the Boston Harbor Light, and the open Atlantic. I watched her pull away. The pilot boat hove into view from behind Little Brewster. I remember it was the *Coquette*, a trim schooner.

This is it, Finn, I thought. You've missed her.

I rested on my oars, exhausted, and watched the two ships approach each other. I didn't even try to hail them, they were that far off. Bound for Africa with Da and Peter.

The wind and waves forced me back to the oars. My little boat was beginning to pitch. I was getting wet. The wind was blowing harder, and colder. This wasn't the quiet harbor; it was the mouth of the ocean. But I couldn't take my eyes off the *Lady Devon* and the pilot boat. Finally, I looked back toward the Narrows, the long row home. Alone.

And there was the *Hang-Jinhe*, beating toward me with a bone in her teeth.

Chapter 20

I COULDN'T BELIEVE MY eyes. The *Hang-Jinhe* had all three of her big sails set, like some manner of strange schooner. She'd looked clumsy at anchor, shaped wrong. But, sure, she could sail, right into the teeth of the wind, it seemed. The eyes painted on her bow made her fierce.

I cheered, I waved, I thanked Mary and Jesus and all the Saints. And someone on her deck waved back. She eased off the wind and headed toward me.

"No!" I cried. "Not me!" I pointed toward the *Lady Devon*. She and the *Coquette* were both hove to. The *Coquette* was lowering her yawl to go pick up the pilot. "Catch her!"

The *Hang-Jinhe* was fast on the wind with her fore-and-aft rig, but a square-rigger like the *Lady Devon* could put on far more sail once she had the wind with her. I grabbed the oars and pulled toward the *Hang-Jinhe* as fast as I could.

She was almost right on me before the helmsman brought her into the wind. The big lug sails, each ribbed like a whale's chest, were tame as kittens in the hands of the crew. They threw me a line and dropped the rope ladder, and I was up the side in a trice. The helmsman was already backing off; the sails came over, and we were away, towing the canoe behind.

But it had all taken time. The pilot yawl was on its way back to the *Coquette*. The *Lady Devon* was making sail.

I scurried up the ladder to the poop deck. Captain Li himself was at the big tiller, with Mr. Lawson beside him. And An-Ming on his other side. Her head was wrapped with a cloth and a plaster that smelled of ginger and hot pepper and looked like a Turkish turban. She had the Malay pirate look in her eyes.

"Can we catch her?" I cried.

"Yes!" she snapped.

"We will damn well try," Mr. Lawson said. He was grim, and not so certain.

Captain Li never took his eyes from our quarry, except to check the set of the sails and the play of the wind in the long pennant that still flew from her main mast. He yelled something in Chinese, and the crew sprang to action, making tiny adjustments to the many lines that controlled the three big sails. The *Hang-Jinhe* seemed to pause at the peak of the next wave, then leapt forward to meet the next. I couldn't stand still. I ran to the side and gripped the rail. An-Ming followed me.

"We catch," she told me, making no effort to sound American. "We chase to Africa and back."

And we were gaining on them. The *Lady Devon* had set her topgallants, but was still heading too close to the wind for topsails and mains. Captain Li adjusted his helm and shouted another command. The crew sprang to the lines. We gained another dozen yards.

"Signal her!" Mr. Lawson yelled.

"*Yes!*" An-Ming called back.

She hurried down the ladder and ran toward the bow. I followed.

We ducked through the companionway and into the forecastle. Four of the crewmen were waiting there, peering out of a square port in the junk's flat bow. They took positions as An-Ming came in, spreading apart to reveal a long, small-bore cannon. I gaped at it. Surely they weren't going to fire on the *Lady Devon*?

But surely they did. An-Ming shouted an order, and the crew grabbed lines and ran the gun out. She shouted another order, and the gun captain took a burning slow-match from a tub. An-Ming grabbed it from him.

"Ears, Finn!" she warned, even as she held the match to the cannon's touch hole.

I got my ears covered and jumped aside. The cannon boomed. The recoil sent it flying back against the ropes. Smoke filled the cabin, but the brisk headwind cleared it quickly. Ears ringing, I peered out the gunport with the rest of them.

"*Wa!*" the gun captain cried, pointing.

I glimpsed the end of the splash as it collapsed back into the waves. The crew cheered. And I heard Mr. Lawson bellow from the deck.

"Ahoy, the *Lady Devon!* Captain Tyler! We need to speak!"

There was no reply at first. An-Ming barked a command, and the crew began to swab the barrel and ready the gun for another shot. Then we heard an answering call, too distant to make out the words. The *Lady Devon* turned into the wind. Her headsails flapped. Her crew manned the sheets and lines to back her topgallants and heave her to. The gun crew cheered again. An-Ming and I raced back on deck.

"I don't recall telling the gunner to load shot!" Mr. Lawson snapped, giving An-Ming the hardest frown I'd ever seen him make.

"It worked," she replied.

But Captain Tyler was none too pleased. He and Mr. Lawson argued through speaking trumpets for ten minutes or so, while Captain Li held the junk about twenty yards off the *Lady Devon's* starboard side. Tyler didn't see how Mr. Lawson had claim to the least one of his crew members, and had no right to fire on him in any case. Lawson was a damned pirate and he and the whole crew would be in irons if this were England. And so on.

Finally, An-Ming grabbed the trumpet and yelled. "He is my fiancé! If you abduct him, I fire again!"

Mr. Lawson snatched the trumpet back. "Please forgive my daughter, Captain," he called. "She was injured when her young man was taken and has not been herself."

I thought she was acting more like herself than ever. But this bit about "fiancé?" I wondered if Peter knew yet.

"I assure you," Mr. Lawson was saying to Tyler, "we will do our best to make amends."

"I doubt you can replace a missing crewman!" Tyler yelled back, still all huffy. "I am short-handed as it is, since your damned Bostonian coppers jailed three of my men. I can ill afford to give up another."

"I will happily replace him!" Mr. Lawson replied. "Anie —"

But she was already hurrying down the ladder to the lower decks.

"I'll go, sir," I said. "In place of Peter and Da."

"That won't be necessary, Finn," he said.

I hardly had time to ask what he meant before An-Ming came back up, followed by Wang. And trailing Wang, hands tied to a lead rope, feet hobbled with bamboo shackles, came Billy Adams and the tall thug. They blinked at the *Lady Devon* in the hard sunlight.

"Finn," Mr. Lawson said, "would you be so good as to row us across to trade these ruffians for Peter and your father."

"With pleasure, sir!" said I.

He turned to Adams and the tall one. "Gentlemen, behold your new home for the next six months or so. She'll be a good berth, I imagine. Captain Tyler seems just the man to deal with the likes of you."

Billy Adams paled. The Brits had a reputation for keeping their crews in line.

"I'll give you one last chance," Mr. Lawson went on. "Tell us who put you up to this abduction, and you can stay here. The judge will be more lenient to witnesses, I'll see to it. Otherwise, you're joining Captain Tyler's ship."

The tall thug didn't blink. Adams swallowed, but held his tongue.

"Very well," Mr. Lawson said. "I'm sure you'll make many good friends on the *Lady Devon*. Particularly any who've stayed at your boarding house before."

That did it. No one hated crimps and boardinghouse runners more than a sailor.

"It was your nephew, the banker," Adams said. "Robert Lawson."

Mr. Lawson looked poleaxed. "Robert?" he said, leaning on the rail to steady himself.

"Nonsense!" An-Ming said. "Cousin Robert is ill, confined to bed. Who deals with you?"

"I tell you—" Adams began.

"Wang," An-Ming snapped.

Wang took a step toward Adams.

"I tell you it was Lawson!" Adams cried. "Sands was just passing on the orders!"

"Sands now? He gave you orders?" An-Ming demanded.

"Yeah, it was Sands. Working for old Lawson. I swear it!" Adams looked wildly from An-Ming to Wang and finally to Mr. Lawson.

"Do you agree with him?" Mr. Lawson asked the tall thug.

"I'll take my chances with Tyler," he said. "You can explain to the boys why you didn't come with me, Adams."

I've never seen a man look more trapped than Adams did then. He shut up, and two of the crewmen took him back to the hold.

I rowed the tall thug over to the *Lady Devon*, with Mr. Lawson, An-Ming, and Wang. Peter was waiting for us. He looked horrible – bruised, cut, black eyes, and a broken nose. He could hardly stand on his own two feet. An-Ming gave a cry and ran to him.

Captain Tyler stared at her in surprise. "Didn't realize a young lady was involved," he said, "particularly, em . . ."

"Her mother was a great Chinese lady," Mr. Lawson replied coldly.

"Of course," Tyler replied quickly.

"I'm afraid I have only one man to trade with you," Mr. Lawson went on. "I need the other for a witness to this . . ." He gestured at Peter. ". . . this violence."

"One will have to do," Captain Tyler replied. "He seems in better condition, at least."

"He's a ruffian, I warn you."

"They all are. We'll whip him into shape, never fear."

"Yes, but you should have two men for me. Mr. Jenkins and his companion, Mr. O'Neill."

"Was that his name?" Tyler said. "I knew he was Irish the minute I laid eyes on him. I wouldn't have him, sir. I sent him back with the runner."

"He's not here?" I cried. "Where did they take him?"

"No idea," Tyler replied. He pointed at the tall thug. "You! Where did you take the Irishman?"

The man glowered back.

The ship's bosun took a firm grip on his arm and give him a hard shake. "Speak smartly, or it'll go hard on you," the bosun growled.

"Deer Island," the tall thug muttered. "Adams paid off a couple of the night watch to take him over."

That evening I had to tell Ma and Bridget what had happened.

"We'll go right to the police," Ma said, reaching for her coat and bonnet.

"Mr. Lawson already did," I told her. "As soon as we were back at anchor. He's still there, arguing with them and the judge about Billy Adams and old Robert and Sands."

"What about Da?" Bridget cried.

"The judge wrote up a release, but they can't send to the island till the steamer goes out tomorrow morning," I explained.

Ma sank back onto her chair. "Poor Mike. It's just like Ireland all over."

"What do you mean?" I asked.

"He was jailed in Dublin for brawling with the police. You know your Da; his soul's out on the water. He like to went mad shut up behind bars."

I knew my Da, all right. Or thought I did. "If he wasn't such a brawler in the first place it wouldn't have happened," I muttered.

"Hush your mouth, Finn O'Neill!" Ma scolded. "He was fighting to keep the police off the backs of women and children and old men, poor folks who couldn't move fast enough when the officers got ugly. It was a rally for O'Connell and repeal of the Act of Union. You were there, hardly just born, and Molly, Grace, and Tim, God bless him. Your da was protecting you, me, and them, and everyone around. He took on a whole squad, all by himself. Knocked two of them right out cold." She shook her head. "They were always onto him after that, trying to make reasons to throw him in jail, and knock him about while they were at it. Your da never went looking for a fight, but he never learned how to turn away from one, either. It was why we left. I couldn't take it, seeing what it did to him. I made him leave. In his heart, he's never stopped fighting."

That was a story Da had never told me.

We had supper, but none of us were too hungry, and we went to bed early. The wind backed to the northeast and blew a small gale, rattling the window sash and spitting showers of hard rain against the panes. The drafts rippled the curtains around my cot, warning that Winter was due soon. Bridget cried in her sleep. The place seemed empty.

Next morning the wind kept up, and the early steamer to Deer Island was delayed till afternoon. It was near dark when it finally returned, and Da wasn't on it. Ma went up to the officers who'd escorted the prisoners. The sergeant was kind enough when he realized who she was. Da wasn't at the house of correction, he said. There was no record of him or anyone else all beaten up coming in the night before.

"He wasn't sent over on the steamer," I said. "He was slipped in by the night watch."

"I was told the story," the officer replied, "and we did a roll call through the wards. No one answered to O'Neill. Sorry, lad, ma'am."

Ma and Bridget and I were left looking at each other.

"He must have been put with the Irish in quarantine," I said. "It's the only place."

"Sweet Blessed Mary, I hope someone's taking care of him," Ma said. "They must have beaten him near to death to get him out there."

I wished I hadn't told her what Peter looked like.

We went back to the police station to see what to do next. They said we needed to speak to the hospital board or the quarantine office at the Customs House. And it was too late for that. We spent another lonely night.

The next day Ma had to go to work, and Bridget back to school. I rowed out to the *Hang-Jinhe*. Peter was staying there, being nursed by An-Ming and Hu-Lan. The clock was put aside until he was well again. He was saying he felt up to it already, but An-Ming wouldn't let him out of bed. He'd not only been beaten senseless by the thugs, they'd poured almost a whole bottle of rum down his throat when he'd come to, so he'd be out cold drunk when they carted him off to the *Lady Devon*. He was still a bit hung over two days later.

I told Mr. Lawson about Da, and he said he'd find out who to go to as soon as he could. That morning he had to be in court again. Billy Adams was coming up before a judge.

There were lawyers to deal with beforehand.

"Don't worry, Finn," he assured me. "Your father is a strong man. He'll be all right, and we'll get him off as soon as we can."

So I rowed him and Wang to Central Wharf and spent the whole day waiting to take them back. The news they brought wasn't good.

Adams had told the same story, which didn't make anyone happy. The judge knew both old Robert and Sands, of course. He determined to make a personal call, with Mr. Lawson and only one police officer, because it wouldn't do to arrest a Brahmin on the word of someone like Billy Adams. They came to the townhouse to find old Robert had taken a turn for the worse. Eleanor Sands was badly shaken, and Sands was by her side. Mr. Lawson was afraid to push any accusations for fear she'd lose the baby.

Mr. Lawson looked awful, he did. He didn't want to lose the old man, his nephew and only living link to his early life. He couldn't bring himself to believe old Robert was behind all the trouble. I didn't care one way of the other right then. I asked if we still had time to go to the quarantine office to see about Da.

Mr. Lawson collected himself and said yes, he hadn't forgotten. We went over to the Customs House together and found the office. They were polite as could be and said they'd look right into it. As soon as the steamer went over the next morning. Perhaps we should speak to the police first.

It was like hearing an echo down a deep well.

I rowed Mr. Lawson and Wang back to the *Hang-Jinhe*. The wind had dropped, leaving behind the chill of the storm and a Heaven full of cloud. The seas were rough but settling. I figured when dark fell I was going to have to go fetch Da off the island myself.

Chapter 21

IT SOUNDS LIKE AN adventure, doesn't it? Rescuing Da. Again.

It wasn't.

I was tired of adventures by then anyway.

I rowed to East Boston that evening and caught Séan Dwyer as he got off the ferry after work. I had him describe, as best he could, the place where Da had hidden the boat when he'd fetched the Dwyers off Deer Island. Dwyer admitted he didn't have much memory of it, not in the dark. He offered to come and show me, but I said no. He had a family, and the little one had taken sick. The wife needed him at home, not risking capture on a fool's errand like this.

I went by myself, picking a way around the back of Governor's Island, then close by Apple Island, where the trees gave some shelter from the wind. I found the spot, near the entrance to Shirley's Gut, a gently sloped bit of shingle that made it easy to pull the boat in without losing your boots in the muck. I did get wet to my thighs. I followed the path Dwyer had described, through some trees and up a bank, and there was the quarantine camp.

There were hospital buildings, of course, but the two of them had never been big enough. Low shanties thrown together with rough boards made up a small village. You could tell the privies by the stench. The sleeping shacks had a different smell, the reek of sweat, vomit, fear, blood, and death. The sound of coughing carried clearly over the wind-blown grumble of surf from the ocean side.

I went to the nearest shed and knocked, then stuck my head in and said to the darkness, "I'm looking for a man named Mike O'Neill."

There was no answer at first, then a voice thick with Irish said, "O'Neill? American?"

"That's right, from Boston. They'd have brought him in three nights ago. Beat up pretty bad, he was." He must have been, and drunk, too, from what Peter'd said.

"Not here," the voice replied. "Maybe next door."

It was that easy. Da was next door, crowded in with more than a dozen. The people lit a candle, so I could see to rouse him. They'd given him his own bed on a bottom bunk, and I could see why. He was gray, shivering, damp from fever sweat, or maybe still wet from when the thugs had dropped him into the harbor. And when I shook him awake, he started coughing, a deep, tearing cough that brought up ugly yellow spit flecked with blood.

"Da!" I was trying to whisper, but it was hard. "Da, wake up! It's me!"

He opened his eyes a slit. They were both ringed with black and blue from the beating. His nose had a dirty plaster over it, and there was another round his head. He squinted at me.

"Finn," he wheezed, then coughed some more. "You came, then," he got out finally.

"I did, Da. I came for you."

"You got the girl away safe?"

"I did."

He took my hand. His knuckles were black with bruises. "Good job. Peter?"

"He's with her."

"Even better." He was having trouble breathing and

coughed up another gob. More blood. Then he closed his eyes and seemed to be drifting off.

"Come on, Da," I said, pulling at his elbow. "Get up now. We've got to be bringing you home. Ma's waiting. Bridget, too."

"I'm coming, lad. Don't rush me." He pushed at my hand and didn't move.

"Da!" I pulled again.

"Bad as your Ma," he muttered.

Two of the other men helped me get him up onto his feet. We stumbled out the door into the cold night. He was hot through his damp clothes, but shivering like his bones had come untied in the wind. I led him out of the shanty town, down the rise and into the trees. I was more his crutch than companion. He had to stop every few steps to breathe and cough, though he fought it, awake enough to know we needed quiet. Getting him into the boat was another story. He slipped in the small waves and almost fell in. I only just held him, and he got wet to his chest. Finally I managed to heave him over the gunwale. He tried to take up the oars, but couldn't lift them into the locks, and fought me when I tried to pry them out of his hands.

"I'll row this time, Da," I said. "You steer."

He gave in and huddled on the stern thwart in the cold wind, dripping water into the bilge. He knew the way, though, I'll give him that; steered us right to the end of Lewis Wharf, dark as it was. I heaved him up the ladder and half carried him home. It was the Devil's own walk up the steep, narrow pitch of Margaret Street. The stairs were worse. We fell through the doorway, both of us brought to our knees beside the kitchen table. It scared poor Bridget half to death.

Ma came flying out of their room, and the three of us got Da stripped down, wrapped in blankets, and into bed. He was past thinking by then. He didn't even recognize us. Ma made hot tea, and Bridget and I held Da's head up while she fed it to him. He kept coughing, spilled half the tea, but Ma had put a towel on his chest. Spots of blood shone ugly in the lamplight.

He settled back, breathing a little more easily, and we kept watch through the night.

Come dawn, he took a little broth and woke enough to greet Ma and Bridget. He couldn't remember how he'd gotten there, so Ma told him. He nodded and fell back to sleep. It was Saturday, a half day for Ma at Tierney's, just six hours. She'd already missed one day that week, so she went. There was no school, so Bridget could stay home with Da. I rowed out to the *Hang-Jinhe* to tell Mr. Lawson Da was home. He wanted to know that Da was all right, and I told him about the bruises. I didn't tell him about the cough. He had enough worries.

"Ma's making him stay in bed," I said. "Like Peter."

Peter was actually out of bed and in the clock room with An-Ming. He was looking more like his old self, if you could ignore the yellowing bruises. He was more worried about his hands. Hu-Lan spoke up from the corner, where she was sitting quietly, being chaparone. She said he'd broken two fingers in the fight. They were wrapped tightly together with a bamboo splint and smeared with some Chinese poultice that smelled like a spice cabinet. It was his left hand, which wasn't so bad, but even his right was bruised and sore. He wasn't working on the clock; An-Ming wouldn't let him. So he'd made her be his hands. When I arrived, he was telling her how to fit in the final gears that linked the five separate clockworks to the main shaft and spring.

"We can still finish the clock on time," Peter said. "Once Anie is done with this last bit of small work, all we'll need is the heart stone to complete the assembly. I believe I could do that with only half a hand, and my eyes closed. I even dreamed about it last night."

Just like Peter to dream about a clock. "And how did

your fiancée take to that, you dreaming about cold metal gears instead of her?"

Peter fired up red as an ember. "Ah, fiancée?" he said, all innocent-like. "Whatever do you mean?" He took a quick glance at An-Ming. She tried to look as calm as Wang, but I could see she was fighting a smile.

"Didn't she tell you?" I asked. "You two got engaged while you were out cold drunk and sleeping with the sailors on the *Lady Devon*."

"Ah, well, that was just a ruse," Peter said. "I haven't even asked Mr. Lawson yet."

"And what's keeping you?" I asked. "She's not getting any younger, you know."

"*Wa!* What does that mean, O'Neill?" An-Ming glared daggers at me.

"Just that time's passing, and faster than you think," I said. "You've seen how Peter is. You'll be an old spinster before he can bring himself to ask for your hand."

"Spinster? What is that?" she demanded.

"Wrinkled," I said. "Old, unmarried, and wrinkled."

"Now see here, Finn," Peter said, "there's no need to be insulting. When the time is right, I'll . . . I'll do it."

"And when will that be?" I asked.

"Yes, when?" An-Ming turned on Peter and scrunched up her face. "Look, I am wrinkling!"

"Well . . . Well . . . When the time is right!" he exclaimed, throwing up his hands. "You can't just walk up and ask, you know."

"Ask what?" It was Mr. Lawson. He'd come in quietly behind Peter. An-Ming and I had both seen him. She'd led Peter on like a well-trained mule. With a little help from me.

Peter's face blanched, even through the bruises. "Well, ah . . ."

"Courage," I said. "There's no time like the now."

"Mr. Lawson," Peter said. "Sir." He squared his shoulders, stood to his full height. "Sir, may I have the hand of your daughter in marriage?"

Mr. Lawson regarded him for a moment. Then he turned to An-Ming. "Anie?" he asked.

She bowed, a big, sweet smile on her face. "I am honored," she said.

"I know I don't have much to offer—," Peter began, but Mr. Lawson cut him off.

"You already offered to sacrifice your life, Peter. That's as much a fortune as any father could hope for." He held out his hand. "Yes. Thank you. We are both honored."

They shook hands, those blessed formal Americans. They'd a thing or two to learn from us Irish about celebrating. But when An-Ming took Peter's hand, their eyes were shining. And I noticed even Hu-Lan was wearing a smile so broad it like to split her face in two.

Mr.Lawson watched fondly as An-Ming rose and gently took Peter's good hand. They were grinning at each other like they were demented. But Mr. Lawson's smile faded, and he slipped out. You could understand why. He had to worry about lawyers and judges and what was going to happen to old Robert and Eleanor and her baby.

I had my own troubles to brood on. We both needed something to distract us. I followed him out.

"Excuse me, sir," I said. "Peter was thinking the heart stone would be ready this week. Would you like me to row into the city to look in on Mr. Feinmann?"

"An excellent idea, Finn," he replied. "And I shall come with you, as Peter is so occupied."

"I doubt he'll notice we're gone till we hail him coming back," I said.

So I rowed Mr. Lawson to Central Wharf. Wang came with us, of course, along with the mate – Mr. Lawson wasn't going to let his guard all the way down so soon. We found a lad to watch the canoe and trooped up to Mr. Feinmann's together. People were staring at us again, after the news had come out in the *Herald* about the attack and abduction and what Billy Adams had testified. Pat Delany had written up a storm. The Harbor Bank had been closed to business for two days, so all the depositors couldn't pull their money out. It was the kind of stir Mr. Lawson had hoped to avoid, but at least it wasn't about the clock.

And the heart stone was ready, a beautiful, round jewel as big as the nail on my little finger. It seemed to shine from its own light. Only it was a white jewel, not a ruby, which seemed somehow less than the clock deserved. Mr. Feinmann was very proud of it. He held it up to the light. And then he surprised the Devil out of me. He pulled the top off the heart stone.

"You see?" he said, showing the two pieces to Mr. Lawson. "It is exactly to the dimension specified. The stopper and the vial mate precisely." He put the top back on, then pulled it off again, and I saw it was a tiny stopper. Just like the stopper to a fancy liquor bottle. And the heart stone was the tiny bottle. It was all I could do to keep my mouth shut while Mr. Lawson praised the work and thanked Mr. Feinmann, then paid him and thanked him again, and finally led the way back to Central Wharf and the boat. I hadn't taken two strokes on the oars when the question burst out of me.

"The heart stone is a bottle, sir. Why is that?"

Mr. Lawson was as bad as Peter. He looked around, as if there might be someone lurking in another boat right beside us, then waited till we were past the end of the wharf in open water.

"It is a bottle of sorts, Finn, yes."

"What would you be putting in such a tiny thing? Some sort of clock oil?" It was all I could think of, but how would it get out to grease the gears?

Mr. Lawson let me row a few strokes, watching with a thoughtful look, as if he wasn't sure quite how to explain it. "Have you ever seen a lover's locket, Finn, where a young woman might keep a lock of her betrothed's hair?"

"I have." Ma had a locket with a snip of hair from each us, braided together in a slender queue.

"The hair in the locket has a special meaning to the wearer," he went on. "Some might say it has more, an essence of the spirit of the person who gave the hair. A tiny spark of the love, as it were. Do you understand?" I nodded, and Mr. Lawson nodded back. "Well, in order to work properly, the clock requires some essence of the person to whom it is linked."

"So you're going to squeeze a wee bit of hair into that jewel?" Even as I said it, I realized it was wrong.

"No, Finn," Mr. Lawson said, "not hair. The heart stone will hold—"

"Blood!" I exclaimed. "It's a bottle for blood!"

"Not so loud, please!" Mr. Lawson warned. "Sound carries over the water."

"Sorry, sir. But that explains why the heart stone in your old clock is so red. And here I've been thinking all along it was a ruby."

Mr. Lawson smiled. "It's worth far more than a ruby to me. I'm surprised Peter didn't tell you about this. There seems to be little else that you haven't managed to worm out of him."

I thought about it. "Well, it is blood, sir. Hair is one thing; you just snip it off. Blood, you have to get it out."

"There is that, but it's not a lot. Three drops precisely. A pinprick will do it."

"But it's the thought, if you see what I mean, sir. Blood makes it . . . well, like a sacrifice." Which is not something a good Christian is supposed to do.

"Does that bother you?" Mr. Lawson asked. He seemed truly worried it might.

"Not me, sir." Three drops would hardly make a blood oath between Irish heroes in the stories Da told. "But Peter, he's a bit more squeamish, I believe."

"Or maybe he thought you would be. Perhaps he was

trying to spare you the gruesome details." Mr. Lawson smiled. "Peter is a considerate man, and far less squeamish than either of us may have believed."

"You're right about that, sir. And I suppose, if he's up to it, you'll be finishing the clock tonight, before the stars and planets move to all the wrong places."

"They've already moved. To be honest, Finn, I don't know how important the heavenly bodies really are." Mr. Lawson sighed. "Wu's manuscript speaks of propitious alignments, but does not name them. He could simply mean favorable moments. Or his own lucky stars. He is often unclear. He wrote down just enough to jog his own memory. Always, I was supposed to find my own path, as he had. So I have set my own deadline."

"Do you mean to say the clock might not even work?"

He chuckled. "Oh, it will mark the time and the heavenly bodies. Peter has done an excellent job with the clockworks. But as to its other purpose? I believe it will work as intended, once it is filled. I simply cannot be certain. What's most important is whose . . . essence is in the heart stone; that I am sure of. In any case, Peter will have a day of rest tomorrow, as the Good Lord intended. If he is up to it on Monday, then we shall finish the clock. As to when the clock is started, I hope it will be next Wednesday."

"Why is that, sir?"

He shook his head. "That is a surprise. And I task you not to mention it to Peter or my daughter. Even they are in the dark on this point." He looked me in the eye. "Can I trust you to silence, Finn?"

"You can, Mr. Lawson," I replied.

I rowed Peter to Central Wharf that afternoon so he could go home to his rooms above Bond's shop. I think he'd have been happy to stay on the junk, but he needed to write a letter to his parents and see Mr. Bond and generally get back to a regular life. Me, I was glad to head home early. For all the excitement of the day, I couldn't take my mind off Da for more than a few minutes at a time.

Ma was home ahead of me. She and Bridget were feeding broth to Da when I came in. He asked me how Peter was, and An-Ming. I told everyone how Peter had finally gotten the courage to ask for her hand, and that brightened the room for a few minutes. I started to tell Da about Billy Adams and what he'd said about Sands and Robert Lawson, but he fell asleep before I could finish. He seemed to be breathing a little more easily. I asked Ma if she'd been to call a doctor.

"I haven't," she said. "You know what your Da's like."

"He's too blessed sick to argue, you know!" I snapped.

"And what'll we do when the doctor sends him back to Deer Island?" Ma replied. That shut me up. "I've been to the chemist, Finn. He gave me some medicine to put in the broth. Your Da's a strong man. We'll keep him warm, keep him fed, and pray. That's all we can do. It's between him and the Lord now."

Da slept on and off through the night. It was the coughing that woke him, and us, too. He just couldn't seem to get his lungs to stay clear. And he kept bringing up blood. His fever came and went. When he was hot, he'd shiver and toss and mumble in his sleep. He called for me, asked me if I'd gotten An-Ming away safe. When I said yes, he asked about Peter. I told him they were both fine, had become engaged. Later he asked me again.

I stayed with him in the morning, while Ma and Bridget went to early mass. Then Bridget went to the telegraph office to send to Molly out in Lawrence, and I went to Beacon Hill to tell Gracie. They came that afternoon, Gracie right after dinner, then Molly about an hour later. We hadn't any of us seen Molly in months, and she looked so much older, more grown up. More like Da. She took one look at him laying there in bed, and her face went near as white as his.

"Oh, Da," she murmured, taking his hand. When she felt the fever, tears came to her eyes.

She sat with him for a few minutes, with Gracie holding his other hand. Then they looked at each other, and I didn't like the way they seemed to be steeling themselves. Molly set her jaw, the way Da would when there was heavy work to be done.

"Have you sent for the priest, Ma?" she asked.

Ma and Bridget and I were all struck dumb.

"Now, how would your father feel if I did that?" Ma asked. "You know how he is. He hasn't been to confession since Easter."

"All the more reason," Molly said.

Ma was shaking her head.

"She's right, Ma," Gracie said. "He needs to confess before . . ." She swallowed and blinked back tears. "While he still can."

"Listen to you!" I cried. "You're acting like he doesn't have a prayer! Give the medicine a chance! He's strong. Ma said so, didn't you, Ma? Strong! He'll be up and about soon enough."

"Then he'll be up and about with a clean soul," Molly said. "Where's the harm in that?"

"I'll go, Ma," Bridget said. "You wait here and visit."

So she went to fetch a priest, and Father McMahon himself came a few hours later. We weren't the first home he'd visited that day. He shooed us out of the room to hear Da's confession, not that he got much. Da was enough himself to talk, but too much himself to tell his all to a priest. Father McMahon blessed him anyway. He let us back into the room for the last rites. Then he hurried off to squeeze in one more dying soul before vespers.

Molly and Gracie lingered longer than they should've, then rushed off. Molly had a train to catch. Gracie had a mistress to tend. Ma and me and Bridget were left by the bedside to wait.

Chapter 22

IT WAS A LONG night, with Da floating in and out of his fever. He talked to himself, to people who weren't really there. He called for Tim, and spoke with him long and earnest. His voice went hoarse. Even the coughing grew faint. Come morning, Ma dozed in her chair, while Bridget and I made a rough breakfast. She and Ma decided to keep the vigil. I went off to let them know at Tierney's, then hurried to get the boat and pick up Peter.

"How is your father?" he asked, right off.

"Still with us," I said.

He took it for a joke and laughed. "I should hope so. Tell him not to linger too long in his bed. Hu-Lan and the cook are missing his talent for a bargain at the market."

I couldn't bring myself to say how bad it was with Da. Peter was too happy at being engaged. "He'll be glad to hear it," I said.

There was a chill wind, with blowing clouds and a stiff chop on the water. Peter clung to his dented hat with his good hand as I rowed us through the shipping in the inner harbor. There was no custom for us there, so we took up station off Castle Island in hopes something would venture in. Mid morning, Peter finally found a welcome on an inbound ship from the West Indies. I followed them to a mooring off Gray's Wharf and had a long, cold wait in the boat, with plenty of time alone to worry about Da. I could see the steeple of the Old North Church and the tops of the trees at the Copp's Hill cemetery. I wondered what I'd find when I returned home that evening.

We went straight out to the *Hang-Jinhe* when Peter was finished, though he admitted his hands were aching and in no shape to work on the clock till they had rested a bit. Mr. Lawson asked after Da, and I said he was still abed. Nothing more. There was the heart stone on Mr. Lawson's mind, and the troubles with Sands and old Robert. And, to be honest, there was my own fear that talking about such things would only make them worse. I couldn't be like Molly and Grace and Ma; I wouldn't admit that Da was dying.

Peter went into the stern house, with An-Ming at his side. And Hu-Lan, of course. It seemed now they were engaged, she was more determined than ever to be a proper chaperone. I rowed back in with Mr. Lawson. He was due in court. I waited with the boat again after setting him and Wang off at Central Wharf. It seemed a day for waiting. I hadn't made up a lunch for myself and had to make do with a bite of salt cod I was able to cadge from one of the fisherman on T Wharf. I found a spot out of the wind behind a stack of bales on Commercial Street, under the bowsprit of some bark rich with the scent of spice wood and foreign places. I was wishing I was far away and warm, reading a letter from Ma telling me how well she and Da were getting on and how Molly had three children now and Gracie two and Bridget was soon to be married. And I didn't have to worry about any of them. It was a fine dream, but a shifty gust of wind got under my collar and brought me back to the cold truth of it.

Mr. Lawson was some hours returning, and he wasn't any happier when he did. Mr. Sands hadn't shown up. He'd sent his lawyer to say old Robert was getting worse, and his wife's emotions were frail, so he had to stay with them. The lawyer had tried to have Billy Adams's testimony thrown out because he was obviously a man of low means and untrustworthy. Well, I could have told you that.

"On this matter, the judge supports us at least," Mr. Lawson reported as I rowed us back to the junk. "But he still refuses to subpoena Sands for an appearance until Robert's condition is resolved. I only hope Robert will rally and be able to speak for himself."

I had a hard time digging up any sympathy. If there was rallying to do, I wanted it to be for Da.

When we were back on board, Mr. Lawson headed for the clock room.

"Come, Finn," he said. "You've seen the clock grow from the start. You should see the final assembly as well."

So I crowded into the little cabin with the rest. Peter was seated at his usual place at the end of the table, with An-Ming on one side and his tools at the other. Hu-Lan was at the other end of the table.. Mr. Lawson stood behind Peter's right shoulder, where he could see everything as it happened. Wang was by the door. I stood behind Hu-Lan, out of the way. Everyone was still, eyes fixed on Peter. You could hear the slap of the chop against the *Hang-Jinhe*'s hull, feel her tug at her mooring. The wind sighed past the quarter window.

Peter had the clock tipped over on the leather mat that he worked on, so the back was up. One of the five faces – the seasons and eclipses of the sun – was turned my way. The back panel was off, revealing the brass base of the clockworks. Now Peter took up the heart stone and handed it to An-Ming. It gleamed in the gray light filtering through the window. An-Ming had lit an oil lamp on the table as well, and its yellow flame picked out a spark of gold that pulsed as she turned the heart stone in her fingers.

"This is the bearing," Peter said, pointing out a dimple in the rounded belly of the jewel, directly beneath the tiny stopper in its top. "The bottom of the main shaft bevels to meet it." He pointed with a fine screwdriver to show us the bevel. It came to a rounded tip that protruded from the works by little more than a hair's breadth. "When the heart stone is, ah, filled, we will fit it into the base plate, over the tip of the main shaft, where it fastens with this clip."

The clip was a narrow slip of brass that pivoted into place and was held by tiny screws at either side. It domed slightly in the middle to fit over the stopper and hold it tightly.

"Father?" An-Ming offered the heart stone to Mr. Lawson.

Mr. Lawson regarded it with a curious expression, as if he couldn't quite believe the time had finally come. But he made no move to take it.

"I can help, Father," An-Ming said. She picked up a short, thin lancet from the table.

Mr. Lawson held up a hand. "Not yet," he said. "Please go ahead and install the heart stone. We can perform the ceremony then to mark the completion of the clockworks."

"The stone isn't filled for the ceremony?" Peter asked.

"That isn't required," Mr. Lawson replied. "It can be filled at any time before the clock is actually set in motion."

"Why wait?" An-Ming asked. "All is ready."

Mr. Lawson shot me a quick glance. "My mind is not yet ready," he said. "Another day or two won't matter." An-Ming scowled, and Peter looked more than a little disappointed. Mr. Lawson chuckled. "Don't worry, Peter, you will see your clock in action very soon. What's important now is that we each finish our part in its making. Then it will be primed for its purpose. I promise you will be there to see it wound and started."

So An-Ming held the empty heart stone in its place, while Peter slid the clip over the stopper and snugged down the two tiny screws. It took hardly a minute, and hardly more to replace the bottom panel and set the clock aright. It was a beautiful thing, but it sat there unfinished, silent and still.

Mr. Lawson checked his pocket watch. "We have just under half an hour till 6:07 PM. At that time, both Jupiter and Saturn will be near their zenith. Over China, that is. It seems as significant a celestial moment as we can hope for. We will perform the ceremony then. Peter, Finn, you may join us, if you like."

Peter looked as surprised as I felt. "Join you?" he stammered. "For the ceremony? But we are not, ah . . ."

"Not Taoists, I know," Mr. Lawson said. "Neither am I, but the ceremony is not precisely religious. In any case, you will be merely spectators." He smiled. "You will not be asked to foreswear your faith or take part in any heathen rituals. However, if it bothers you, you may wait here. Anie and I will understand."

An-Ming gave Peter a look that almost dared him to say no.

"I would be honored," he said. "Fascinated, in fact."

"Good. You have much to learn about your betrothed's culture. Much to accept." Mr. Lawson turned to me. "Finn?"

I was thinking it was time I rowed Peter home, so I could see to Da. But Peter had said yes and, I admit, I wanted to see the ceremony myself, even if the bit I'd already snuck a listen to had scared the Devil out of me. "I'll watch," I said. "I won't be able to understand a word of it anyway, so what's the harm?"

"Harm? Anie and I will be singing. That might be hard on the ears, I suppose."

"Don't blame me for bad voices," An-Ming chided. "Finn knows I sing like nightingale."

It was a pale joke on both parts, but it eased the tension.

Peter and I waited with the clock while Mr. Lawson and An-Ming went across the companionway to his cabin to make ready. When Mr. Lawson came back for us a few minutes later, he was wearing a long, dark Chinese robe, with a light collar and cuffs and embroidered all over with symbols in different bright colors. Some of them I'd seen before on the clock faces, others were new. There was a crane, a turtle, a tiger, and several dragons, along with Chinese letters and patterns that didn't make any sense to me at all. He was also wearing a funny round hat with a tassel at the peak. It was no more elaborate than Father McMahon would wear for high mass, I suppose, but I was used to that.

Peter looked nervous. When he lifted the clock, his hands were shaking a little. He steadied himself and followed Mr. Lawson across the companionway to set the clock on a small, carved table in the middle of Mr. Lawson's cabin. An-Ming had put on a robe like her father's, only it was light with dark trim and the symbols were only on the borders. She was lighting a charcoal fire in a small brass bowl, what they call a brazier. She had already lit the incense, and the sweet-spicy smell was starting to tickle my nose, just like before. I rubbed it hard. I was a little nervous, myself, and the scent didn't help. The hairs on the back of my neck started to prickle from the memory.

There were curtains pulled across the window, and the cabin was lit only by two small brass lanterns, the tiny charcoal fire, and the glowing sparks on the incense sticks. Squares of silk, embroidered with some of the same symbols Mr. Lawson and An-Ming were wearing, hung in a vertical row on the bulkhead behind the table. But all this was set up in a room that was obviously the cabin on a ship, with a cot, a small desk, a chest for clothing, a hook for Mr. Lawson's coat. It was odd and foreign and stank of incense, but it also had the closed-in feeling of a chapel. There was something there you couldn't see or smell or touch. A mystery that made your heart rise like the hairs on your neck. You wanted to explain it, but you couldn't, so you blamed it on God. Or gods. Or magic.

Mr. Lawson had Peter and me sit on his cot. He stationed himself beside the table holding the clock. An-Ming stood across from him, by the desk. He looked at her a long time, all serious. She waited, looking back. Finally, he took a deep breath and nodded. An-Ming struck a round, brass chime on the desk. Three times. *Ting. Ting. Ting.* Mr. Lawson began to chant.

He was reading from a book laid open on the table beside the clock. Wu's manuscript, it was. An-Ming struck the chime again – *Ting* – and joined him in the high, whining voice that had set my neck hairs straight out the last time. It did it again. Her eyes were closed, her brow creased. Her lips curled and twisted around the sing-song words. Her teeth flashed in the flickering light.

Mr. Lawson turned a page in the book. An-Ming struck the chime. *Ting.* The clear note rang through their mingled voices. An-Ming began to sing.

It was like no hymn I'd ever heard before. It wasn't the foreign words – after all, I got Latin in church – it was the melody. The notes weren't the right distance apart. They didn't blend the way I expected. But I could hear the call and the question in them. The prayer. She was asking for help, from something that had to be treated right.

Now Mr. Lawson came in, deep voiced, powerful as a priest. The ruddy light made his nose jut forward, his eyes sink into his face. There was no harmony in his words. He pronounced, she sang the next question, he answered, she sang. And each time he spoke, at some word or other, she struck the chime. *Ting.*

Smoke from the brazier began to fill the room. The incense clouded my nose. My vision blurred. I could only see their faces. And the clock: its top face and two of the sides. I felt a little dizzy. Things were moving, more than the wind and sea could explain. The clock faces turned. No, the symbols moved on their own. The turtle, a dragon, the crane – I swear they looked at me.

Ting!

I blinked, swallowed hard. Now there were just flickering highlights. The lamps, the brazier, the incense. An-Ming's teeth. Mr. Lawson's dark, deep-set eyes. The faces of the clock. They flickered. From inside.

Then the singing stopped.

Ting! Ting! Ting!

I think every hair on my body was standing on end. I stared at the clock, saw the lights flicker out with the fading notes of the chime. But I did see them. Whoever or whatever An-Ming had called to, it had answered. Not through Mr. Lawson's voice. Through the clock. It sat there on the table, waiting. Alive. No, not alive itself. A channel to life, it was. For as long as it ran.

The scent of low tide eddied around the flower stench of incense: salt and seaweed and mud. Everyday smells taking back the room. An-Ming had pushed aside the curtains and opened one of the stern windows. The smoke began to clear. Now she lit a lantern, and the place was a ship's cabin again. Mr. Lawson doffed his robe and funny hat and laid them in the sea chest.

My throat was stiff, dry. But I had a question I had to ask. I swallowed hard.

"Sir? What happens when you put your blood into the heart stone and start the clock? What does it feel like?"

He considered a few moments. "It is too subtle to describe," he said. "Too personal. My heart was racing the first time, so I noticed nothing. The second time, I expected nothing, and so I did feel it, a faint . . . quickening, but in the broader sense. Not at all a change in the pace of my heart. It was a lifting of spirit, an exhilaration, as if I had stumbled onto the beginnings of an understanding of some deep knowledge. An insight into how life should be lived. But that was me. My wife – Anie's mother, that is – she said it felt as though she had just fallen in love. Whoever fills the heart stone in this clock will feel something similar, but very much their own."

"Anyone could fill the heart stone?" I asked. "I thought it was made just for you."

"Only one person can use it," he said, "but that could be anyone. If it were you, whatever humor lay in your blood as it dripped into the stone would regenerate with each tick and tock of the clock. You would feel it, faintly, in every heartbeat." He smiled, but I could see his mind was somewhere else. "If you'll excuse me, I need to rest for a moment."

"Yes, sir. Thank you," I replied.

Peter had been watching An-Ming as she put away the chimes and lamps and such. "I'll put the clock back," he said, lifting it carefully, so An-Ming could fold up and stow the little table. They went out together. I followed them into the companionway. As I shut the door behind me, I saw Mr. Lawson staring through the stern window toward the lights of Boston. I wondered if he was brooding about old Robert again.

I stuck my head into the clock room. "Ready to be leaving?" I asked Peter.

He glanced at An-Ming. "Ah, in a minute, Finn. I just have a few things—"

"We wish to say goodnight," An-Ming said. Peter blushed.

"I'll leave you to it, then," I said.

"We go on deck. Under the stars," she said. Peter's blush spread.

"Then I guess I'll wait here."

"No need. We find shadows." She took his hand.

"Ah, we shan't be too very long," Peter stammered as she led him past me, out the companionway.

"Don't rush on my account," I told him.

I wondered if Ma and Da had been like that. More likely reversed, with Da doing the pulling. My eyes were suddenly hot. I blinked hard and looked away. As my sight cleared, I was looking at the clock. There it was, all polished wood and painted faces. And magical gears. Waiting for three drops of blood.

I didn't have to think about it, I just did it.

I took it.

Chapter 23

BY THE TIME AN-Ming let Peter go, the clock was wrapped in rags and tucked behind the bailer under the forward thwart in the canoe.

"I, uh, I'm sorry to keep you waiting," Peter said, as he came down the ladder.

"Whenever you're ready." I tried to sound calm, but I was more anxious than ever to get home now.

It was a long pull back to Central Wharf in the growing dark. I kept expecting to see lights flare on the *Hang-Jinhe*, to hear a hail come over the water, calling us back. Peter was in a mood, too, wanting to talk about the ceremony and the clock. The most I could give him was a grunt and a nod, but his head was too lost in the clouds to notice.

"See you tomorrow, bright and early," he called, as he climbed up to the wharf.

"Tomorrow," I replied. I had no idea what the morrow would bring.

I raced back to Lewis Wharf and eased the clock up the ladder as though it were a sleeping baby. I kept it wrapped in the rags. There were plenty of people about, hurrying this way and that in the lamplight, and I knew the sight of a clock in the arms of the likes of me would attract attention.

I skirted Hurley's on the opposite side of the street, ducked into a doorway to let the watch stroll past, and hid the clock under the stairs before skipping up to the apartment.

"How is he?" I asked, right off.

Bridget was at the stove. Her eyes were red, her face tired enough to look old. For a moment I feared the worst. But she shushed me and managed a brave smile. "Still fighting," she said. "He's slept most of the day."

"Is he better then?" I asked, my fears swinging wildly to hope.

Her smile fell and she gave her head a little shake. "No. He hasn't spoken or eaten. Ma's been with him the whole time."

"Has she slept herself?"

Another shake. "Nor eaten a bite. I'm making some soup, if they'll take it."

I went into their room. Ma was by the window in one of our two chairs. She had hold of Da's hand, but she turned to give me a faint smile. The curtain made a picture of their faces, hers drooped with weariness, him pale and drawn on the pillow. She was almost as gray as he was.

"Good evening, Finn," she said. "He's waited for you, I think."

I doubted it was for me, but I was glad of it anyway. And I prayed he'd wait a little longer. He looked like he could go any minute. His breath came short and shallow, each one a gasp, as though there was no room in his chest for it. He didn't seem to have the energy to drag more in, even to cough up the mess that was choking him. He was drowning in the open air.

"Speak to him," Ma said. "Let him know you're here."

I was afraid to, afraid it was all he needed to let go, the final goodbye. And then where would I be? Where would any of us be? I got angry. It was foolish, I knew it even then, and I felt small for it. But I still got angry. He was leaving us to fend for ourselves. It seemed the most selfish thing I could think of.

Ma saw something was bothering me, but she guessed wrong. "Don't blame yourself, Finn," she said. "You got him off the island as quickly as you could. He's grateful for that, he told me so."

It only made me feel worse, because she hadn't guessed wrong. The anger had been helping me hide all along from the feeling that I'd let him down. Now I was both angry and guilty.

I went to the bed and took Da's other hand. It was hot and dry, and the bruises had gone an ugly yellow-gray. I didn't dare press it hard.

"Hello, Da," I said. "It's me. Finn."

His eyes opened the tiniest bit and glanced toward me. His fingers curled. He had big hands, he did. Mine was lost in it, but there was no strength left in his grasp.

He tried to say something, but he didn't have the wind. He started coughing, and it pained me to watch him heave and gasp. Ma caught the phlegm in a cup. It was more blood than spit. She wiped his chin.

"You got the girl away, then?" he said to me.

"I did, sir. She's safe. Peter, too. They're engaged to be married, Da."

"Good. Good work. Tim—"

He couldn't finish for coughing, but I'd heard enough. He doesn't even recognize me, I thought. And now I had another reason to be angry, and another anger to be guilty about. I started to draw away, but he wouldn't let go of me. So I sat there holding his hand, my head and my heart caught up in a blessed row. He doesn't know what he's saying, I told myself. He says what matters to him, I replied. And it isn't me.

Finally Bridget came in with the soup and took my place to feed him. I cleaned up the kitchen for her, straightened the room. Sat by the window looking out at the clouds scudding across the stars, what I could glimpse of them beyond the rooftops and through the glow of the street lamps. I worried about the clock. Would it really work? What if Mr. Lawson had the stars wrong? What if Peter had made one of the gears wrong? What if it didn't take to Da's blood? What if it was a sin to use?

Well, the sin was on me, not Da. And there was nothing to lose by trying, as Da himself would have said. The evening wore on. Ma and Bridget waited for Da to die. I waited for them to fall asleep. Bridget did first, worn out by worry. I carried her to her cot.

"I'll keep watch," I said to Ma. And then I lied to her. "I don't have to row Peter tomorrow. Mr. Lawson is having one of the crewmen do it. He told me to stay here with Da. You should sleep. I'll wake you if anything changes."

Finally Ma went out and lay down on my cot. A while later I heard her breathing slow. I waited a bit longer, to be sure. Then I snuck out downstairs and fetched back the clock. I set it on the chair by Da's bed. Turned it over. Slid out the bottom panel. The heart stone gleamed in the light of our single, dim lamp. I stared at the clockworks a moment.

"You're going to work," I told it. "Peter made you, Mr. Lawson blessed you. Or whatever it was he did. That doesn't matter; all that matters is you're going to work."

I had taken Peter's tiny screwdriver with the clock. And I had my jackknife. I pulled them from my pocket and set them on the chair, knife open and ready. I rubbed my hands to warm them. Then I picked up the screwdriver and went to work.

I had the clip free in a moment. Almost too free; one of the screws fell loose, and I had to scrabble for it before it got lost between the floorboards. I took a breath to steady myself, and lifted the heart stone from its bed. It was smooth and light and lay cool in my palm. I drew out the little stopper and placed it carefully beside the clock. I picked up the knife. I turned to Da. His eyes were open, staring right at me. My heart skipped a beat. But he wasn't seeing anything. He was hardly breathing.

"Da!" I whispered. "Da, hold on!"

He blinked and drew in a hard, wheezing gasp. Then another, a little easier. Then a third. He muttered something, but I couldn't make it out.

"That's right, Da," I said. "Stay with me."

I set the heart stone on his chest. Picked up his hand – dear Lord, it was hot – and jabbed the tip of my knife into his palm. It wasn't the best place. He had calluses as thick as a boot heel. But I managed to draw blood. I dropped the knife and picked up the heart stone. I held it to the cut and squeezed his hand. A drop fell into the jewel. Then another, but the second didn't want to go in. I shook the heart stone. Tapped it with my fingernail. The blood clung to the opening. I blew on it, and most went in. Some ran down the side. Did it count as a drop? Did a half drop matter?

I didn't know, and I couldn't ask, so I squeezed out a third drop and forced it into the heart stone. I grabbed the little stopper and used it to scrape the blood over the edges and into the hole. I pushed the stopper home. I wiped the sides of the heart stone on the bed sheet, already stained with Da's blood. As I set the jewel into the clockworks, I noticed the white circle of the fifth face, down near the bottom inside. It was smaller than I'd expected, and very simple: a curved line, one dark side dark, one light, and one symbol that I couldn't hope to read.

Work, I whispered. *Work!*

I fit the bearing point in the heart stone over the tip of the slender brass shaft and carefully fastened the clip. I had hardly drawn a breath the whole time. I was dizzy, and my hands were shaking. But the job wasn't done.

I slid the back panel back into place and righted the clock. It looked so strange in our little, shabby room, on that battered chair. The dragons and cranes and symbols seemed perched on the polished faces, ready to leap into motion.

The key was held in a slot in the top corner. I drew it out and set it in the hole and wound. Slowly, steadily, as Peter would do with one of his chronometers. When I felt the spring tighten, I stopped. It wouldn't do to overwind it and break the spring.

I slid the key back into its slot, took a breath, and twisted the catch that freed the works.

An instant later the clock began to tick. It was a light sound, quick and easy. Two to a heartbeat. I stared at the moon phase face, until I could see that it was truly moving. I hadn't set the faces, didn't know how, but I didn't think it mattered. Not for Da. It only had to run.

I looked from the clock face to the bed. Da's eyes were closed. His breathing was still quick and shallow and hard. His face still gray. I touched his hand, and it still burned with fever.

Give it time, I thought. It's only been a minute. He'll need time to heal.

I fetched a clean rag from the kitchen and wiped the blood from Da's palm. He opened his eyes a moment when I touched him, but nothing else changed. I wiped my knife blade and folded it back into my pocket. I got a drink a water for myself, and tried to give some to Da. He choked down a little. I wiped his forehead and cheeks with a cool, damp cloth. Nothing changed. Nothing changed all night. Except the turning faces on the clock.

Ma stirred before the sun was up. I was half asleep, slumped on the side of the bed. Holding Da's hand. I jerked awake and felt the heat in my palm. Heard his labored breath. He was still alive, there was that.

I heard the clock, too, ticking softly on the chair.

Ma stirred again, threw off the blanket. I grabbed the clock, and almost dropped it. It was as warm as Da's hand. But Ma was coming. I stooped and slid the clock under the bed, then carefully laid a cloth over it. The ticking dimmed.

Ma came in just as I straightened. "How is he?" she whispered.

"No change," I said.

She came to the bedside and looked down on him. She put her arm around my shoulders and leaned against me. "The waiting is hard, Finn, isn't it," she said. "He's such a stubborn one. He can't let go."

"He just needs time to heal, Ma."

She squeezed my shoulder, but she had no words for me.

Da woke then and spoke her name. She let go of me and went to him, took his hand. She spoke to him and he answered, and he managed not to cough too much. It drowned the ticking of the clock, at least.

I woke Bridget and we got water and wood, started the fire and the kettle, just like any other morning. Ma even came out to make some breakfast, and she told Bridget to go to school. Bridget tried to argue, but Ma wouldn't hear it.

"You've missed two days already," she said. "Your da wouldn't rest if he knew it. You know how he feels about school."

So Bridget left, and Ma had to go to work, too. Mr. Tierney wouldn't have minded her staying home, but she couldn't afford to lose the pay.

"Don't forget to give him the tonic," she told me. "It seems to be helping a little. Makes him sleep at least." She squeezed her eyes shut, shook her head. "It's the waiting, Finn. God knows how he lasted the night. Send Mrs. Ryan when . . . when things change."

I promised I would.

She left then, and I was alone with Da and the clock. I pulled it out to make sure the cloth wasn't sagging onto the faces. It seemed to be running fine, so I pushed it back under and propped the cloth around it properly. I could hear the ticking when I listened for it, regular as any heart could need.

The sun was rising, and Da stirred. I got the tonic and tried to give him a spoonful, but he pushed it aside with a weak shove on my wrist.

"Makes me sleep," he muttered. He cleared his throat and spat up more ugly phlegm. I held the glass to catch it and wiped his chin.

"You're supposed to sleep," I said, offering the spoonful of tonic again.

He turned his head away from it. "S'like being drunk. Swore I'd never die drunk."

"You're not going to die, Da," I told him.

He managed a smile for me. "We all die, Finn. Don't worry, I'm not afraid to walk home in the dark."

"Blessed saints, Da, you shouldn't have to!"

"Don't swear, boy. You how your Ma feels about it."

"I'm sorry, Da." And I was, for so many things. "I should have stayed to fight by you. I could have helped. Maybe—"

He grabbed my wrist, with a grip so weak I almost cried. "Don't talk like that, boy. If you'd stayed, we might both be dying."

"I ran away when you needed me. You made me run." Guilt and anger, both at once.

"You got the girl away, didn't you? Well, who else was going to do it?"

"Peter," I said. "He's her lover, after all."

"Too clumsy on his pins," Da said. "You were always the quick one, Finn. Quick mind, quick feet. You did what you were meant to."

"But—"

"Hush. We did what we each had to. That's what life's about, isn't it?" He started coughing again. More blood came up. "Gonna sleep now," he mumbled afterward.

I sat by him, watching the sky grow brighter. Listening to the wind blow past the leaky window. Listening to the faint ticking of the clock.

I heard the front door open, footsteps on the stairs, a

knock. Another. The door opened.

"Finn?" It was Peter. I knew it would be.

"In here," I said.

He came in, took one look at Da, and gasped. "Heavens, Finn, what's happened?"

"It's his lungs," I said. "When Billy Adams dropped him in the water, took him to Deer Island." I couldn't say any more, not without cursing. Or crying. I held onto both.

"Why didn't you tell me?" Peter said.

"You had enough on your mind. You were hurt yourself. You . . ." I shrugged.

"But I might have been able to help. I still can. Is there anything you need? Has he been to a doctor?"

"We're doing what we can, Peter," I said. "You should be getting out to the junk."

All I wanted was for him to leave. I could hear the clock clearly.

"I've no one to row me. Come, Finn. Surely there's something I can do to help?"

"You can go out and make some tea." I figured that'd tie him up for awhile, and cover the sound of the ticking.

"Of course. Anything." He hurried back into the kitchen.

Before the pot could boil, there were more footsteps on the stairs, another knock on the door. Peter answered it.

"Mr. Lawson!" he exclaimed. "Anie! What are you doing here?"

Just a bit longer, I thought. Why couldn't they have taken just a bit longer?

I heard Mr. Lawson say something, and Peter cried, "What?" He led them into the room. "Finn, do you know what's happened to the clock?" he asked.

"I do. I took it," I said.

"But whatever fo—? Oh." He looked from me to Da and back. "I see." He turned to Mr. Lawson. "Sir, ah, Mr. O'Neill is . . . not very well. I fear Finn has taken the clock in hopes that it would cure him."

"*Aiyo*," An-Ming muttered.

Mr. Lawson was looking at me. It was all I could do to meet his eyes. I could see the anger in them. "Did you take the clock for your father?" he asked.

I nodded. I reached under the bed and brought it out, set it on the chair. When I pulled off the cloth, its ticking filled the room.

"You filled the heart stone with his blood?"

I nodded, and his face filled with the saddest look.

"He was dying," I said. "I was going to bring it back afterward. After he heals."

Mr. Lawson sat on the edge of the bed. He took off his hat and ran his hand through his thick, white hair. "You can't bring it back," he said. "And he is still dying."

I looked at An-Ming and Peter. They looked like they were already at the funeral. "What do you mean?" I asked.

"The clock does not heal," Mr. Lawson said. "It simply maintains."

"Anie explained it to us weeks ago, Finn," Peter said. "Don't you remember? She said—"

"The clock stops you," An-Ming said. "Your father is ill all the time the clock runs."

I looked at Da. "He won't get better?"

"Never," she said. "Just like that, while the clock ticks."

"He won't die?"

"He will always be dying."

"You must stop the clock, Finn," Mr. Lawson said.

"But he'll die!"

"We all must die eventually," he said.

"You won't!" I cried. "You'll have your blessed clock!"

"The clock wasn't for me," Mr. Lawson said. "It was for An-Ming."

"What?" Peter said. He turned to An-Ming. "You never told me—"

"I didn't know!" she exclaimed.

"I meant the clock to be yours, Anie," Mr. Lawson said. "Tomorrow is your birthday. I planned to tell you then, to fill the heart stone then, on your lucky day."

"I was going to give it back," I said again.

"The clock can't be used twice," Peter said. "Once the heart stone has been filled—"

"Then make another one!" I shouted. "Make one apiece!"

"No!" An-Ming said. "I do not want one."

We all stared at her.

"Why ever not?" Peter asked.

"To see all about me grow old?" An-Ming replied. "How could I stay young and watch that? We three would have clocks, yes. What of Wang and Hu-Lan? What of Finn and his mother and Bridget? Could you make clocks for all? For Li? For crew? For their families? You could not! Then how to decide who has a clock? I cannot make that decision. I will not."

"Do not be so hasty," Mr. Lawson said. "When you have lost someone you love—"

"I have lost Mother and Grandfather," she said, "and I remember how. I have thought on this a long time."

"Well," he said. "Well, that's an argument for another day perhaps. Finn? Your father?"

I realized I was holding Da's hand. Sometime in the fuss I had taken it, like he had taken mine when I was a child, to keep me safe by him. I looked at him, and he was looking back at me.

"Da?"

"I heard," he replied. "Stop it for me, Son. I'll have my time run its own course, if you don't mind."

"I will do it if you like," Peter offered.

"No," I said. "But if you'd go fetch my ma from Tierney's, and Bridget from school?"

"Certainly," he said. He hurried out.

I held onto Da's hand and pushed the curled brass lever

on the top of the clock case. The catch slid into the gears. The ticking stopped.

Da squeezed my hand gently. "You got the girl away," he said. "Good job, boy."

"I'm Finn, Da. Not Tim." I finally had the courage to say it.

"I know you're Finn. I named you, didn't I? Named you after a hero. Got that one thing right, I did."

Then we waited together till Ma and Bridget were there.

Epilogue

DA'S ENDING WAS HARD, but it wasn't the end of the story. This isn't his story only. You could just say his chapter ended hard, like the tale of Ossian, who grew old and died when his feet touched the Earth after coming back from *Tir na nÓg*. Others fared worse, and others more happily. Not fairy-tale happy, I suppose, but bright enough to spin a tale around.

Jacob Sands hid in his house for four more days. Then the Harbor Bank failed, the day after we buried Da. It turned out Sands had been losing money at the race track for a long time, and making bad investments to cover his own debts, trying to hide it all with clever bookkeeping. The newspapers had already made a great deal of Billy Adam's claims, and now they went wild. The judge ordered Sands into court the next day. Mr. Lawson himself went with the officer to deliver the summons. And I went with him. Peter and An-Ming wanted to come, but Mr. Lawson said it wouldn't be proper to make such a show of it. I was only along to row, he said.

But he was the one who found a boy to watch the boat so I could come up to Beacon Hill with him. I think he knew how I felt, how I needed to be there. For what had happened to Da.

Wang came along, too. And I had my own escort, it turned out. Pat Delany had been watching for Mr. Lawson to come ashore from the moment he heard the bank had failed. He slipped along a ways behind us. I didn't even notice him.

We went up past the state house, then cut over the two blocks to Pickney Street. It wasn't busy: a few carriages, a few passersby, a maid pushing a pram. We were about halfway down when a cab swung onto Pinkney from Louisburg Square and pulled up at the curbside. The horse hardly had time to stop before a man in a top hat and traveling cloak scurried out the door of a row house, down the steps, and across the sidewalk. He yanked open the door of the cab, threw a small valise inside, and scrambled in. The cabbie gave his reins a quick shake, and the horse pulled away. It was all done in an instant.

Mr. Lawson slowed. "Was that . . .?"

He was walking in front, with the officer. I was behind him, with Wang. I hadn't gotten a good look at the man. "Who?" I asked.

Mr. Lawson stopped, uncertain.

"Who?" I asked again, but it could only have been one person. "Was that Mr. Sands?"

Mr. Lawson shook his head. "No, he wouldn't." But he didn't move.

The horse was stepping smartly now. The cab rattled up the street toward us. We all watched as it neared, trying to see who was inside. A pale face, half hidden by a high collar and a scarf. Mr. Lawson and I recognized him at the same time.

"No!" he exclaimed, his face stricken.

"It's him!" I shouted.

And then the cab was rolling past.

"Wait! Stop!" Mr. Lawson cried. "Stop that cab!"

I dashed into the street after it. The officer and Wang

were both right behind me. I was quicker off the mark, and gaining. I'm sure I would have caught up.

But Pat Delany saw what was happening. He jumped into the street right in front of the horse, waving and yelling like a banshee. The horse shied, hooves skidding on the cobbles. The driver cursed and snapped his whip at Pat, but Pat held his ground and made a grab for the horse's halter. He almost got trampled. Mr. Lawson was shouting behind me, and the officer finally blew his whistle, three sharp blasts, just as I reached the back of the cab.

It jerked to a stop. I leapt onto the step and yanked the door open. Sands was trying to get out the other side. He glanced back at me, his face bent in a snarl that was more fear than rage. I threw myself across the bench, grabbing for him, and the door burst open. We tumbled out onto the hard street. He gave a cry and tried to push me off.

And there I had him, under me. The pale eyes, big mustache, thin nose. The sneer. I drove my knees into his belly, knotted my left hand into the dark wool throat of his cloak, and drew back my right fist. To punch him. To smash his face. To pound him bloody. Like Da could have done before—

Wang grabbed my wrist. Pat threw an arm around my chest.

"No, Finn!" he cried. "That's not the way!"

"Damn you! Let me go!" Oh, I cursed, I did. But not at Wang and not Pat, not really. They were right. Punching Sands would have made me feel good for a few moments, but it wouldn't have done a thing for Da. It was Sands I was cursing. He was cowering under me, not looking for a fight. He set others to do his fighting. Da wouldn't have wasted his time on Sands.

I let them pull me off, and stood there watching as the officer collared Sands and delivered the summons. He even put the cuffs on and commandeered the cab to take Sands to jail, so he couldn't try to escape again. It wasn't till they were driving off that I felt my leg stinging. My new pants were cut, and blood was oozing from a small slice on my shin. There was glass on the road from a broken green bottle, lying in a pool of thick yellow stuff. Wang carefully picked up the top half of the bottle and sniffed. His eyes widened.

"Robert Lawson medicine," he said.

Old Robert's medicine had been poisoned. Not a quick poison – my leg didn't sting much, and not very long. It was the kind that killed slowly, the more you took. Poor Hedi, the cook, was the first suspect, but it came out Mr. Sands himself was the poisoner. He'd been trying to get rid of old Robert so he wouldn't catch on to the fraud. And he'd tried to get rid of An-Ming for the same reason. Sands broke down and confessed everything. He was charged with attempted murder and fraud and embezzling and a few other things that didn't matter to me at all. He was never charged with Da's death, not even as an accomplice. He got twenty years in jail. Only twenty.

He didn't serve much of it, though. Eleanor Sands sued him for divorce, for trying to kill her father. Two nights later, Sands tore his prison blanket into strips and hung himself in his cell. I like to think that's when he started serving his real sentence.

So old Robert was innocent, and he got a little better once he stopped taking the bad medicine. Eleanor Sands recovered, too, though it was all a shock. She'd have lost the baby, I'm sure, if it hadn't been for Hu-Lan, who knew a thing or two about Chinese midwife lore. Eleanor Sands bore a pretty girl, and they named her Ann Lawson Sands.

Mr. Lawson finally moved off the *Hang-Jinhe*. He bought a nice row house on Belknap Street, so he could be near to old Robert and Eleanor. He and An-Ming spent the winter closing down the bank, finding new investments, and paying off Sands's debts. Somehow, they kept the family out of the poorhouse. That spring, Peter and An-Ming were married. A month later, they sailed for China on the *Hang-Jinhe*. Wang and Hu-Lan went with them. It was a raw, blustery day, clear as a bell. They had all their flags flying, including the big banner with the golden cranes. We followed them out on the *Peabody* as far as the lighthouse island, then watched till they were no more than a dot on the water.

Gracie became Mr. Lawson's maid, and wound up marrying his new manservant. Ma stayed on at Tierney's, and Bridget worked there, too, after she finished school. When Tierney got old, the two of them took over the business, and ran it well. There was always plenty of Brahmin ladies who wanted hand-sewn gowns. When Ma's eyes started to fail . . . But you don't need to hear all that.

Me, I left for San Francisco in September of 1854, right after my 15th birthday. And despite all my dreaming, I went by steamer instead of sail. Mr. Lawson paid my fare, and I had saved enough money from the fair wage he'd been paying me that I could afford to have a good pulling boat built when I arrived. I was a boatman on San Francisco harbor for the rest of my working life. At one time I ran a fleet of seven boats. Never for the boarding houses, and we never crimped a single man as long as I was in charge.

Robert Lawson died the year after I left. Eleanor Sands never remarried. When her daughter moved away to Texas or some such place after the Civil War, Eleanor went with her. Her brother, Simon, was killed in that same war. So Mr. Lawson was left alone, except for Gracie and her husband. Ma moved in with them. Bridget and her husband and five children lived above the tailor shop. They're all gone now, and the great-grandchildren back East don't write. The only person who ever wrote regular like was Pat Delany. He did finally become a real reporter, and did well by it. But he's long gone now, too.

I've seen the world change in those years. Steamers rule

the seas now. Trains reach every corner of the country. So does the telegraph, and the telephone is spreading fast. And there's radio, the motorcar, even airplanes. In that time, I've seen not just the Civil War, but two or three more, depending on how you count them. I lost two grandsons to war, a daughter to the earthquake and fire, and my wife to old age, after a life spent well.

I'm ninety-one today, the same age Mr. Lawson was when I first met him. And I'm not done yet. My chapter hasn't ended, though I doubt I'll live another twenty years, which is how long he lasted after turning off his clock. I don't have a clock, never did and never will. Just the ticking of my own stubborn heart, and a great desire to see what will happen next. I've seen Irishmen become mayors and governors, and I don't doubt someday one will be President. I've seen the Italians arrive, and be treated almost as bad as the Irish. I suppose they might say worse. But they're part of the country now, and have a shot at President, too. Maybe even a woman will one day. They've had the vote for over a decade, after all. Maybe even the blacks will be treated right some day. Maybe even the Chinese. I think An-Ming would have made a very good President, even a great one.

I think of her a lot these days, her and Peter. Mr. Lawson received one letter, to say they had reached Canton. That was all. I tried to contact them myself some years ago, but Mr. Lawson was dead by then, and I couldn't remember the name of the town, only that it was somewhere upriver from Canton. No one here in Chinatown could help me, no one at our embassy. China has been through as many wars and revolutions as any other country. Plagues and famines. Earthquakes. And there are all the little ways to die. I like to think they simply didn't have time to write: too many children to tend to, too many investments to manage, a living to be made. Lord knows I was never good at writing letters myself. But I do wonder. Peter took his clock-making tools with him. I wonder if An-Ming might have changed her mind.

Her father did. He stopped his clock shortly before I left. I still remember what he said when he told me he'd done it.

"We were once people of the sun. In these modern times, we have become creatures of the clock. The rich few have gained in material comfort, but we measure the rest by their toil, to the merest minute, even to the second. What sort of measure is that? A life should be more than bright clockwork put up for show on a mantle, and much more than the span of hours it took to cut the gears. I have had a long life in this clock, but I have spent too much of it watching the pendulum, afraid it would stop. Some day, it will, no matter how many jewels are in the works.

"Let your heart be your clock, Finn. Live for the moments when it runs full tilt for joy, or slows to the gentle tick of contentment. Treasure it. There is not enough time in life for clocks."

Da said it more simply: "Do what you're meant to. Let your life run its own course. That's what it's about, isn't it?"

Coming Next: The Bell Cannon!

From Chapter 12

So far . . . Ewan Gilmore, a cabin steward on the Scots-American Line steamship Isle of Lewis, is traveling as a passenger in order to act as a secret bodyguard for Professor Jakub Skovajsa and his daughter, Tereza Skovajsovà. They have been forced to leave the U.S. after a mysterious but deadly accident the previous May of 1878. Rumor has it that the professor had been building an unimaginably powerful weapon for the Army, but during a test had killed a squad of soldiers, the assistant Secretary of War, two U.S Senators, and his own wife in a horrible way. The press has vilified the professor, and death threats have come from many directions. No other steamship line would take the professor aboard. Now Ewan's task is to keep him alive. On the second night of the passage from New York to Glasgow, Ewan discovers a murdered passenger in the Ladies' cabin above the saloon – a man who, from the rear, looked very much like Professor Skovajsa. Ewan's suspicions fall on one of his cabin mates, a young man named Derek Reid, who befriended him early on and spends most of his time in the company of the professor.

Tereza and the professor spent almost three hours touring the engine room, Ewan with them. By the time they finally clambered up the ladder and back into the chilly evening, he felt as sweaty and sooty as the stokers and trimmers looked. He blessed the gray skies and cold wind and vowed never to become an engineer. Tereza, on the other hand, was glowing through the soot that dusted her face, hands, hat, and clothes. She thanked him again and again for arranging the visit. He felt no guilt at all accepting her gratitude; in the past three hours he had sweated enough to earn it.

The others, led by the count, had left after only a brief glimpse at the engine, and Ewan wasn't surprised to find Derek sound asleep in his berth. Keane was just leaving, having barely awoken, it seemed. When Ewan asked if he was all right, he mumbled something about the effort of so many mesmeric inductions and stumbled out. Ewan thought it looked more like the world's worst hangover.

Alone now in the cabin with sleeping Derek, Ewan studied the young man's boyish face. If Derek was plotting something against the professor, it certainly didn't show in sleep. His valise, on the other hand, might yield more. It was tucked under the berth.

Ewan knelt and carefully slid it out. Derek had left the buckles undone, and the latch was unlocked. It opened with a loud *snap* when Ewan pressed the catch. He froze, but Derek didn't move. Ewan slowly lifted the lid. Two poetry books lay on top of the clothes, next to a shaving kit and a small flannel bag that turned out to hold a second pair of shoes. A pocket inside the lid held a writing set, papers covered with scribbled poems, and a thin leather wallet with a few small bills and a draft on a Kentucky bank for fifty dollars more – hardly enough to tour the Continent. Ewan smiled grimly. Ranald Morrison wouldn't see much of a tip from Derek.

Unless he had means to get more. Someone to slip him

cash when he needed it. An accomplice. A master.

Ewan dug through the clothing: shirts, handkerchiefs, trousers, underthings, socks, and finally felt, beneath it all, the rasp of very coarse cloth. A burlap sack. Hiding a rough jacket, with trousers to match. And squashed between the sack and the bottom of the valise was a battered, wide-brimmed hat.

The memory clicked on like an electric light: Coming up from steerage. A man at the saloon hatchway. A thick immigrant accent. A glimpse of blonde hair beneath his hat. This hat.

Ewan sat back on his heels. If he'd needed more proof that Derek was a stowaway, he had it now. But it still didn't prove that Derek was stalking the professor. Or had murdered the reverend. It still seemed so unlikely. Ewan finished ransacking the valise but found nothing more that could be called evidence. No club or any other weapon. He stood and checked Derek's jacket and overcoat, too, draped atop the spare upper berth. They held nothing more than a handkerchief and a thin pair of gloves. That left the trousers, but Derek was wearing them.

Ewan carefully tidied the contents of the valise, shut the lid, and slid it back under the berth. He studied Derek's sleeping form one last time. Finally, he leaned over and slowly, carefully, slid his hand under Derek's pillow.

Nothing there.

Derek's eyes fluttered. He drew in a deep, wet breath and rolled onto his side. Ewan slipped his hand out, stepped back, and turned around, grabbing at his tie and shrugging off his coat. Derek sighed and went quiet.

Ewan let out his own slow, sigh of relief and tip-toed over to Keane's berth, where the much labeled valise was lying right on top, unlatched, with the end of a necktie sticking out from under the lid. Ewan opened it and began searching inside. Clothes, colored scarves, packets of playing cards, a slender wand, a pair of phony roses, a paper-mâché thumb, a Chinese puzzle box. Ewan shook the box and tried to figure out the trick, but it wouldn't open. He muttered a curse and tucked it back in with the rest of the gear, trying to arrange it the way he'd found it, making sure to leave the end of the necktie sticking out.

When he turned away, Derek was watching him with bleary, puzzled eyes.

Ewan smiled. "Woke up, did you? You were thrashing about there so much I was sure a bad dream had swallowed you whole. Sorry if I disturbed you. Just getting into bed here. Don't mind me, I'll be quiet as a mouse." He forced himself to stop babbling and started getting undressed.

Derek grunted and rolled onto his side, still facing Ewan. He closed his eyes, but Ewan could tell he didn't fall right back to sleep. Ewan turned off the light, crawled into his berth, and lay still, listening. After a minute, he shifted and tried to breathe more slowly, feigning sleep. He almost did fall asleep. Derek's next movement brought him back from the edge of the abyss.

Ewan forced himself to lie still and keep his breathing slow and steady. He kept his eyes closed, trying to see with his ears. Derek slid out from between the sheets. His feet landed softly on the deck. His valise whispered out from under the berth. Clicked open. Clothes shifted. The lid clicked shut. Then more stealthy movements: Derek getting dressed! Ewan stiffened and Derek froze.

Ewan snorted, swallowed, and went still again. After a long few minutes, Derek finished dressing. The door clicked open, admitting a brief gleam of light, then shut again. Ewan counted to fifteen, then threw off the covers and hurried to listen at the door. Nothing. Maybe Derek had just gone to the head, but maybe not. Ewan wasn't going to wait to find out. He pulled on his clothes, grabbed his hat, and slipped out into the companionway. It was empty. So were the heads and the baths. Ewan hurried forward, listening for voices behind the cabin doors. He paused a second at the silent stairs, then decided to check the saloon first. It was empty, too – odd, because Keane was still out and about. Ewan wondered if he and Derek had planned to meet. If so, it would have to be in the smoking cabin.

Ewan hurried up the companionway and paused to check the ladies cabin first. A chill went down his neck as he shuffled into the dark room, half expecting to trip over another body. But the cabin was empty. With a foolish surge of relief, Ewan went out on deck.

He found the ship mantled in fog. The horn sounded just as Ewan stepped out, and he realized he'd been hearing it belowdecks the whole time. He'd been so focused on Derek's movements that he hadn't even noticed the deep-throated moan. The sounds of the sea and the wake were muffled, too. There was part of a moon somewhere up in the sky, but the drifting fog hoarded light. The ship's running lights glowed dimly, red and green orbs of gauze. The side of the deckhouse was dark gray velvet. The lifeboats hovered like distant clouds. The rail was all but invisible.

Ewan stood a moment to let his eyes and ears adjust. He started aft, toward the smoking cabin, then heard something the other way, footsteps maybe. He turned, peering into the gloom. He went forward. His footsteps tapped dully on the damp planks. The horn sounded again. Ewan passed the end of the deckhouse. He could just make out the engine room skylights beside him and the bulk of the funnel, looming overhead. He took one more step, when an arm looped around his neck and jerked him backward, choking off his startled cry.

* * * * *

Vermont author Dean Whitlock writes fantasy and science fiction for young and not-so-young adults. His stories have appeared in Asimov's, Fantasy & Science Fiction, and Aboriginal SF, as well as in anthologies in the United States and abroad. His first two YA fantasy novels were originally published by Clarion Books, but now he publishes independently under the Boatman Press imprint. Dean is currently working on a new novel, The Arrow Rune, a rescue quest set on alternate worlds, one of them now, the other a planet where the tale of Beowulf is newly composed and fully believed, a world where there be not just dragons but *thyrs*, *scuccas*, *nicors* and giant *wyrms* whose venom sears flesh like lye. A world where mad harpers can pluck illusions from their strings, and bullying warriors will challenge you to a duel at the drop of the wrong word. A world where a young archer from today will find more than magic and battle.

An Air Force brat, Dean has lived in a dozen states and three foreign countries, a life of travel that gave him plenty of time to read in the car and now enriches his writing. You can find out more about Dean and his books at www.deanwhitlock.com.

CPSIA information can be obtained
at www.ICGtesting.com
Printed in the USA
FFOW03n1442060218
44939824-45196FF